The Killer Bee

LULU HART

The Killer Bee

Cover Design by Hannah Reinhard of HannarchyStudios

Editing by L.D. Butler

First Edition

 Created with Vellum

Content Warning

Graphic Sex

Potential Triggers
Assault & Violence
Murder

Playlist

"Sweater Weather" by The Neighborhood
"Summertime Sadness" by Lana Del Rey
"In for the Kill" by LaRoux
"Numb" by Marshmellow and Kahlid
"Get Low" by Dillon Francis
"APT" by Rosé and Bruno
"Automatic" by Brothers Conti
"Cake by the Ocean" by Bossa Nova Covers
"Mad Hatter" by Melanie Martinez
"Dangerous" by Sleep Token
"Forever in Love" by A1
Mingle Game Song (Merry Go Round)
"Space Song" by Beach House
"Yo, Ho" by Blood on the Dance Floor
"Ascensionism" by Sleep Token
"Even in Arcadia" (Piano Version) by Sleep Token
"Flying Without Wings" by Westlife

Contents

Chapter One

LUKE

IT TURNS OUT, interviewing strangers to live in your home is a lot like dating—awkward, slightly desperate, and full of red flags.

"Alright, thanks for coming by. We'll let you know what we decide," Chase says as he ushers a disaster of a potential roommate to the front door.

The moment the guy is gone, I roll my eyes and collapse onto the worn leather sofa in our living room.

"Jesus Christ," I groan, "Did you smell him? He must have bathed in Axe body spray, then rolled around in weed."

"Forget the smell," Wes snorts, leaning against the wall. "Did you hear his answer to the chore schedule? 'I'm more of a free spirit when it comes to cleaning.' Translation: I'll leave my shit everywhere until you clean it up."

Chase joins us, shaking his head. "And those references? His mom and his gaming buddy? Hard pass."

"Plus," I add, sitting straighter, "He mentioned he

'practices drums' at night to 'channel his creativity.' Our neighbors already hate us."

Wes scrolls through his phone. "That's the fifth disaster interview today."

"Maybe we should just put up with one of these losers," Chase sighs. "I appreciated the guy who brought his headshot and star chart..."

"You know what?" I throw my hands up. "I'm calling it. This roommate search is officially over."

Wes raises an eyebrow. "We still have one more interview in fifteen—."

"Cancel it," I say firmly. "Getting a roommate was never mandatory. I'd rather eat ramen for every meal than share our space with some random weirdo we can't stand."

Chase frowns. "But dad's allowance cuts—"

"Are bullshit," I interrupt. "So we failed some stupid societal aptitude test that determines if we're 'contributing appropriately to Keeper standards.' Big deal. Half the initiates failed."

"Yeah, but they don't have Wesley Sullivan Senior breathing down their necks," Wes points out, tossing his phone onto the coffee table. "The extra rent money would cover the luxuries—beer, parties, paintball..."

"And our sanity?" I counter. "Dad's trying to teach us another lesson. Remember when he made us get jobs at the country club after we crashed his car?"

Chase snickers. "You looked ridiculous in that uniform."

"Exactly. And we survived it, didn't we?" I stand, ready to call this whole thing off, when the doorbell rings. "Oh, for fuck's sake," I mutter.

"Last one," Wes says, already heading toward the door. "Just be nice for ten minutes. That's all I'm asking."

I collapse back onto the sofa, rubbing circles on my temples. Five interviews are enough to drain anyone's social battery, and mine's been running on empty since the third guy showed up with his "emotional support" snake.

I hear Wes's voice from the foyer, unusually warm and animated. "Guys, this is Bebe," he announces, stepping into the living room with an unexpected smile. "She's here about the room."

She?

Standing next to my brother is the most intriguing girl I've ever seen. She's tiny—barely reaching Wes's shoulder, with cinnamon brown hair lying down her back, catching the light like it was spun from honeyed silk. We make eye contact, and I'm caught off guard. It should have been jarring. Instead, it was like seeing something rare and magical. Her eyes. They're mismatched—one green, one partially brown with a pop of blue—framed by naturally long lashes that brush her cheekbones when she blinks. Her skin is sun-kissed, like she's spent just enough time outdoors to glow without burning.

Her worn black Converse have little doodles on the white rubber parts; her light denim jeans expose torn knees that appear naturally frayed rather than factory-distressed. Everything about her seems effortless, but when you really look closely, you can see that her beauty was anything but. Her natural beauty is the kind that will stay with you long after she's left a room.

I realize I've been gaping at her like an idiot and quickly sit straighter as she hovers in the doorway, looking simultaneously confident and shy.

"Why don't you have a seat?" Wes gestures toward the dining chair we've strategically placed in the center of the living room—our little intimidation tactic for the interviews.

She nods and crosses the room with light, deliberate steps. I catch her perfume. It's sweet and floral, vanilla and roses maybe.

I watch as she takes in our place, which allows me to view it through an outsider's eyes. Our house is a prime example of what happens when three brothers with zero design sense move in together. The living room flows directly into the kitchen and dining area in that open-concept style realtors love, but that actually means you can see the mountain of dishes from every angle.

The living room has a leather sofa and loveseat set, paired with a sleek glass coffee table that's currently littered with empty pizza boxes and alcoholic beverages, a massive flat-screen TV mounted on the wall, surrounded by an impressive collection of gaming consoles and tangled cords. The walls remain mostly bare except for a neon beer sign Wes "borrowed" from a bar downtown.

The dining area has a half wall separating it from the living room with an archway. Inside sits a rectangular oak table. One chair has a wobbly leg we've fixed with a stack of coasters, and the surface is permanently stained from a sangria incident.

The kitchen is in the back corner of the space, separated by a breakfast bar cluttered with mail, but it has a large marble island.

As she settles into the chair, we instinctively move to the sofa across from her, taking our unassigned but understood positions—Wes in the middle as the oldest, me on his right, Chase on his left.

"So," Wes begins, leaning forward, "we were expecting a Bobby to show up today." He glances at his phone. "That's what was in the email."

Her full lips curve into a small, apologetic smile. Her hands rest neatly folded in her lap, not a single nervous fidget betraying her composure.

"I apologize for the deception," she says, her voice soft but unwavering. There's something melodic about it, like she's used to being listened to despite its quietness. "I noticed your ad specified a male roommate, but..." she pauses, meeting each of our eyes directly. "I'm a late acceptance at Dalton University. All the dorms and student housing were full by the time my letter arrived. I've been searching for weeks with no luck. I figured showing up in person would at least give me a chance."

"Clever girl," Chase comments, with a note of admiration in his voice.

"Look," she says, leaning forward slightly, "I know living with a girl probably wasn't your plan, but I was raised by my three older brothers. I'm used to guy stuff—the mess, the noise, the way you all communicate with grunts sometimes." A ghost of a smile crosses her face. "I won't try to be your mother or anything. I'll clean up after myself, stay out of your way, and honestly, you'll barely notice I'm here."

I almost snort at that. *I will.* I will definitely notice she's here. There's no way she'd blend into the background. While that might not be a bad thing, we've never lived with a woman other than our mother.

"We have parties," Wes says bluntly. "Loud ones."

"That's okay," she counters without missing a beat.

"And what about rent?" Chase asks, cutting to what's really important.

"I can pay four months upfront," she states, reaching into her messenger bag and pulling out an envelope. "Cash."

My brothers and I exchange glances. That would solve our immediate financial problems.

"So," Bebe says. "Could you tell me a bit about yourselves?"

I blink in surprise. None of the other applicants had bothered asking about us. They'd been too busy trying to sell themselves or acting like they were doing us a favor by gracing us with their presence.

Wes immediately sits straighter, his smile widening as he slips into the charm I've seen him use on countless women.

"Well, we're the Sullivan brothers. I'm Wesley, or Wes, the oldest," he says with an easy confidence that makes professors grant him extensions and girls give him their numbers. "Senior at Dalton U, quarterback for the Dragons." He flashes his signature smile. "Three-time regional champs, will go pro after graduation."

I resist rolling my eyes. Brag much?

Chase jumps in next, his entire demeanor shifting into what we call his "golden boy mode." He leans forward, making direct eye contact with her.

"I'm Chase, a sophomore at Dalton U. I'm studying law," he says with a smile. "I'm also the family chef, so if you'd like homemade pasta at midnight after a night out, I've got you covered." He winks, and I notice Bebe's lips quirk upward slightly.

Everyone's glances turn to me expectantly, and suddenly my mouth goes dry. Those mismatched eyes focus directly on me, patient and attentive. I clear my throat, trying to channel my brothers' effortless charm.

"I'm, uh, Luke. Junior at Dalton U," I pause, uncharacteristically tongue-tied. Something about the way she's looking at me—like she's genuinely interested in what I have to say. I swallow and continue. "Business major. Will probably inherit the family business."

She nods. "Thank you all for sharing. It's nice to meet you properly." She tucks a strand of hair behind her ear. "I should probably tell you a bit more about myself, too."

"Please do," Wes says, leaning back into the couch.

"Well, I mentioned my brothers. They're a bit older than me, so I grew up as the baby of the family—hence the name Bebe—French for baby." She smiles fondly. "I actually spend a lot of time in the kitchen, too. I'm a pretty decent chef, though I'm more into baking," she continues, glancing at Chase. He catches her eye and winks, a signature move that usually has freshman girls giggling in the quad. She doesn't giggle, but a soft blush colors her cheeks. "I'm undecided on my major, just going to explore different departments my first semester. Philosophy, art history, maybe even business." At this, she shoots me a quick look. "I'm just looking forward to the college experience, you know? Join a couple of clubs, attend football games, study in the library until it closes—the whole normal college thing."

The way she says "normal" catches my attention. Like normalcy is something she's observed from a distance rather than lived. It makes me wonder what kind of life she's had until now.

Chase clears his throat and stands. "Would you excuse us

for a minute?" he says, then turns to Wes and me. "Guys—sidebar."

My brothers and I file into the kitchen, huddling together near the refrigerator.

"What do you think?" he whispers, glancing over his shoulder to make sure she can't hear us.

"I think she's perfect," Wes says immediately, not bothering to hide his enthusiasm. "She's got cash upfront, she's lived with guys, and she's..." he trails off, searching for the right word.

"Cute?" Chase says with a smirk.

I elbow him in the ribs. "Dude, we're not looking for a hookup. We need someone who won't drive us insane."

"Fine," Wes holds up his hands. "But you can't deny she's different from the losers we've seen today. Plus, she seems... I don't know, self-contained? Like she won't be all in our business."

I nod slowly, thinking about the way she carries herself—confident, but not intrusive. "I agree. There's something about her that feels... right."

Chapter Two

BEBE

I'VE BEEN TRAINED in interview tactics, though that was more for interrogation, but the principles are still the same. Keep your breathing steady, maintain a mental anchor and make eye contact.

From my chair positioned in the living room, I see them huddled in the kitchen, talking about me, obviously.

I smile to myself, knowing I've given them exactly what they wanted to see—the charming, capable girl who'd make a perfect roommate. Not that I was being fake, per se. I showed them the real me, just... the polished version. The version who knows how to laugh at the right moments and create meaningful eye contact that says "trustworthy" without saying a word.

I need to rent this room. These nine months—this school year—are all I have left before being sentenced to a life I never wanted.

"Well, Bebe," Wes announces with a grin as they enter

back into the living room. "You've got yourself a new place to live."

"Really?" I stand, genuine relief washing over me.

Chase nods. "The vote was unanimous. When can you move in?"

Luke stands behind them, his impossibly blue eyes meeting mine with quiet approval.

I take in the Sullivan brothers, standing here as though they've stepped out of a magazine spread—all towering over my 5'4" frame with varying shades of blond hair.

Luke's blond is lighter, more sun-kissed. It's shorter on the sides but with enough length on top to show a hint of natural curl. While his brothers exude obvious charm, there's something more reserved about him, a quieter intensity behind those startling blue eyes.

They're all in jeans, but that's where the uniformity ends. Wes wears his denim low on his hips, paired with a faded Dalton U t-shirt that's just tight enough to showcase the muscles that earned him quarterback status.

Chase's jeans are darker, with a crisp hem that speaks to a methodical nature. His light blue button-down shirt has its sleeves casually rolled up, showing his tanned forearms. It's the kind of casual-but-put-together look that says, "I might be studying law, but I'm not stuffy about it."

And then there's Luke. He has a more lived-in style. His plain black t-shirt is simple but fits him perfectly across broad shoulders that taper to a narrow waist. No logos, no statements—just like him, straightforward but somehow still mysterious. Around his wrist is a leather band, the kind of accessory that looks meaningful rather than fashionable.

My heart does a stupid little flip that I immediately try to suppress.

"I could move in tomorrow," I say, trying not to sound too eager. "If that timing works for you."

Luke steps forward. "Tomorrow will be great."

I tuck a strand of hair behind my ear, feeling oddly nervous. "And as a thank you, I could cook dinner tomorrow night."

"Dinner sounds perfect," Chase adds.

After exchanging numbers and working out the details and time, I thank them again and head for the door. Luke walks me out, taking a few steps with me outside the threshold.

"See you tomorrow, Bebe," he says, and the way my name sounds on his lips makes something flutter in my chest.

"Tomorrow," I echo, offering a smile that feels more genuine than I intended.

I walk down the tree-lined street their home is on, the fall breeze rustling the leaves overhead. I check over my shoulder once to make sure he's gone back inside before I quicken my pace.

I round the corner to where Dominic, my family's driver, waits in the sleek black Bentley, engine idling. His eyes meet mine in the rearview mirror as I slide into the backseat.

"How did it go, Miss Laurent?" he asks, his tone formal as always.

"I move in tomorrow." I exhale, releasing the tension I've been holding all afternoon.

"Congratulations." His expression remains neutral. "Where to now?"

"The penthouse, please." I lean back against the leather

seat as we pull away from the curb, leaving behind the modest neighborhood.

As we drive from Ambrose, the small college town a little over an hour outside the City of Los Angeles, the scenery transforms to progressively taller buildings where glass towers scrape the sky. I stare out the window, wondering what my new roommates would think if they could see where I'm heading. What they'd say if they knew the truth.

The elevator doors slide open with a soft chime, revealing the marble foyer of the penthouse. Two men from security nod respectfully as I pass. They never smile. They're not paid to.

I head down the hallway, my Converse shoes squeaking on the polished floor. Family portraits line the walls—carefully staged photos that project unity and power rather than actual warmth. In most of them, I'm standing slightly behind my oldest brother, Gabriel, his hand on my shoulder. Positioning that speaks volumes.

I pause outside Gabriel's office door, taking a deep breath before knocking.

"Come in," his voice commands from the other side.

He sits at his massive desk, phone pressed to his ear. He holds up a finger, signaling me to wait while he finishes his conversation. At forty-years-old, my brother carries our father's legacy with authority. Same dark eyes, same ability to make people feel small with just a look. It's a quality you need if you're going to run an empire in organized crime or what some would call—the mafia.

"Call me back when you have that information," he says into the phone before hanging up. "Bebe."

"I found a place," I announce, taking a seat across from him.

His jaw tightens. "With those three guys?"

"Yes. They seem normal. Safe. You vetted them..."

One condition of the agreement between Gabriel and me was that he had to approve of where I lived, and that included background checks on potential roommates.

He leans back in his chair. "I still don't like this. We have plenty of properties where you could stay. Dominic is happy to—"

"That's exactly why I need to go," I say, meeting his gaze directly. "I want these months to myself before—"

"Nine months," he sighs. "That is all I can give you before the arrangement becomes unavoidable."

I nod, relief mingling with the dread that has become my constant companion. "I know. Nine months of freedom in exchange for a lifetime of duty."

"It's not just duty, Bebe. It's survival. The Calabreses want more than just business ties. Alessandro wants blood—our blood—and this marriage."

At least Gabe is giving me this—one academic year at a university, living like a normal eighteen-year-old before I become Mrs. Calabrese. The thought of my "fiancé" makes my stomach clench. He's Gabriel's age with cold eyes that assess me like livestock at auction. A necessary alliance between families, he explained. My opinion was never part of the equation.

I stand, ready to leave before the conversation veers into

territory I'm not emotionally prepared to handle. "I should go pack."

"Hold on," he says. "I have a job for you."

My hand freezes on the doorknob. "Gabe, I—"

"Just because I'm allowing you this college fantasy doesn't mean you're relieved of your immediate family responsibilities." His eyes harden, familiar steel replacing the brief glimpse of the brother I once knew. "You're still The Killer Bee."

The nickname lands like a slap.

"I thought we agreed—"

"The agreement was nine months of college, not nine months of abandoning your family." He stands, coming around the desk.

My jaw clenches. "Who's the mark?"

"An auto mechanic."

"Fine," I concede, years of conditioning making my spine straighten. "Where and when?"

He slides a folder across the desk. "Tonight. He has an apartment over Roger's Garage. The details are all there." He studies me for a moment, something like pride or regret flickering across his features. "No mistakes, Bebe."

"There never are," I reply coldly.

I leave his office without another word; the folder clutched tightly in my hand. The penthouse suddenly feels suffocating, the marble and crystal chandeliers a gilded cage I've dreamed of escaping my entire life.

In my bedroom suite, I toss the file onto the bed and stare at my reflection in the floor-length mirror. The girl who stared back at three potential roommates hours ago—the one with the easy smile and casual clothes—seems like a stranger now.

The black fabric clings to my body like a second skin, the reinforced spandex blend stretching with each movement. It's not unlike what you'd imagine Catwoman wearing, minus all the leather and impractical latex. This suit is engineered for efficiency—breathable mesh panels along the sides allow for proper ventilation while the weave offers protection without sacrificing mobility. The matte finish absorbs light rather than reflects it, perfect for blending into shadows.

I secure the utility belt around my waist. Inside is a syringe of toxin blended with honey. Our signature creation—sweet, untraceable and devastatingly deadly.

I pull my hair back into a tight bun, securing it with pins that double as lock picks. No loose strands to leave behind, no DNA to trace.

Lastly, I reach for the small contact lens case on my vanity. They will erase my most identifiable feature. I place the azure-colored lenses over both irises. The color reminds me of Luke's eyes, which sends a pang through my chest.

The tabloids would have a field day if they discovered the true identity of their sensationalized "Killer Bee." Four years of carefully orchestrated deaths, all traced back to the honey residue found in the victims' bloodstreams. The honey is merely a carrier, infused with a compound that degrades completely within hours of administration, leaving only nature's most innocent sweetener behind.

I check my reflection one last time. The girl staring back at me isn't Bebe Laurent, future university student with roommates and homework. She isn't even Bebe Laurent, reluctant fiancée to a man twice her age. She's simply The Bee

—Gabriel's most efficient weapon. The one they never see coming—deployed only when necessary. Precise. Lethal.

He started training me when I was seven years old. While other kids were learning to ride bikes without training wheels, I was learning how to break a man's wrist with a simple twist of my hands. By ten, I could disarm someone twice my size. By twelve, I could fight blindfolded, relying on sound and air displacement to track my opponent.

"Your size is an advantage, not a weakness," he would say during our dawn training sessions in the penthouse gym. "They'll underestimate you. That's when you strike."

The honey was his idea too, though it started innocently enough. When I was little, before our parents died, I had an obsession with honey. I'd drizzle it on everything: toast, yogurt, even my chicken nuggets, much to our mother's horror. Gabriel would sneak me honeycomb from the farmer's market, watching with amusement as I sucked the golden sweetness from each hexagonal cell.

He channeled my childhood preference into something sinister and brought in chemists, toxicologists, people who owed the family favors, to develop the compound.

"Memorable enough to send a message, untraceable enough to keep you safe," he'd explained when he first handed me the specialized syringe four years ago. The irony isn't lost on me—how something so sweet could be so deadly.

Chapter Three

BEBE

The apartment over the garage is exactly what I expected —dingy with peeling paint and security that's laughable at best. The fire escape creaks under my weight as I climb to the second floor.

I find the window Gabriel's intel indicated would be the easiest entry point. The lock is simple, a basic latch mechanism that takes me less than ten seconds to disengage with one of my hairpins. I slide the pane up slowly, testing for squeaks before easing my body through the narrow opening.

I land silently on the worn carpet, my eyes quickly adjusting to the darkness. The apartment smells of stale cigarettes and cheap takeout. According to the file, John Abel lives alone. No pets, no girlfriend, no complications. A lonely auto mechanic with a side hustle of using luxury cars as drug mules on unknowing owners. The owner brings in his Maserati for an oil change and leaves with bricks of drugs hidden in the vehicle's panels. Days later, your car gets jacked from a Whole Foods parking lot, and when you report it to the police—they do not know the crime was drug related. Recently, Mr. Abel has been using cars from the wrong people. My people. We don't tolerate drugs—ever.

A thin strip of light spills from beneath the door at the end of the hallway. Strange. It's nearly two in the morning. He should be asleep by now. There's a reason I hit my marks in the middle of the night.

I move through the shadows, my footsteps soundless as I approach the living room. That's when I hear it—the distinctive sound of someone snorting, followed by a sharp inhale and a soft curse. I press myself against the wall, just outside the doorway, and peer around the corner.

John sits on his couch, hunched over the coffee table. His back is to me, shoulders moving rhythmically as he leans down, straightens up, then leans down again. The television casts a bluish glow across the room, illuminating the neat lines of white powder arranged on the glass surface.

Perfect. The coke will make this easier—his heart already racing, his system primed for the toxin to work faster.

I step into the room, silent as a ghost, the syringe palmed in my right hand. Three more steps and this will be over. Two more steps. One.

His head jerks up suddenly. On the dark TV screen, our eyes meet. He spins around with surprising speed, diving for the space between the couch cushions.

My instincts kick in before my mind fully processes what's happening. A pistol appears in his hand, but I'm already moving. My leg snaps out in a precise arc, and my boot connects with his wrist with a crack, causing the gun to fly across the room.

He presses his palm to his chest, eyes bloodshot and wild with panic while dilated from the drugs. "What the fuck?" he shouts, scrambling backward, knees on the floor, until his back hits the coffee table, sending the remaining lines of cocaine flying into the air like toxic snow. "Who—who are you?" he stammers, voice cracking with fear. His eyes dart around frantically, searching for an escape route or another weapon.

I maintain my silence, studying him with clinical detachment. This is the moment they always try to connect, to humanize themselves. To make me see them as people rather than targets. I've learned that lesson the hard way. Words create bonds. Bonds create hesitation. Hesitation creates mistakes.

Wordlessly, I move around the couch, approaching him with measured steps. Despite my small stature, he shrinks back against the coffee table, eyes widening in recognition. Perhaps he's heard the whispers about The Killer Bee. Maybe he's realizing why I'm here.

His mouth opens and closes, forming pleas I refuse to acknowledge. I step forward, pressing my boot against his chest to pin him to the floor. I remove the cap from the syringe, watching as his pulse hammers visibly at his throat— the perfect injection site.

"Please," he begs, voice cracking. "Whatever they're paying you, I can double it. I—I've got money stashed—"

His struggle intensifies as I lower myself, one knee on his sternum. His pleas turn to gurgles as the needle pierces skin and I depress the plunger in a single smooth motion. The effect is almost instantaneous. His body tenses, then goes slack beneath me. I watch as the light fades from his eyes, pupils dilating one final time before the lids flutter closed.

I wait exactly sixty seconds, counting each beat in my head while monitoring his pulse until it stops completely. I reach for my belt bag, fingers finding the small protective case containing my signature. The honeycomb gleams amber in the dim light, perfectly preserved hexagonal cells still holding traces of natural sweetness.

Gently, I pry his jaw open, noting the slight resistance of early rigor mortis, and place the honeycomb fragment on his tongue. It will dissolve slowly, and by morning, the police will find only another victim of the mysterious Killer Bee.

I stand, surveying the scene. The room falls silent except for the low murmur of the television still playing in the background—some late-night infomercial about knives that never need sharpening.

Nothing out of place, nothing to connect me to this room or this man. I'm careful not to disturb anything else, and exit the way I came.

The streets are empty at this hour, with only the occasional car rushing by. I keep to the shadows out of habit, making my way to where Dominic waits three blocks away, engine idling.

He doesn't speak when I slide into the backseat, just meets my eyes briefly in the rearview mirror before pulling away from the curb. We've done this dance so many times that words are unnecessary.

The city blurs outside my window, streetlights smearing into streams of gold against the night. I strip off my gloves, tucking them into a specially lined compartment in my belt. They'll be incinerated later, along with the empty syringe.

Dominic pulls into the private underground garage, the security gate sliding shut behind us with a soft mechanical whir. I exit without a word, taking the exclusive elevator directly to the penthouse.

It's quiet at this hour, and I make my way down the hallway, my footsteps barely audible on the marble floors. The adrenaline that fueled me earlier is fading, leaving behind a familiar hollowness that settles in my chest after each job.

I walk to Gabriel's office. He's still awake, always working for our family. I stop in the doorway and nod to him. A silent acknowledgement that the job is complete.

He looks up from his laptop, the blue light casting harsh shadows across his face, making him appear older than his years. He returns my nod, a barely perceptible dip of his chin. No congratulations, no questions—just quiet acceptance of a task efficiently executed. This is our ritual, perfected over years. The unspoken language of killers.

"There's tea in the kitchen," he says, his voice cutting through the silence, surprising me. "Chamomile. It might help you sleep. There is also a gift on the counter."

The unexpected gesture of kindness catches me off guard. For a moment, I glimpse the brother who used to make me honey toast when I couldn't sleep after our parents died.

I smile at him and walk toward the kitchen. Like he said, there's a hot kettle on the stove, a mug with tea bags and a bottle of honey waiting for me. Next to it, an unexpected gift —a set of car keys for a Volkswagen tied with a red bow. I take a seat at the kitchen island thinking about Gabriel's generous gesture. Is it just a car, though? It's his way of support or another form of control. Either way, I'll take it.

I prepare the tea how I like it. The irony doesn't escape me as I stir a generous spoonful of honey into my cup, watching it dissolve into golden ribbons. The same substance that brings me comfort is what I leave behind as my calling card. Sweet death.

I wrap my hands around the warm mug, letting the heat seep into my fingers. Nine months of freedom, then marriage to Alessandro—a man who runs his family's empire with the same ruthless efficiency that Gabriel runs ours—if not more. The engagement was announced in hushed meetings between family heads, my future sealed with handshakes while I stood silently in the corner, an asset being transferred.

I wonder if Alessandro knows who I am, what I've done. Does he expect his young bride to continue being Gabriel's weapon? Or will I become a different kind of asset?

Chapter Four

LUKE

THE GRAND MASTER rises from his ornate chair, and the circular chamber falls silent. Wes nudges me with his elbow, and I stop fidgeting with the hem of my velvety dark blue ceremonial robe I'm wearing. Society meetings are so boring.

I glance around, taking in the ancient stone walls that still bear the faint scent of fermented grapes. Decades ago, this cellar housed rows of oak barrels aging fine wines; now it's home to forty of Dalton University's alumni. All men who have formed a brotherhood; a secret society for them to pass on to their sons. To me—we're guys in matching robes pretending we're part of something profound. Although the organization has hundreds of Chapters throughout the country—we're the headquarters since we reside in the same city as the university.

The original barrel racks have been converted into benches that line the perimeter, each one uncomfortable as hell.

Wrought iron sconces contain flickering candles, casting dramatic shadows across the vaulted ceiling, but do little to dispel the perpetual dampness that clings to everything.

Why we can't hold these meetings in the winery's beautiful courtyard is beyond me. The estate's upper level has a stone terrace surrounded by cypress trees and rose bushes. There's actual sunshine up there, fresh air that doesn't smell like mildew. But no. Tradition demands we gather in this underground tomb like we're medieval monks instead of semi-privileged college students with access to perfectly good outdoor furniture.

The Grand Master, or as I know him, Professor Vicnent from Economics 301—clears his throat dramatically. "The Keepers have three objectives for the coming quarter," he announces. "First, we must secure the artifacts from the Wellington estate before they go to auction."

Poor old man Wellington died three days ago, and instead of mourning the loss of their friend, they're thinking about what they need to take from him.

Chase leans forward, his eyes wide with interest. Wes and I are whatever about the society. We take part as expected and go along with the motions. Chase, however, shows real engagement.

"Second," continues the Grand Master, stroking his gray beard, "it is necessary that we strengthen our alliance with the Los Angeles Chapter. Too long have we operated in isolation."

The assembly murmurs in agreement. My father, seated among the council of five, nods solemnly.

"Which brings us to our final goal," the Grand Master's voice drops to a grave whisper. "We must identify the individual known as The Killer Bee."

A collective gasp ripples through the chamber. Chase's posture stiffens beside me.

"The L.A. Chapter's Grand Master, Maxwell, has formally requested our help," he continues, his hands gripping the podium he stands in front of. "Three of their members have been found dead in the last six months, each killed with honey toxin and given the signature hexagon placed on their tongues."

Wes shoots me a wide-eyed glance. *The Killer Bee is targeting Keepers? Why?*

"This is now our highest priority," the Grand Master declares. "We cannot allow this threat to continue eliminating our brethren."

"I volunteer to form an investigative committee," my father says as he rises from his seat.

I scoff internally. The Killer Bee has been headline news for a couple of years now. If the entire state police force, FBI, and who knows what other agencies can't catch this guy, what chance do we have? We're a glorified brotherhood in fancy robes—not detectives.

After the meeting adjourns, I slip away to the courtyard, needing air that isn't thick with pretension and paranoia.

"You looked like you were about to burst in there," Wes's voice comes from behind me. I turn to find him leaning against a wall, his robe discarded.

"Can you blame me?" I ask, pulling off my own stuffy robe. "The Keepers weren't always this way, remember?" My voice drops lower, more intimate. "Grandfather told us stories about the original purpose. A network of people across different professions—doctors, lawyers, politicians, artists—all working together, sharing knowledge, creating opportunities, helping each other succeed. So what happened to that?" I ask, genuinely curious.

"Success corrupts," he says simply, running a hand through his sandy blond hair. "What started as mutual aid turned into trading favors, then greed."

"Now look at us. Planning to raid a dead man's belongings before his body's even in the ground."

"And crime-solving, apparently," Wes jokes.

I'm about to respond when the sound of heavy footsteps grates on the concrete. Our father appears, his ceremonial robe discarded but his Keeper medallion still hanging around his neck.

"Boys," he calls out, his voice carrying an authoritative tone we've known since childhood. "Family meeting. Now."

He disappears, clearly expecting us to follow.

I glance at my watch. It's 4:30pm. "Shit," I mutter under my breath.

"What?" Wes asks.

"I wonder how long this'll take. Bebe. She's supposed to be moving in right now, then making us dinner. Listen," I say, lowering my voice and leaning closer, "we probably shouldn't tell dad about our new roommate."

"Yeah, okay," he agrees. "If he sees her there, we can tell him she's one of our girlfriends."

The family meeting drags on for nearly two hours, dad talking in circles about our "sacred responsibilities" and the need for "heightened vigilance" given The Killer Bee situation. Chase nods along seriously while Wes and I exchange glances, silently counting the minutes.

By the time we finally escape, the sun has already set. We pile into Wes's Jeep Wrangler, Chase claiming shotgun before I even have a chance to reach for the door.

The Jeep looks badass with its rugged exterior and open-air design—the kind of vehicle that screams adventure and makes heads turn when you cruise through campus. I fold myself into the backseat. It's nothing more than a glorified bench with minimal cushioning, designed for occasional use or very small humans—neither of which applies to me.

"Can you push your seat up?" I ask Jake, who pretends not to hear me as he fiddles with the radio.

"Sorry, bro. Driver picks the music, shotgun adjusts the volume, backseat suffers in silence," Marc says with a grin, catching my eye in the rearview mirror while the engine roars to life.

"Dad really thinks The Keepers can solve the Bee case," Chase says, scrolling through his phone.

"Congratulations," I say flatly. "Now you can play detective while the actual detectives do their jobs."

Wes snorts. "Be nice. Chase is living his dream."

"Whatever," I mutter, staring out the Jeep as streetlights flicker past. "I'm just ready to get home. I'm starving."

The Jeep turns onto our street twenty minutes later, and we notice a white VW Jetta parked in our driveway.

"Looks like she made it," Wes says, pulling in next to her car.

As soon as Chase unlocks the front door, a heavenly aroma hits us. Rich garlic, sizzling meat and the unmistakable scent of bacon wafted through the air. My stomach growls, reminding me we haven't eaten since breakfast.

"Hello?" I call out.

"In here!" Bebe's voice floats from the kitchen.

Bebe stands at the stove, stirring something in a large pot. She's wearing an apron tied snugly around her waist and these tiny shorts that barely cover anything; the lower curves of her ass peek out beneath the hem.

Her cinnamon-brown hair, twisted up in a messy bun, gives her this effortless, just-rolled-out-of-bed sexiness that makes my mouth go dry.

"Perfect timing, guys!" she chirps, her expression lighting up with a smile. She switches off the burner. "Carbonara with pancetta and steak. My specialty." She twirls pasta onto three plates, then adds a fourth for herself. "I hope you don't mind," she says, gesturing toward the dining room. "I found some place settings in the cabinet and set the table. Figured we could have a proper first dinner as roommates."

"Not at all," I say. "It's... really nice."

We each grab a plate and follow her to the dining space where she's arranged everything perfectly—cloth napkins I didn't know we owned, glasses filled with ice water, and even a small vase with fresh flowers as a centerpiece.

Wes doesn't waste a second. His fork is loaded and in his mouth before his chair stops scraping against the floor. His eyes roll back dramatically as he chews.

"Oh my God, Bebe," he moans, pressing a hand to his heart. "I'm in love with you. Will you marry me? This is the best thing I've ever tasted."

Her cheeks flush a deep pink, and her mismatched eyes flick to mine for just a second before darting away. That look

—like she's checking if I noticed her reaction—sends an unexpected jolt through my chest.

I twirl the noodles around my fork and take a bite. *Holy shit.* The creamy sauce coats my tongue, the perfectly cooked pasta with a slight resistance, the savory pancetta, the tender steak—it's a goddamn religious experience.

"You know what?" I say, locking eyes with Bebe. "If Wes's proposal doesn't work out, I'd be more than happy to step in. Seriously, this is delicious."

Her blush deepens. She bites her lower lip, her eyes darting between me and her plate with a shyness that seems at odds with the confident way she was when we first arrived. The reaction is much more intense than when Wes made his joke. And I feel a strange flutter of satisfaction.

"Don't listen to either of them," Chase chimes in, waving his fork. "I'll marry you right now. We can drive to Vegas tonight." He's grinning, but there's something in his eyes that makes me think he's half-joking.

She laughs, the sound light and musical. "Three proposals in one night? That's got to be some kind of record." She tucks a loose strand of hair behind her ear. "I think I'll hold off on accepting any marriage proposals until we've lived together for at least a week."

I notice Bebe's expression shift. Her smile remains, but her eyes take on a more solemn quality. She places her fork down gently and straightens in her chair.

"Seriously though, guys," she says, her voice no longer carrying a playful lilt, "Thank you." She gestures around the table. "For enjoying the food, for letting me move in here with you. This whole experience..." She pauses, seeming to search for the right words. "it means more to me than you could possibly know."

Experience. The word catches in my mind. Something about the way she says it, like living in a home with roommates is some kind of exotic adventure.

I can't help but wonder what sort of life she's been living where basic human interaction feels novel.

Chapter Five

BEBE

MY CONTROL IS CRUMBLING. My plan to charm these men is backfiring as they are doing it to me—naturally.

Wes has a magnetic confidence that reminds me of Gabriel; knowing exactly what he wants and how to get it. His quarterback swagger isn't an act; it's earned through years of being put on a pedestal. I can see how women would fall for him instantly, with that simple charm designed to disarm. In my world, I'd classify him as dangerous.

Chase is the baby-faced charmer with innocent eyes. There's something genuinely sweet about him that makes me want to trust him, which is exactly why I shouldn't.

Then there's Luke. *God, Luke.* Those piercing blue eyes that seem to look straight through my carefully constructed persona. His presence fills the room differently than his brothers—less flashy but somehow more substantial. When he speaks, I actually want to listen. The way his t-shirt stretches across his shoulders when he reaches for his water. The way his strong hands handle his fork with unexpected delicacy, how his smile reaches his eyes. *I've got a crush—bad.*

I force myself to look away from him after I catch myself staring, focusing instead on twirling pasta around my fork. This is dangerous territory. I'm not here to develop feelings for—.

"Bebe," Luke's voice breaks through my thoughts, "did you run into any problems moving in today? Everything go smoothly?"

"No issues at all," I reply. "The key was right where you said it would be. And since the room came mostly furnished, I didn't need to bring much. Just clothes, bedding, and a few personal items. My younger brother helped me carry all of it in. He was in and out in less than an hour."

"That was nice of him to help," Chase says.

Wes takes a sip of water, then sets his glass down. "So, Bebe," he says, leaning forward, "do you have a boyfriend? Anyone special we should know about?"

Luke's fork clatters against his plate. "Wes, seriously? That's not our business."

"What?" he shrugs. "I'm just wondering if we'll be having other guys hanging around. It's a reasonable roommate question."

Heat creeps up my neck as three pairs of eyes fix on me, waiting—curious about my response. "No boyfriend," I answer.

"Good to know," Wes says with a smile that's just a touch too satisfied.

Chase clears his throat. "Though, you know, if you had girlfriends who wanted to come over, that would be totally fine. I mean, whatever your preference is, we're cool with that."

I can't help the laugh that bubbles. "Thank you, Chase."

I take a small drink of water, gathering my courage.

"What about you guys?" I ask, trying to sound casual. "Anyone special in your life? Girlfriends I should know about?"

Chase shakes his head. "Not at the moment. Had something going with this girl from my criminal justice class last semester, but it fizzled out over summer break."

I give him a weak smile, unsure if he's happy about that or not.

"Single and loving it," Wes announces. "Football season keeps me busy, and I like to keep my options open."

I nod, then turn to Luke, my heart inexplicably picking up speed. "And you?"

He meets my gaze, those blue eyes making my stomach flutter. "No," he says simply.

Relief washes through me, which is ridiculous. I have no right to feel anything about his relationship status. In nine months, I'll be married to Alessandro Calabrese, sealing a pact between families. Yet here I am, secretly pleased that Luke is single, smiling like some lovesick teenager.

"So, what are your favorite foods?" Chase asks, redirecting the conversation as he helps himself to seconds at the stove. "Besides making incredible pasta, what do you like to eat?"

"I'm a sucker for simple comfort food," I admit. "Grilled cheese sandwiches with tomato soup. My brother, Beau, makes these amazing breakfast burritos."

"I make a mean grilled cheese with three kinds of cheese and sourdough bread," Chase says with a grin.

"You'll have to show me sometime," I say, surprised by how much I mean it.

Luke watches our exchange with an unreadable expression. "What about movies? What kind do you like?"

"I'm embarrassingly behind on pop culture," I confess. "If you showed me a picture of an A-list celebrity, I couldn't even tell you who it is. I might be able to name a few Disney princesses. Oh, and I've never even seen Star Wars."

All three brothers stare at me in horror.

"That's it," Wes declares, pointing his fork at me. "Movie marathon this weekend. Non-negotiable roommate bonding activity."

I laugh, feeling a strange warmth spread through my chest. Is this what normal friendship feels like? Easy conversation over dinner, making plans?

I notice Luke stealing glances at me when he thinks I'm not looking, and each time our eyes meet, I glance away, pretending to be fascinated by my pasta.

"So," Wes says, "what made you decide on Dalton University?"

"I wanted something... normal. Somewhere I could blend in, have real experiences without too much pressure," I answer truthfully.

Chase nods enthusiastically. "That's what college is all about. Speaking of experiences," he sets down his fork with a decisive clink, "we should all go to Ambrose Pins after dinner."

"Ambrose Pins?" I ask, my brow furrowing.

"The bowling alley," Luke explains, his eyes lighting up. "On Thursday nights they do cosmic bowling with black lights and music. It's actually pretty fun."

I twist my napkin in my lap, suddenly feeling self-conscious. "I've never been bowling before," I admit, the confession slipping out before I can stop it.

Their eyes widen simultaneously.

"Never?" Chase gasps, as though I've just told him I've never breathed oxygen.

"First Star Wars, now bowling?" Wes adds, pressing a hand to his chest in mock horror. "What kind of deprived childhood did you have?"

A small laugh escapes me. "My brothers were more into... different activities."

Luke leans forward, his blue eyes sparkling with something that looks like genuine delight. "Then you absolutely have to come. First-time bowling experience? That's something I wouldn't miss seeing for the world."

The warmth in his voice makes my resolve crumble. This is why I'm here. Nine months, I remind myself. I have nine months before my life belongs to someone else.

"Okay," I agree, surprising myself with how much I'm looking forward to it. "Let's go bowling."

Wes claps his hands together. "Perfect! I need to shower first."

"Same," Chase adds, as he stands and collects his plate.

"I'll help you clean up," Luke offers, already stacking dishes as Wes and Chase disappear upstairs, their footsteps thundering on the wooden staircase.

Suddenly, the kitchen feels smaller with just the two of us. I gather silverware, hyperaware of Luke's presence as he carries plates to the sink. The domesticity of the moment strikes me—something so ordinary for most people feels precious to me.

"You don't have to help," I say, turning on the faucet. "You can get ready too."

"I'm good," he replies, rolling up his sleeves to reveal tanned forearms with a light dusting of golden hair. "Besides, it's only fair since you cooked."

We fall into a rhythm—I wash, he dries. The silence between us isn't uncomfortable, but charged with something I can't quite name. As he goes for a glass I'm rinsing, our fingers brush under the water. A jolt of electricity shoots up my arm, and I nearly drop the cup.

"Sorry," we both say in unison, then laugh.

He takes the glass, his fingertips lingering against mine a moment longer than necessary. His eyes meet mine, and suddenly I'm drowning in blue. Everything else fades away— the running water, the clink of dishes, the distant sound of Wes's off-key singing from upstairs in the shower.

"Your eyes," he murmurs, a kind of awe in his voice. "They're incredible."

A strange feeling washes over me—warm and fluttery, settling low in my stomach. I recognize it from books I've read but have never experienced it myself. This pull toward another person, this awareness of every inch of space between us.

"I love them," he continues, "the way the brown and blue blend in your right eye..." he adds with a self-conscious laugh, "You probably hear that all the time, though. The heterochromia thing."

I shake my head, surprised by my honesty. "I actually don't," I tell him. "Most people just stare, saying nothing. They find it... unsettling. Weird."

He steps closer, his gaze never leaving mine. "I don't find them weird at all. I think they're stunning. You're beautiful."

The words hang in the air between us, sincere and unexpected. My heart stutters in my chest. No one has ever called me beautiful before—not like this, not with this gentle reverence in their voice. Gabriel's associates have called me pretty, cute, even sexy in ways that made my skin crawl. *But beautiful?* Never.

I part my lips, but no words come out. *Should I thank him?* No, that seems inadequate.

I'm saved from having to respond when thundering footsteps announce Chase's arrival. "Alright, who's ready to bowl?" His voice cuts through the tension as he bounces into the kitchen, freshly showered and practically vibrating with excitement. His hair is still damp, and he's wearing a fresh t-shirt and jeans. "I called ahead and got us a lane reserved. Cosmic bowling starts in thirty minutes!"

Luke steps back, the spell broken. He runs a hand through his blond hair, a slight flush coloring his cheeks. "Yeah, I should probably get ready, too. Let me grab my wallet upstairs, and I'll be right back."

He backs away, his eyes lingering on mine for a heartbeat longer before he turns and heads toward the stairs. I watch him go, my fingers still tingling where they brushed against his.

Alone in the kitchen with Chase, I dry my hands on a dish towel, trying to compose myself. My heart continues racing from that intense moment with Luke, and I need to get it under control.

"You okay?" he asks, leaning against the counter. "You look a little flushed."

"Just the hot water," I lie, gesturing vaguely toward the sink. "Should I change before we go?"

He glances at my outfit—the casual shorts and tank top I'd thrown on after moving in. "You look great, but the bowling alley can get cold with the air conditioning. Maybe bring a sweater? And you'll need socks."

I nod, grateful for the excuse to escape upstairs. "I'll be quick," I promise, already heading toward the staircase.

I slip into my room and close the door behind me, leaning against it for a moment to catch my breath. *What is happening to me?* One dinner, one touched hand, and I'm completely thrown off balance. This isn't part of the plan. I'm not supposed to have any feelings for these men.

I push away from the door and rummage through my dresser for a pair of socks, finding them easily. But as I scan my luggage for something to wear over my tank top, I realize I didn't bring any sweatshirts or jackets.

"Bebe?" Luke's voice comes through the wood with a soft knock. "Are you ready to go?"

I open the door, finding him standing here. The scent of his cologne—a fragrance woodsy and clean—drifts toward me.

"I just realized I don't have a sweatshirt," I admit.

"You can borrow one of mine," he says without hesitation, his eyes warm. "Give me a second."

He disappears down the hall. I hear drawers opening and closing, then his footsteps returning. He reappears carrying a navy blue Dalton U sweatshirt, the university's dragon mascot emblazoned across the chest in silver.

"Here," he says, holding it out to me. "It'll be big, but it'll keep you warm inside."

I take it, my fingers brushing against his again. The sweatshirt is soft, worn from countless washes, and when I pull it over my head, it engulfs me completely. The sleeves hang past my fingertips, and the hem reaches mid-thigh. But more than that, it smells like him.

"Thanks," I say, rolling up the sleeves to free my hands. "I'll wash it before I give it back."

His eyes travel over me, something shifting in his expression. "Keep it," he says, his voice lower than before. "It looks better on you anyway."

Chapter Six

LUKE

Seeing Bebe's face light up when we step inside the bowling alley is priceless. She looks at everything with awe and amazement.

Her eyes widen as they take in the neon lanes glowing under black lights, the fluorescent pins casting an otherworldly glow at the end of each alley. The darkness is punctuated by streaks of electric blue, hot pink, and lime green that transforms the mundane bowling alley into something magical. The speakers blast upbeat tunes, creating a lively and energetic atmosphere, accompanied by the clatter and whoosh of bowling balls hitting the pins. When the disco ball spins, sending fractals of color dancing across her face, she actually gasps.

"This is... awesome," she breathes, her voice barely audible over the pulsing music. She looks like a child experiencing Christmas morning for the first time—pure, unfiltered joy radiating from her entire being.

I can't take my eyes off her. Something about witnessing her experience this simple pleasure makes my chest tighten. Her mouth parts slightly, reaching out to touch a beam of light as if it might be tangible. What kind of life had she lived where cosmic bowling could inspire such wonder?

"Come on," I say, gently touching her elbow to guide her toward our lane. "Wait until you try it."

Wes is already at the counter getting our shoes, while Chase programs our names into the scoring system. Bebe follows me, still gazing around. My sweatshirt hangs off her shoulders, making her look even smaller and more delicate than she is. The sight of her in my clothes sends a strange possessive thrill through me that I immediately try to suppress. *She's your roommate.*

"Bebe," Chase calls her over, gesturing to the control panel. "Do you want bumpers for your first time bowling?"

She looks at him blankly, clearly having no idea what he means. Her eyes dart to me with vulnerable uncertainty.

"No bumpers," I answer for her, giving her a reassuring smile. "She'll do fine without training wheels."

"You sure?" he asks her directly. "There's no shame in using them when you're a beginner."

"I trust Luke's judgment," she replies, her voice soft but certain.

Wes appears with an armful of bowling shoes. "Got everyone's sizes. Bebe, come with me to find you a ball. We need to get you something that fits your fingers properly."

He places his hand gently on her lower back, guiding her toward the ball racks. I watch them go, noticing how she looks back over her shoulder at me once before disappearing into the crowd.

Chase slides next to me, nudging my arm with his.

"Dude," he says, a knowing smirk spreading across his face. "You've got it bad."

"What are you talking about?" I scoff, trying to sound dismissive while watching Wes help her test the weight of different bowling balls.

"Come on," he says, lowering his voice. "I see how she looks at you. How you look at her. It's different from how Wes and I look at her."

I tear my eyes away from Bebe to face my brother. "Different how?"

"Don't play dumb." His expression softens. "We all think she's cute and fucking hot—that's obvious. But with you, it's something else. The way you watch her, how you offered her your sweatshirt, that whole moment in the kitchen I walked in on..."

Heat rises to my face. "You don't know what you're talking about."

"I know you better than you think, Luke."

I sigh, running a hand through my hair. "It doesn't matter, Chase. She lives with us. That could get weird real fast."

"So?"

"So what if it didn't work out? We'd still have to live together. It would be a disaster."

He shrugs. "Or it could be the best thing to happen to either of you," he finishes, but I don't have time to respond.

Wes and Bebe appear before us, her tiny hands cradling a neon pink bowling ball that glows like radioactive bubblegum under the black lights. Her face is practically luminous with excitement.

"Found the perfect one," he announces proudly, his hand still resting on her shoulder. "Eight pounds."

She holds it up like a trophy. "It's so bright! And it has glitter inside!"

"So, who's going first?" Wes asks, clapping his hands together as he surveys our little group.

We all turn to look at Bebe, the obvious choice for the inaugural roll. Her eyes widen slightly, and she clutches the pink ball closer to her chest.

"Actually," she says, her voice dropping, "I'd like to watch you guys go first. Just to see how it's done properly."

"I'll go first," Chase volunteers, grabbing his electric blue ball from the rack. "Pay attention, Bebe. This is how the pros do it."

He approaches the lane with an exaggerated swagger, positioning himself. Chase has always been a show-off, especially when there's a pretty girl watching. He takes three measured steps, swings his arm back, and releases the ball with a dramatic flourish of his wrist. It curves elegantly down the lane, spinning with impressive control before crashing into the pins with a satisfying crack.

Eight pins topple instantly, leaving two standing at opposite corners. Chase turns back to us with a triumphant grin, bowing theatrically.

Her jaw drops, her mismatched eyes wide with astonishment. "That was amazing!" she exclaims, clapping her hands together. "How did you make it curve like that?"

He winks at her. "Years of practice, sweetheart. It's all in the wrist."

He retrieves his ball for the second roll, looking confident as he lines up to take out the remaining pins. With another flourish, he sends the ball spinning down the lane—but this time it veers too sharply, sliding into the gutter. Chase's shoulders slump dramatically as he returns with an exaggerated pout.

"The lane's uneven," he mutters, trudging back to our seats amid Wes's merciless laughter.

"My turn," I announce, selecting my midnight black ball with silver flecks that catch the neon lights. I can feel Bebe's eyes on me as I approach the lane, her attention making my skin tingle with heightened awareness.

I position myself at the starting mark, taking a deep breath to center my focus. Normally, I wouldn't care this much about a casual game, but knowing she's watching my every move makes me determined to impress her. I take three steps forward, the ball swinging in perfect pendulum motion before I release it with a controlled flick of my wrist.

It spins down the center of the lane, curving slightly at the last moment to hit exactly between the headpin and the three-pin—the pocket. The impact creates a chain reaction, with pins flying in all directions until not a single one remains standing. The screen above flashes "STRIKE!"

Bebe leaps to her feet, her face lit with excitement, bouncing on her toes. "Luke!" she squeals, clapping rapidly. "That was perfect! How did you do it?" Her enthusiasm is so genuine, so uninhibited, that I can't help but grin back at her.

"Luck," I say with mock modesty, even as warmth spreads through my chest at her reaction.

"Psh, whatever," Wes scoffs, rising from his seat. "If you're through fangirling over my little brother's lucky shot, let me show you how it's done. Watch and learn, little roomie."

He saunters up the lane with his typical swagger, twirling

his neon green ball between his fingers like it weighs nothing. Unlike Chase's theatrical approach or my focused one, Wes treats the lane like he's walking onto a football field—confident, loose-limbed, and utterly in his element.

Without much setup, he launches the ball hurtling down the lane with raw power. It rockets straight toward the pins, smashing into them with such force that they scatter as if a grenade has hit them. Another STRIKE! flashes on the screen, and Wes turns with his arms raised in victory.

He saunters back to our group with a cocky grin plastered across his face, his hand raised high toward Bebe, who has a stunned smile on her face. "That's how it's done! High five, roomie!"

She hesitates for a second, looking at his hand like she's trying to remember what the appropriate response is, before slapping her palm against his. The sound is louder than I expected from her small frame, and Wes actually winces a little.

"Damn, the girl's got some power," he laughs, shaking his hand out.

"Sorry," she murmurs, then straightens her shoulders. "I guess it's my turn now." There's determination in her voice, despite the nervous way she fidgets with the sleeves of my sweatshirt.

She carefully picks up her glittering pink ball, cradling it against her chest as she approaches the lane. She takes a tentative step forward, then stops, looking down at her feet.

"Wait, hold on," Wes calls out, jumping up from his seat. "Let me help you."

He positions himself behind Bebe, his chest nearly pressed against her back. His hands slide around her waist, fingers splaying across the fabric of my sweatshirt as he adjusts her stance.

"You need to stand like this," he instructs as he guides her hips into position.

I glance at Chase, finding his eyes already on me. His expression is an obvious challenge—a raised eyebrow that silently asks if I'm really going to sit here while Wes gets his hands all over her.

His hands move to her shoulders, lingering there longer than necessary. Something possessive and unfamiliar floods through me. I'm on my feet before I can even process what I'm doing.

"Actually," I say, my voice coming out more commanding than I intended, "I'll show you."

Wes's eyes meet mine over Bebe's head, a smirk playing at his lips. He steps back with exaggerated graciousness, hands raised in surrender.

"By all means, little brother," he says, winking at Chase as he returns to his seat. "She's all yours."

I realize immediately that I've walked right into their trap. The conspiratorial look between my brothers confirms it— they've played me perfectly, using my obvious attraction to manipulate me into action. But now that I'm here, standing behind Bebe with her looking at me expectantly, those mismatched eyes wide and trusting, I can't bring myself to regret it.

Chapter Seven

BEBE

LUKE TAKES Wes's place behind me, and I'm even more nervous than before; like I'm going to embarrass myself.

"First, let's adjust your stance," he says, his voice low near my ear. Unlike Wes's showy instructions, Luke's approach is methodical. His hands settle on my shoulders with gentle pressure, turning me slightly. "Face the pins directly, feet shoulder-width apart."

I follow his guidance, hyperaware of his proximity.

"Now, hold the ball like this." His arms encircle me from behind, his hands covering mine on the bowling ball. I feel the solid warmth of his chest against my back, his breath stirring in my hair. "Three fingers in the holes, not too tight."

My heart hammers as he adjusts my grip, his fingertips brushing against mine with deliberate care. The technical instruction is clear, but there's an undeniable electricity at each point of contact between us.

"When you approach," he continues, one hand sliding to

my waist to guide me forward, "keep your steps smooth and even."

We move together, his body shadowing mine as we take three synchronized steps toward the lane. His hand stays at my waist, thumb brushing against the fabric of his sweatshirt.

"Now, on your final step, swing the ball back like this," he guides my arm through the motion, our bodies swaying together, "and release at the bottom of your swing, aiming for the arrows on the lane."

After we complete the practice motion, he steps back, his warmth suddenly gone. I nearly stumble at the loss of contact.

"You've got this, Bebe," he says, those blue eyes locked on mine. "Try it on your own now."

Something shifts inside me at his words. Not just the encouragement, but the genuine belief behind it. He thinks I can do this. And suddenly, I *know* I can.

I square my shoulders, a familiar sense of focus washing over me. This is no different from the countless skills Gabriel made me master. If I can field strip a Glock 19 blindfolded in under thirty seconds, I can certainly roll a ball down a wooden lane.

Taking a deep breath, I position myself exactly as he showed me. Three steps forward, smooth swing back, eyes on the arrows. I release the ball with perfect timing, my wrist flicking slightly to add just a hint of spin. The pink ball glides down the center of the lane, maintaining a perfect trajectory toward the pins.

CRASH!

Nine pins explode in a spectacular cascade, leaving one stubborn pin wobbling at the far right before steadying itself, refusing to fall.

I spin around, startled by the eruption of noise behind me. Wes and Chase are on their feet, whooping and hollering like they've just witnessed a miracle.

"Holy shit!" Chase exclaims, hands raised above his head in celebration.

"Are you kidding me?" Wes shouts, his voice carrying over the music. "First time ever? That's insane!"

Their enthusiasm is infectious, and I find myself breaking into a wide, genuine smile. My eyes instinctively search for Luke, finding him already moving toward me. His face is lit with pride. Before I can process what's happening, his arms are around me, lifting me slightly off the ground in a spontaneous embrace.

"That was incredible," he murmurs against my hair, his voice vibrating through my entire body.

For a second, I freeze; physical affection isn't something I'm accustomed to. In my world, touch is usually calculated—a means to an end, whether in combat training or the rare formal events for family pictures—for show. But something about the warmth of Luke's arms around me feels... right. I relax into his embrace, allowing myself this moment of pure joy.

"Thanks to you," I say as he sets me down, suddenly shy.

His hands linger at my waist before he steps back, a smile still lighting his face. "That was all you."

I slide my Converses back on, feeling a strange nostalgia as I hand the bowling shoes to the attendant. The night passed in a blur of laughter, friendly competition, and more genuine fun than I've experienced in... maybe ever.

I kneel to tie my laces slowly, savoring these last moments before we head back to the house. Tonight felt like something from another life—a glimpse into what normal could feel like. No assassination targets, no family obligations, no impending arranged marriage.

As I straighten, I spot them across the alley—Chase and Luke huddled with two girls at lane twelve. The blonde leans toward Luke, tossing her hair over her shoulder as she laughs at something he's said. Her friend, a tall brunette, has her hand on Chase's arm, standing close enough that their shoulders touch.

Something cold and unfamiliar twists in my stomach. I watch as the blonde reaches out to touch Luke's chest.

"They know practically everyone here," Wes's voice startles me as he appears at my side, two bottles of water in hand. He follows my gaze, a knowing look crossing his face. "Don't worry about them, little roomie."

I take the water he offers, trying to look casual. "Oh, them?"

He raises an eyebrow, unconvinced. "The blonde is Ashley. She's been attempting to hook up with one of us, especially Luke, since freshman year. He's not interested." He takes a swig from his bottle.

"It's none of my business," I say.

He chuckles, his eyes gleaming with mischief. "Oh, I think it is. Come on."

Before I can protest, his warm hand wraps around mine, fingers interlacing with surprising gentleness. With confident strides, he pulls me across the bowling alley toward Luke and Chase's little social circle.

"Ladies, have you met our new roommate?" Wes announces as we approach, his voice carrying a natural authority that makes people instinctively turn their heads.

Four pairs of eyes snap to us—Chase's curious, the two girls' assessing, and Luke's... something I can't quite decipher flashes across those blue depths when his gaze drops to our joined hands.

The blonde—Ashley—gives me a quick once-over, her smile tightening at the corners. "Roommate? I thought you were looking for another guy."

"We were," Chase jumps in, "but Bebe blew all the competition away."

The brunette's gaze narrows as she studies me more closely, her eyes lingering on the Dalton U sweatshirt I'm wearing.

"Do you go to Dalton? I've never seen you around campus before," she says, her tone casual but with an unmistakable edge of territorial suspicion.

I open my mouth to explain, but Luke steps forward, moving slightly between us. His shoulder brushes against mine as he answers for me, and Wes releases my hand.

"She's wearing my sweatshirt," he says, his voice calm but carrying a subtle note of possessiveness that sends a small thrill through me. "Bebe's starting at Dalton on Monday."

Something flickers across the brunette's face—surprise, maybe disappointment, before she masks it with a polite smile. "Oh, cool."

"Yeah, we'll have to show you around campus," Ashley says, her eyes darting between Luke and me. She steps closer to him, her manicured hand about to find its way to his arm. "We could all grab coffee sometime."

Luke clears his throat intentionally. "We should probably head out," he announces, already turning me toward the exit.

"It was nice meeting you," I call over my shoulder, not entirely sure if I meant it.

As Luke guides me through the crowd, his hand remains firmly at my waist. Wes follows close behind. Chase catches up quickly, falling into step beside me, his arm lightly touching mine with each stride.

Outside the bowling alley, the night air feels refreshingly cool against my flushed skin as we walk toward the parking lot.

"That was really fun," I admit as we approach the Jeep. "Thank you for taking me."

"Your first bowling experience was a success?" Luke asks.

"Definitely," I nod, smiling at him.

Chase gives my shoulder a gentle bump with his. "You're a quick learner."

Wes unlocks the Jeep with a beep, the headlights flashing twice in the darkness. "All aboard the Sullivan express," he announces with exaggerated grandeur, sliding into the driver's seat.

Chase claims shotgun with a triumphant "Called it!" leaving me to share the back seat with Luke. The Jeep's open-air design means we're exposed to the elements, with only roll bars and the windshield.

Luke's thigh presses against mine as Wes backs out of the parking space. The contact sends a shiver through me that has nothing to do with the night air. I try to shift, giving him more room, but the Jeep's back seat is designed for groceries, not people, and there's nowhere to go.

"Sorry," Luke murmurs, his breath warm against my ear. "Not much space back here."

"It's okay," I whisper, hyperaware of every inch where our bodies touch.

Chase cranks up the radio as we pull onto the main road, some upbeat pop song blasting through the speakers. The acceleration pushes me slightly into Luke's side, and his arm instinctively comes around my shoulders to steady me.

As we hit the highway, the wind whips around us and I tug at my carefully secured ponytail. Strands of hair come loose, dancing wildly around my face as we speed by on the empty roads. The wind's roar drowns out most conversation, creating a private bubble in the backseat. I tilt my head back, gazing at the distant stars that blur above us through the open roof, feeling strangely free.

I feel Luke's eyes on me before I turn to meet his gaze. He's been watching me; studying my profile against the passing streetlights, the way the wind plays with my hair, the smile I can't suppress. When our eyes lock, he doesn't look away. Instead, his lips curve into a soft, genuine smile that makes his eyes crinkle at the corners. Without breaking eye contact, he places his warm hand over my bare knee.

My breath catches. This isn't the casual bumping of shoulders or the practical guidance at the bowling alley. This is intentional—a silent acknowledgment of whatever has been building between us all evening.

I should move his hand—establish boundaries. I should remember that in nine months, I'll belong to someone else.

Instead, I let my hand rest on top of his. He turns his palm upwards; our hands come together, his long fingers sliding between mine, finding their perfect fit. The simple gesture feels more intimate than any touch I've experienced before. My pulse quickens, and I can't help but look down at our joined hands resting on my knee, marveling at how right it feels.

When I glance back up, Luke is still watching me. There's a question in them, a silent seeking of permission that makes my heart skip. I answer by tightening my grip ever so slightly.

Chapter Eight

LUKE

A THUD, followed by what sounds like something hitting the wall, comes from Bebe's room. I pause outside her door, my hand hovering over the knob.

It's been three days since we've been bowling, and while we've fallen into an easy rhythm around the house, that moment in the Jeep with our hands intertwined hasn't been mentioned. Just comfortable smiles and lingering glances across the dinner table.

"Motherfucking piece of shit!" Her voice carries through the cracked door, frustration clear in every syllable.

I can't help but smile. Hearing those words in her sweet voice is oddly adorable.

"Son of a bitch," she mutters, followed by another thud. "I am going to cut you limb by limb."

Concerned and admittedly curious, I knock gently on her door. What could be causing her this much distress?

"Come in," she calls, sounding defeated.

I push the door open to find Bebe sitting cross-legged on the floor surrounded by wood boards, pegs, screws, and what appears to be the remnants of an IKEA desk. Various pieces are scattered around her in no discernible order, and she's holding a hex key in one hand and a crumpled instruction sheet in the other. Her hair is piled messily on top of her head, and there's a smudge of something—dust or maybe wood stain—across her cheek.

"What's going on here?" I ask, attempting to suppress my amusement at the chaos surrounding her. "I came to see what all the cursing was about."

She looks up at me with those mismatched eyes, her bottom lip jutting out in the most adorable pout I've ever seen. "I'm trying to put this stupid desk together," she huffs, blowing a stray strand of hair from her face. "But it's impossible. Look at this!" She thrusts the instruction sheet up toward me. "There are no words, Luke. Just pictures. How is anyone supposed to understand this?"

I bite back a laugh as I take the paper from her. The familiar IKEA pictograms stare back at me. "Do you want some help with this?" I offer, gesturing to the furniture disaster zone around her.

Her eyes light up instantly. She presses her palms together in front of her chest like she's praying. "Please," she says with such genuine relief I find endearing. "I was hoping it would assemble itself through intimidation." She huffs. "But that's clearly not working."

I raise an eyebrow. "You? Intimidating?"

"I have my moments," she says with a smirk.

I laugh. "Scoot over a bit."

She shifts to make room for me on the floor, clearing away

some screws and wooden dowels. I settle in beside her, our knees almost touching as I survey the battlefield of parts.

"First things first," I say, picking up what should be the desktop. "I think you've got this upside down. See these pre-drilled holes? They should face the other way."

"Oh," she says, with a hint of embarrassment coloring her cheeks. "That... would explain a lot."

I start by undoing some pieces she's already assembled incorrectly, carefully removing the screws without stripping them. She watches intently, learning from my movements.

"Can you hand me that longer screw? The one with the flat head," I ask, pointing to a piece beyond my reach.

She quickly locates it and places it in my palm, our fingers brushing briefly.

"Thanks," I say, inserting it into the pre-drilled hole. As I twist it in place, my gaze drifts to her nightstand, where a small silver frame sits. The photograph inside shows an attractive couple in their forties—the woman with Bebe's same cinnamon-colored hair.

"Are those your parents?" I ask, nodding toward the picture.

She follows my stare, her expression softening. "Yeah," she says quietly, reaching over to pick up the frame. Her thumb traces the edge of the photo with gentle reverence. "They died when I was six."

I stop working on the desk, the screw half-turned. "I'm sorry, Bebe. That's... I can't imagine losing both parents so young."

And now I understand why her brothers raised her.

She shrugs. "It was a long time ago." She sets the frame back on the nightstand, carefully adjusting its position.

"What about you?" she asks, her voice taking on a deliberately lighter tone. "Are your parents still around? Together?"

"Yeah, they live here in Ambrose. My dad's a property manager in town."

She tilts her head, studying me. "So you've lived here your whole life?"

"Born at Ambrose General, raised five miles from here," I confirm, returning to the desk assembly. "Sullivan men have been attending Dalton University for generations. My great-grandfather, grandfather, my dad, and all my uncles. It's practically a family tradition at this point."

What I don't mention is how deeply that tradition runs—the secret meetings in wine cellars, the oaths taken by candlelight, the network that extends far beyond graduation. The Keepers aren't something you discuss with outsiders, no matter how captivating their mismatched eyes might be.

"What about you?" I ask, changing the subject as I align two pieces of wood. "Where are you from?"

"Los Angeles," she says, handing me another screw. "Born and raised."

"City girl, huh? Quite a change, coming to a small college town like Ambrose."

"That was kind of the point," she admits, her eyes flickering to where our knees almost touch. "I needed something different."

"Did you go to one of those fancy private schools in L.A.?"

She hesitates, tucking a loose strand of hair behind her ear. "Actually, I was homeschooled."

"That explains it," I say with a smile, connecting another piece to the frame.

"Explains what?" she asks, her brow furrowing.

"Your excitement about bowling," I reply, glancing up to meet her gaze. "Most people take things like that for granted, but you looked at it like it was the most amazing thing you'd ever seen."

A blush creeps across her cheeks, and she busies herself with organizing the remaining screws. "Was it that obvious?"

"In the best possible way," I assure her. "So how was homeschooling? I've always wondered what that would be like."

She's quiet for a moment, weighing her response. "It had its advantages. The one-on-one teaching was incredible. My brother made sure I had excellent tutors, so I learned much more than I would have in a regular school. But I missed out on all the normal stuff. Prom, field trips, friends to go bowling with..." Her voice softens. "Sometimes I wonder if that's why my social skills are so... awkward. Interacting with people my age doesn't come naturally to me."

I have noticed the way she sometimes hesitates before responding, like she's calculating the correct reaction.

"That's why Dalton is so important to you," I say, understanding dawning. College isn't just education for her; it's the life she never had.

She nods, a spark of appreciation lighting her eyes that I understand. "This is my chance to experience all those things I read about in books but never actually lived."

Our gazes lock, the air between us suddenly charged with something I can't quite name. Her eyes hold mine, the green one catching the light from her bedside lamp while the brown-blue one seems to absorb it. I notice flecks of gold near her pupil that I hadn't seen before, like tiny sunbursts radiating outward.

I can't look away, drawn into their depths like they contain secrets I desperately want to uncover. The desk parts lay forgotten between us as seconds stretch into a moment that feels significant, weighted with unspoken words.

"Sorry," I murmur, realizing I've been staring too intently. "I just can't get over your eyes. They're... mesmerizing."

A pink flush spreads across her cheeks while a mischievous smile tugs at the corners of her lips.

"If we're being honest," she says, her voice dropping to a whisper, "I might find myself staring at you sometimes too."

"What? No way," I reply, feeling a ridiculous grin spread across my face.

"It's true," she says with a small shrug, looking down at the desk pieces scattered around us. "You're... distracting."

My heart rate kicks up several notches, and warmth blooms in my chest. She's attracted to me. The way she says it—like an admission of guilt—makes me want to reach across the half-built desk and touch her face, trace the curve of her jaw with my fingertips.

I wonder if she feels this electric current between us—this pull that's been there since the moment she walked into our house. The chemistry that makes every accidental brush of our hands feel like touching a live wire.

"Well, make that two of us being distracted then," I say, reaching for another piece of the desk, channeling my nervous energy into productivity. "Let's finish this, shall we?"

The air between us remains charged as we work together, our fingers occasionally brushing as we pass tools back and forth. I guide her through the process, showing her how to align the drawer rails and secure the desktop to the frame. Her quick mind catches on rapidly, and soon she's anticipating which pieces I need before I ask.

"Last screw," I announce, tightening it with a final twist of the hex key. "And... we're done."

I stand, dusting off my jeans before offering her my hand. She takes it, her small palm warm against mine as I pull her to her feet. Together, we lift the completed desk and position it in the corner by the window.

Bebe immediately wheels her computer chair over, pulling it up to her new workspace. She sits with a satisfied smile and tucks her legs up to her chest, wrapping her arms around her knees. The late afternoon sunlight streams through the window, highlighting the gold strands in her cinnamon hair. She looks so perfectly at home—like she belongs in this room, in our house, in my life.

"Thank you, Luke," she says, turning her head to look up at me, those mismatched eyes filled with gratitude. "I would have been at this all night without you."

Something about her sitting here, bathed in sunlight, looking at me with a soft expression, breaks through my last shred of restraint. I reach for the chair and spin it gently until she faces me directly, my hands grip the armrests as I lean down toward her. Her eyes widen slightly, but she doesn't pull away.

My lips brush against her forehead, a feather-light kiss that lingers just long enough to breathe in the scent of her hair— vanilla.

When I straighten, her eyes are closed, her lips parted. Her eyes flutter open, blinking at me with an expression I can't quite read—surprise, wonder, and something else that makes my heart race.

"I should probably let you enjoy your new desk," I say, taking a step back, my voice unexpectedly hoarse. My heart hammers in my chest as I try to process what just happened— what I just did.

Her fingers drift up to touch the spot where my lips pressed against her skin, a small smile curving her mouth. "Luke..." she breathes, my name almost spoken like a question.

I take another step backward, suddenly uncertain. Did I cross a line? Move too fast? The moment had felt so right, but now doubt creeps in. We're roommates. This could complicate everything.

"I'll see you at dinner," I say, continuing my retreat toward the door. "Chase is making his famous meatballs tonight."

I close the door behind me and lean against it, exhaling slowly. What am I doing? One minute I'm holding her hand— helping her build a desk the next, and now, I'm kissing her forehead like we're... what exactly?

Chapter Nine

BEBE

COLLEGE IS HELL. The first day of school was rougher than I expected.

The lecture hall was packed wall-to-wall with students, some looking just as disoriented as I felt. Philosophy 101 seemed like a good foundational course, but I wasn't expecting Professor Murray to be a human tornado. The moment he entered the room, he launched into Aristotle's ethics without so much as a "good morning," somehow cramming what felt like five entire chapters into our hour and a half slot.

By the thirty-minute mark, my hand was cramping from taking notes. He'd already covered the entire history of Greek philosophy. I glanced at the whiteboard, now completely filled with his spidery cursive handwriting.

It had become a chaotic tapestry of philosophical concepts, arrows connecting seemingly random ideas, and underlined phrases that apparently held special significance. In some sections, his handwriting deteriorated until it resembled electrocardiogram readings more than actual words.

The guy sitting next to me had his head thrown back, mouth open, emitting soft snores that occasionally hitched into a snort. He hadn't even bothered to take out a notebook. A thin line of drool glistened at the corner of his lips, and he'd been asleep since approximately minute seven of the lecture.

I stared at him in disbelief. How could anyone sleep through a class when they pay money to go here?

When the lecture finally ended, I gathered my notes—a mess of half-finished sentences and question marks.

College 1, Bebe 0

I stumbled out of the hall in desperate need of caffeine. I felt like someone had put my brain through a blender and poured it back into my skull.

The campus coffee stand wasn't far from the philosophy building, a wooden kiosk with a cheerful blue awning that read "Dalton Brews" in curling white script. The line was mercifully short, just two people ahead of me, both looking as shell-shocked as I felt.

"Medium Americano, please," I said when it was my turn, fishing in my bag for my wallet.

The barista, a guy with blue spiked hair, gave a sympathetic nod. "Murray's 101 class?" he asked, already reaching for the largest cup they offered.

I blinked in surprise. "How did you know?"

"That thousand-yard stare," he chuckled, filling my cup. "I get at least ten of you every Monday. First semester?"

I nodded, handing over my card.

Two minutes later, I had my prize—steaming hot coffee in

a paper cup that promised to restore at least some of my cognitive function after surviving philosophical whiplash. The warmth radiated through my hands, promising the alertness I desperately needed. I brought the cup to my lips and took that first heavenly sip, closing my eyes as the bitter warmth spread through me. *Perfection.*

I closed my eyes, savoring the moment of peace before my next class. Just as I tilted the cup for another sip, something solid collided with my shoulder. The impact wasn't hard, but it was enough. My coffee tilted in slow motion, the lid popping off as scalding liquid cascaded down my front, soaking my white t-shirt and leaving a spreading brown stain.

"Sorry!" a guy on a mountain bike called over his shoulder, already pedaling away. He didn't even slow down. Just continued weaving through the crowded pathway, narrowly missing other students.

"Are you kidding me?" I gasped, more from shock than pain, though the heat against my skin was quickly becoming uncomfortable. I looked down at myself—the damage was impressive. My once-white shirt now featured a Rorschach test of coffee, perfectly showcasing what appeared to be a sad face if you tilted your head just right.

Several students turned to stare; some with sympathy, others barely concealing their giggles.

"Great. Just great," I mutter, plucking the soaked fabric away from my skin.

College 2, Bebe 0.

After trying to salvage and dry my t-shirt in the women's room, I stepped back outside. I spotted a campus store across the quad. As I made my way toward it, I noticed the main pathway had transformed. Where it had been relatively empty earlier, now it was lined with tables draped in colorful banners —Greek letters prominently displayed on each one.

Rush week. I'd completely forgotten.

I wandered to the displays, drawn by curiosity more than anything else. Each table was meticulously decorated with photo collages of smiling girls at formals, charity events, and beach retreats. The word "sisterhood" appeared on nearly every poster and pamphlet.

I paused at a table adorned with pink and silver balloons, where three young women stood behind a pristine white tablecloth. Their matching pale blue blazers and pearl necklaces create an image of polished perfection. Each of them had the same sleek blowout, as if they had visited the same salon this morning.

Sisterhood. The word echoes in my mind as I approach. What would it be like to have sisters instead of brothers? To share clothes? To have late-night talks about crushes?

"Hi!" I said, trying to sound enthusiastic despite my disheveled appearance. "I'm new here and—"

The tallest girl's smile freezes as her gaze dropped to my coffee-stained shirt. The other two exchanged a quick glance, their perfectly glossed lips twitching slightly.

"Oh, honey," said the one with highlighted blonde hair, not bothering to hide her disdain. "Did you have a little accident?"

I looked down at my shirt, suddenly self-conscious. "Yeah, some guy on a bike—"

"Kappa Epsilon is looking for girls who represent our values of elegance and poise, in fact," the blonde continued, tilting her head with a fake smile, "I think Lambda Chi might be more your... speed." She pointed vaguely toward the end of the row. "They're less particular about appearances."

The deliberate insult landed like a slap. Heat crept up my neck as the three of them shared barely concealed smirks. I opened my mouth to respond—though whether with an apology or a cutting remark, I'm not sure—when a familiar voice called out behind me.

"Bebe? Thought it was you."

Wes appeared at my side, his gym bag slung over one shoulder, hair still damp from what must have been a post-workout shower. The sorority girls instantly transformed—backs straightening, smiles widening, eyes brightening with recognition.

"Oh my God, Wes Sullivan!" The tallest one practically purred. "Are you ready for Saturday's game?"

He doesn't even glance their way, his attention focused entirely on me. He notices my stained shirt and frowns. "What happened?"

"Bike collision," I mumbled, embarrassment making my cheeks burn hotter. "Coffee casualty."

Without hesitation, he dropped his gym bag onto the ground and unzipped it. "Here," he said, rummaging through his things before pulling out a neatly folded gray t-shirt with the Dalton Dragons logo across the chest. "Always keep extras. Comes with being an athlete—you never know when you'll need a change."

The sorority girls' expressions shifted from dismissive to impressed as they watched our interaction, clearly reassessing me considering Wes's obvious familiarity.

"Thanks," I said gratefully, accepting the soft cotton

fabric. "You're a lifesaver." It'll be huge on me, but anything's better than walking around in a coffee-stained disaster all day.

His eyes drifted to the table beside us, taking in the decorations, the glossy recruitment pamphlets. A teasing grin spreads across his face.

"Sorority rush, huh?" he asked, eyebrows raised. "Already planning on leaving me and my brothers for a house full of sisters?"

My cheeks warmed. "No, just curious," I reply. "I was heading to the campus store when I got... sidetracked."

He nodded, understanding softening his features. "Good. We'd miss our little roomie." He gave me a gentle nudge with his shoulder. "Can't have these girls stealing you from us." He picked up his gym bag, slinging it back over his shoulder. "I've got a team meeting, but I'll see you at home later, yeah?"

"Yeah, thanks again for the shirt."

As Wes walked away, the three sorority girls immediately swarmed closer.

"So," the blonde one said, her voice dripping with newfound interest, "you live with Wes Sullivan?"

"We're having a mixer this Friday," another one added eagerly, pushing a flyer into my hands. "You should totally come! We'd love to have you!"

I glanced at the glossy paper, then back up at their fake smiles. The same girls who seconds ago couldn't be bothered to introduce themselves are now looking at me like I'm their ticket to Wes.

"Sorry," I said, handing the flyer back with a polite smile. "I have to get to class." I paused, unable to resist adding, "After class, I'll be heading home. To where I live with Wes and his brothers. Gotta run!" I called over my shoulder, walking away.

The petty satisfaction I feel is probably beneath me, but after their earlier dismissal, I can't help but enjoy their shock.

College 2, Bebe 1

The rest of the day passes in a blur of syllabi reviews and awkward icebreakers. By the time my last class ends, my brain feels like mush, and my feet ache from traveling across the sprawling campus.

I trudge up the sidewalk to our house, my shoulders hunched under the weight of my backpack and first-day exhaustion. Fumbling with my keys, I finally manage to unlock the door and practically fall inside.

Luke and Chase look up from the couch where they're playing a video game, controllers in hand. Their faces shift from concentration to amusement as they watch me dramatically drop my backpack with a thud.

"I'm quitting," I announce, dragging myself across the living room. "One day of college is enough for me. I've experienced it. I'm good."

I collapse between them on the couch, letting my head fall back against the cushions. Chase pauses the game, both brothers turning to look at me with matching expressions of sympathy and humor.

"That bad, huh?" Luke asks.

"Worse," I groan. "Professor Thompson might actually be Satan. And some jerk on a bike ruined my shirt. And I'm pretty sure I signed up for a math class that requires knowledge I definitely don't have."

"Welcome to college," Luke laughs. "Trust me, every

freshman goes through this," he says, his smile genuine and reassuring. "I spent my entire first week convinced I'd accidentally registered for graduate-level courses."

"Seriously," Chase chimes in, leaning forward to grab his water bottle from the coffee table. "Last year I walked into the wrong classroom and sat through twenty minutes of Advanced Biochemistry before realizing I was supposed to be in English Lit. The professor continued talking about molecular structures, and I kept thinking it was some weird metaphor for Shakespeare."

I laugh at the mental image of him frantically trying to connect DNA helixes to Hamlet's soliloquies.

"It gets better," Luke promises, his voice softening. His hand comes to rest on my thigh, warm and steady through the fabric of my jeans.

The weight of his palm sends a flutter through my stomach. His thumb moves in a small, comforting circle, and something inside me shifts. Before I can overthink it, I slide closer to him on the couch, tucking myself against his side. The faint scent of Luke's cologne fills my senses, making me feel at ease.

He stiffens momentarily, then relaxes, his arm sliding around my shoulders and pulling me closer. The warmth of his body, the feeling of his steady heartbeat under his thin t-shirt, is exactly what I need after this exhausting day.

"Would you guys mind if I took a nap right here while you play?" I murmur against the soft cotton of his t-shirt. "I don't think I can make it to my bedroom."

Luke and Chase both laugh, the sound vibrating through Luke's chest against my cheek.

"Make yourself comfortable," Chase says, his voice tinged

with amusement. "But fair warning—we get pretty competitive. There might be shouting."

"I don't care," I mumble, my eyes already drifting closed. "I could sleep through a 7.0 earthquake right now."

Luke's arm tightens around me, his fingers absently tracing patterns on my shoulder. "Sleep all you want," he whispers. "I've got you."

Chapter Ten

LUKE

"THE L.A. CHAPTER IS GETTING DESPERATE," Wes says, leaning back in his chair. His plate of half-eaten pasta salad sits forgotten as he taps his fingers against the polished wood. "The police don't seem to know the connection between the three victims—being Keepers."

I take a swig of my beer, letting the cold liquid wash down my throat. "And they're certain it's The Killer Bee?"

Chase nods. "All the hallmarks were there—honey residue in the bloodstream, the hexagon token on their tongues. The Elders are convinced we're being hunted."

"But why? Why would The Bee want to kill Keepers?" I ask, running a hand through my hair. "We're hardly worth assassinating."

Wes shrugs.

Chase shifts in his seat, his expression serious as always when it comes to Keeper business. "We just have to find the connection between them other than being Keepers."

"How would we know?" I ask. "Grand Master Maxwell is the one in charge of his Chapter. He hasn't found a connection or shared with dad anything on his belief of why The Bee would kill Keepers? I mean, come on..."

"No," Chase confirms. "He has shared no reason his Chapters members are being targeted."

The front door opens suddenly, and we all tense. Bebe appears in the doorway, her arms carrying grocery bags. She freezes when she notices our serious expressions.

"I'm sorry," she says, her voice soft with genuine apology. "I didn't mean to interrupt."

Her eyes dart between us as she shifts the weight of the grocery bags, clearly sensing the unease in the room.

"It's fine," I say quickly, watching as she moves past our little gathering toward the kitchen.

Chase immediately pushes back from the table. "Let me help with those," he offers, rising to follow her.

I can't help but notice how she's dressed today. A cropped cream-colored sweater that reveals inches of her midriff, low-waisted jean shorts that accentuate the curve of her hips, and those beat-up Converse she seems to live in. It's such a simple outfit, but on her it looks like something from a magazine spread. Her hair flows down her back, with wispy tendrils framing her face that make me want to reach out and tuck them behind her ear.

I push out my chair from the table as she comes to stand by me and pull her down on my lap, and she sits sideways.

Her small frame tenses momentarily in surprise before relaxing against me. The subtle scent of her vanilla shampoo fills my senses as her hair brushes my cheek.

Her eyes dart to Wes, who's watching us with a raised eyebrow and that infuriating, knowing smirk of his.

"We were talking about that serial killer," I say casually, as if having her perched on my lap is the most natural thing in the world. My arm slides around her waist, steadying her. "The Killer Bee."

"Oh," she breathes and straightens her back. "That's... quite the conversation topic. Why the interest?"

"Chase is writing about it for one of his criminal justice classes," Wes lies. We can't tell her about the society.

"Yeah," Chase chimes in quickly, picking up Wes's lie. "Professor Derry assigned this case study. The psychological profile is fascinating."

Bebe shifts slightly, and I tighten my grip instinctively. It strikes me that this is the first time I've touched her since the start of the semester two weeks ago.

I guess she was serious about how we wouldn't notice she was here. Because classes started a few days after she moved in, we hadn't seen her much except in passing. Ten—maybe fifteen minutes here and there—a few dinners. We all have our schedules, I suppose.

"What do you think about The Killer Bee?" Wes asks her.

"I've read a little about it in the papers. It's terrifying to imagine someone like that being out there. But... doesn't he only kill bad people?"

Chase reclines in his chair. "That's what everyone thought at first. The initial victims were all connected to organized crime in some way—drug dealers, money launderers, even a hitman."

"To me, he's taking out the trash the legal system can't touch," Wes adds with a slight smirk.

"But three of his recent targets don't fit the pattern at all," Chase continues. "They were completely clean—no criminal records, not even parking tickets. One was an investment banker, another taught history at a private school, and the third worked for a non-profit."

Her mismatched eyes widen. "Oh, really?"

Chase nods solemnly. "That's what has law enforcement scrambling. The killer's either changing their M.O.—"

"Or," Wes interrupts, "they're targeting people with a different connection no one has figured out yet."

I find my attention drifting away from the conversation. The weight of Bebe on my lap, the softness of her skin beneath my fingertips is far more interesting than theories about some killer. My hand at her waist slides slightly lower, fingers caressing her skin just below the waistband of her shorts. Her body arches almost imperceptibly against my touch, but she doesn't shy away. And it tells me she's okay with it. But I notice Wes's eye watching my fingers. His gaze lingers a beat too long, and when he looks up, our eyes lock.

"Eyes up, brother," I say, my voice low but carrying enough edge that Chase glances between us with raised eyebrows.

Wes's mouth curls into a teasing smirk. "Your fingers are getting dangerously low, *brother*. Just waiting to see if we could catch a glimpse of what Bebe's got going on down there."

She shifts subtly. Her fingertips find mine at her waist, not pushing away but lightly resting over them, acknowledging the contact.

"Doesn't every woman look all the same?" she asks shyly.

"I mean, not *exactly* the same. But I thought it was like... elbows or knees. Just a standard issue."

That's... weirdly innocent. Kinda sweet though.

"Oh sweet Bebe, definitely not," Chase answers immediately, his eyes widening at her question.

Wes shakes his head emphatically. "Every woman is like... a unique snowflake down there."

"Hair for starters—some women shave completely," Chase explains, leaning forward with interest. "Others trim, or go Brazilian. I've seen some creative—shaped like a heart, and some go full natural, resembling a 70s retro situation."

"Then there's the whole symmetry factor," Wes continues, warming to the topic with concerning enthusiasm. "Lips can be different sizes, different colors—"

"And texture," Chase adds, gesturing vaguely with his hands. "Some are smooth, others more... ruffled."

"Jesus Christ," I mutter, shaking my head. *Are we really having this conversation?*

"She asked," Wes shrugs, a mischievous glint in his eyes. "We're just being educational."

"What about you, Bebe?" Chase asks with a smirk and a hint of a challenge. "What's your... hair situation?"

I expect her to be mortified, to jump off my lap and flee the room, but not before slapping him across the face. Instead, she surprises me by tilting her head thoughtfully.

"Um..." she pauses, her fingers still laced with mine. "It's a stripe, I guess..."

Chase nearly chokes on his beer. Wes's eyebrows shoot up, clearly not expecting such a direct response. Then both of them nod and groan with approval.

"The landing strip—perfect choice..." Chase says.

I, too, am quietly pleased. The mental image her words conjure makes me shift uncomfortably beneath her.

"What about..." Bebe hesitates, her voice dropping lower. "Do guys have preferences? For how women look... everywhere?"

"Some do," Wes says, leaning forward with interest. "But it entirely depends on the guy."

"What about breasts?" she asks.

"Well," Chase rubs the back of his neck, "I don't mind small chests. I'm more of an ass man myself. The perfect curve, you know? That's what catches my eye first."

Wes nods enthusiastically. "True, though I appreciate a nice chest, too. But D-cups can be too much. Most guys just want a handful." He holds his palms out, cupping invisible breasts. "Not too big, not too small."

I notice her glance down at her chest as she subtly assesses herself through her sweater.

I lean forward, my lips brushing against the shell of her ear. "You're perfect," I whisper.

A shiver runs through her body, and she relaxes against me. Her cheeks flush pink, but there's a small, private smile playing at the corners of her mouth.

"What about you, Luke?" Wes asks, his eyes dancing with mischief. "What's your preference?"

I hesitate, considering my answer. The truth is, I'm drawn to a very specific type of woman these days—one with mismatched eyes and cinnamon hair who's currently sitting on my lap.

"I like—"

The doorbell's shrill ring cuts through the tension, making Bebe jump against me.

"I'll get it," Chase says, rising from the table and heading toward the front door.

Bebe scrambles off my lap, her face flushed as she straightens her sweater. The sudden absence of her warmth leaves me feeling oddly lonely, but also gives me a chance to adjust myself beneath the table. Wes notices and smirks, making an obscene gesture when Bebe's back is turned. I flip him off.

I shift in my chair, tugging my t-shirt down as footsteps approach. Chase returns with a grim expression, followed by a familiar figure.

"Dad," Wes says, immediately standing. "We weren't expecting you."

Our father stands in the archway, impeccably dressed as always in a tailored charcoal suit despite the casual weekend.

"Who's this?" My father fixes on Bebe with laser-like intensity, his eyes narrowing as he takes in her appearance.

"This is Bebe, Luke's girlfriend, visiting from campus," Wes says smoothly, not missing a beat.

Bebe blinks a few times before standing perfectly still under his gaze, her posture shifting almost imperceptibly— shoulders straightening, chin lifting slightly. The transformation is subtle, but striking. Suddenly she doesn't look like the carefree college girl from moments ago, but someone poised and composed, accustomed to being examined.

"It's relatively new, Mr. Sullivan," she says, her voice carrying a polished quality I haven't heard before.

Dad's eyebrows rise as he gives her a slow once-over, his expression unreadable but undeniably assessing.

"Is that so?" he says, his tone carefully neutral. He extends his hand. "Wesley Sullivan Sr. Pleasure to meet you, young lady."

She steps forward, grasping his palm with surprising composure. "The pleasure is mine."

I step closer to her, my hand finding the small of her back.

"I need to discuss some family business with my sons," my father continues. "Privately. Please go home, dear."

The tension in the room thickens. She stiffens under my touch, though her face remains perfectly composed.

"Of course," she says with a polite smile.

I turn to look at her, my hand still resting on her back. Our eyes meet, and I try to convey everything I can't say out loud—that I'm sorry for the interruption, that I wish she could stay, that I'll explain everything, and that this whole girlfriend charade isn't entirely unwelcome.

"I'll call you later," I tell her, my voice low and intimate.

She nods, understanding passing between us without words. She walks to the front door, plucks her keys from the bowl, and slips out into the afternoon sunshine.

Chapter Eleven

BEBE

I GET into the driver's seat of my Jetta and think about what just happened.

I was just temporarily kicked out of my home... Does their dad not know I live there?

And Mr. Sullivan...

Mr. Sullivan's dismissal—the authoritative way he commanded the room, the expectant pause as he waited for me to leave; it's eerily familiar. Gabriel uses the same tone when he needs to clear a space for "business."

I drum my fingers against the steering wheel, not starting the engine yet. The Sullivan patriarch carries himself with the same calculated power as my brother—shoulders squared, chin slightly elevated, eyes that assess everything in milliseconds. It's the posture of someone accustomed to being obeyed without question.

My mind flashes to countless childhood memories of standing in doorways as Gabriel would say, "Bebe, give us the room," whenever associates arrived for meetings. The same polite but firm dismissal, the same understanding that whatever followed was not for my ears.

What kind of "family business" could the Sullivans be discussing? Something about the way Mr. Sullivan appeared unannounced, the tension that instantly filled the room—it wasn't normal. Not that I know what 'normal' is—but that—isn't it.

I start the car, watching the house through my windshield, and shake my head, clearing my thoughts. This isn't the time to analyze the Sullivan family dynamics. I have more pressing concerns.

The three victims weren't criminals. The words echo in my mind as I shift into reverse and back out of the driveway.

The investment banker. The history teacher. The non-profit guy. Clean records, Chase had said. Not even parking tickets.

My stomach churns as I accelerate down the tree-lined street.

I remember those jobs, and they were all drug related, like most of them have been lately. There's an epidemic of it going around Los Angeles. *But Gabriel wouldn't lie to me about targets... would he?* Each mission has always been presented to me with the documentation as it relates to completing the job with a brief summary of their illicit actions. But I know nothing about the proof of crimes, evidence of corruption, details that justified their elimination.

I merge onto the highway toward the city, gripping the steering wheel so tightly my knuckles turn white.

But if Chase was right... if those three people were innocent...

I need answers.

Traffic thickens as I approach the city's center, towering glass buildings reflecting the late afternoon light.

The parking garage beneath my family's building is cool and dim as I pull into my designated spot. The security guard nods in recognition, pressing the button that summons the private elevator.

"Miss Laurent," he acknowledges.

The ride up feels endless, each floor ticking by as my questions multiply.

I step directly into the penthouse foyer, the marble floor gleaming under recessed lighting. The usual security detail is absent—unusual for a Saturday afternoon. Instead of Gabriel's imposing presence, I'm greeted by the familiar sound of gunfire and explosions coming from the living area.

Rounding the corner, I find my youngest brother, Henri, sprawled across the Italian leather sofa. At thirty, he's all untamed energy, his dark hair falling into his eyes as he frantically works the controller in his hands. The massive screen before him displays a war game where he's currently decimating a line of enemies with a sniper rifle. He glances up at my approach, a wide grin splitting his face.

"Well, if it isn't my Honey Bee," he says, pausing the game. "Come to visit the hive?"

"What are you doing here? Gabriel lives here, not you."

He tosses the controller aside and stretches his long limbs across the sofa. "Marissa's on my case again. Something about attending her parents' anniversary dinner tonight." He rolls his eyes. "Two years of marriage and I'm still not used to having a wife who thinks she can tell me what to do."

I wince at the reminder of his situation. He'd been married

off too—another "necessary alliance" orchestrated by Gabriel. Unlike my impending arrangement with Alessandro, Henri's bride had at least been close to his age.

I plop down beside him, sinking into the plush leather. "Does Gabriel know you're hiding out here?"

"Of course. Big brother's the one who suggested it. What are you doing here? Aren't you supposed to be living the college life right now?"

I sigh, settling deeper into the sofa. "I need to talk to Gabriel about something."

"The college thing was brilliant, you know. Buy as much time as you can."

I look at my brother's profile in the dimming penthouse light. The question burns in my throat, threatening to choke me.

"Henri," I say quietly, "do you think he would ever ask me to... handle someone who wasn't deserving? Someone who wasn't a criminal?"

His playful demeanor vanishes instantly. He sits straight as he turns to face me fully. His eyes, like Gabriel's, narrow with sudden intensity.

"Bebe," he says, his voice dropping to a serious tone I rarely hear from him, "everything he does is for a reason. Every target, every mission—there's a purpose behind it all." He studies my face carefully. "Why are you asking this?"

"I heard something today. About three of The Bee jobs... that the victims were clean. Normal people with no criminal records."

"Listen to me," he says firmly, covering my hand with his. "Gabriel protects this family. He wouldn't send you after anyone without cause, even if that cause isn't immediately obvious to you."

I nod slowly, letting his words sink in. He's right—Gabriel has always protected us and the city. If there were reasons those three people had to die, reasons that weren't in their official records, he would have known.

"You're right," I mumble. "I just wish he'd tell me everything sometimes."

"Need-to-know basis, Bee." He squeezes my hand once before releasing it.

My phone vibrates in my back pocket, the screen lighting up with Luke's name and a photo I snapped of him smiling at dinner last week. My thumb hovers over the screen for a moment before I decline the call.

I turn back to Henri, something cracking open inside me. He's always been the most approachable of my brothers.

"I think I'm in trouble." I whisper.

His eyebrows lift. "What kind of trouble?"

"The kind where I'm crushing on one of my roommates." The confession spits out.

His face instantly crumples. "Oh, Bee," he says, wincing. "That's not good. You know that can only end in heartbreak, right? "

The truth I've been trying to ignore crashes over me in waves. My eyes fill with tears that spill over before I can blink them away. I nod, unable to speak past the lump in my throat.

"Hey, hey," he murmurs, sliding closer on the sofa. His arm wraps around my shoulders, pulling me against his chest. "Come here."

I collapse against him, burying my face in his shirt as quiet sobs shake my body. His hand strokes my hair gently, the way he used to when we were children and I'd skinned my knee or had a nightmare.

"I didn't mean to," I choke out between sobs. "It just happened... he's different. He makes me feel normal."

He pulls me tighter against him, his chin resting on top of my head. "Normal is overrated and temporary."

I nod against his chest, trying to compose myself. His familiar scent—expensive cologne mixed with the faint metallic hint of gun oil—reminds me of home, of who I really am beneath this college girl facade.

"Alessandro is old," I say. "And creepy." I wipe tears from my eyes with my knuckles. "I don't like the way he looks at me."

"I know," Henri says, rubbing his hand down my arm. "I've mentioned it to Gabe. But he just perceives Alessandro to be attracted to you—and that's not a bad thing in his mind."

"Ugh." I pretend to gag, although I might just throw up for real.

"Besides," he continues, "we've all had arranged marriages, and while they are uncomfortable at first, it'll get better."

I huff. "All three of you can't stand your wives," I point out.

Gabriel's wife and kids live in a luxurious suburb outside of Los Angeles, while he remains in the penthouse. Beau and his wife have a child together, but sleep in separate bedrooms. And now here's Henri, hiding from his wife at Gabe's home.

"What?" Henri protests. "I love Marissa... I just need a break now and then; she can be a lot... We're trying now, you know?"

I look at my brother and smile. "That's great." He's trying

to have a baby. Henri would make a wonderful father and would be involved in every way possible.

"Falling for someone isn't the end of the world," he continues. "Just don't let it get serious. Have fun, enjoy whatever it is, but keep your heart locked up tight."

I pull back, wiping tears with the back of my hand. "That's the problem. I don't know if I can." I take a shaky breath.

His expression shifts, the worry lines between his brows softening into something more playful. He sits up straighter, gripping my shoulders.

"Look at me, Bebe," he says. "Who are you?"

I sniffle. "What?"

"You're Bebe fucking Laurent," he declares, giving me a gentle shake. "Mafia princess extraordinaire."

I roll my eyes, already knowing where this is going.

"Don't give me that look," he continues, undeterred. "You're not just some college girl with a crush. You're a badass who's taken down some of the most dangerous men in Los Angeles without breaking a sweat. You think a college boy is going to be your undoing?"

"Henri—"

"No, listen. You've spent your entire life being told what you can and can't do. These nine months? They're yours. All yours." His eyes light up with mischief. "So you like this guy? Great. Have fun with him. Break his heart. Break ten hearts across campus if you want."

"That's not what I—"

"The point is," he interrupts, squeezing my shoulders gently, "you get to choose. For once in your life, you get to be free. Use this time however you want."

"You make it sound so simple," I say, wiping away the last of my tears. "But thank you. You've always had my back when I needed it most."

"Team Bebe forever," he says, nudging my shoulder with his. "So... since you're already here, what do you say? I'll order us a pizza from that place on Wilshire you love, and I can kick your ass in a round of Call of Duty?"

I glance at my phone—my missed call from Luke. I should go back, face whatever is happening between us, and deal with the reality of my situation. But the thought of a few more hours with Henri is too tempting, and maybe, I'm a little homesick.

Chapter Twelve

LUKE

It's almost midnight, and she's still not home nor returned my call.

I roll over again, punching my pillow into a more comfortable shape for what must be the fifteenth time tonight. The red numbers on my alarm clock mock me: 11:47 PM. My phone lies dark and silent on the nightstand where I've been checking it obsessively.

"Where the hell is she?" I mutter into the darkness.

After dad left, I tried calling Bebe, but her phone went to voicemail. At first, I figured she was driving or studying at the library. But as the hours passed with no word, worry crept in.

I throw off the covers and sit up, running my hands through my hair. *What if she's pissed about the girlfriend lie?* It had seemed like a good idea at the moment; dad would never approve of us having a female roommate—but I never got to explain that to her.

The house creaks as I pad down the hallway to check her room again. The door is still open, the bed still made, everything untouched since this morning.

"Luke?"

I nearly jumped at Chase's voice behind me. He's standing in his doorway, rubbing sleep from his eyes, his hair sticking up in all directions.

"You're still up?" he asks, though it's obvious. He leans against his doorframe, studying my face. "You're really worried about her, aren't you?"

I exhale heavily, not bothering to deny it. "It's been hours, Chase."

He crosses his arms, his expression softening. "Have you considered that maybe she just needed space? We kind of threw her into an awkward situation."

"But all night? Without a text or call?" I check my phone again—nothing.

"Look," he says, pushing off from the doorframe and stepping closer, "we barely know her. Maybe this is normal for her. She's not required to check in with any of us."

I sigh. "I know."

He studies me for a long moment. "You really like her, don't you?"

"Yeah," I admit quietly. "I do."

Just as Chase opens his mouth to respond, the distinctive click of the front door lock echoes through the quiet house. My heart leaps in my chest.

"Thank God," I breathe, already moving toward the stairs.

Chase follows close behind as we reach the top of the staircase. The hallway light casts our elongated shadows down the steps as she appears below, climbing slowly. When she glances up and sees me standing there, her entire face transforms—her eyes brightening, lips curving into a smile that chases away the tension I've been carrying for hours.

"Hey," she says softly, continuing up the stairs toward us.

"I was worried about you," I respond, my voice embarrassingly rough with emotion.

She reaches the top step, pausing inches from me. "I'm sorry. My phone died, and I lost track of time. Went to the city and had dinner with my brother."

Chase clears his throat beside me. "Well, now that we know you're not dead in a ditch somewhere, I'm going back to bed," he says. "Night, Bebe, glad you're safe."

"Goodnight, Chase," she whispers, her eyes still fixed on mine as he retreats to his room.

The moment his door clicks shut, her fingers wrap around my wrist. She tugs me toward her bedroom, pulling me inside before quietly closing the door behind us. She leans back against the door, her eyes searching mine.

"I'm sorry, Luke," she murmurs. "I should have called or texted. I didn't mean to worry you."

"It's fine," I say, though we both know it isn't. "I was just... concerned."

She pushes away from the door, closing the distance between us. Her fingers reach up to brush a strand of hair from my forehead, the touch featherlight but electric.

"I'm tired," she says, her eyes never leaving mine. "It's been a long day."

I nod, taking a reluctant step back. "Of course. I'll let you get some rest."

I turn toward the door, my hand reaching for the knob when I feel her fingers tighten on my wrist. The gentle pressure stops me instantly.

"Luke," she whispers, with a hint of vulnerability in her voice I've never heard before. "Would you... would you like to stay with me tonight?"

My breath catches in my throat as the words register. Time seems to suspend between us, the air charged with possibility.

"Yes," I whisper.

Her lips curve into a soft smile, illuminating her face with a warmth that makes my heart stutter. She releases my hand and moves to her dresser, sliding open the top drawer. Her fingers skim over neatly folded clothes before selecting what appears to be a silky pajama set.

"Get in," she says over her shoulder as she pads toward the bathroom. "I'll just be a minute." The door closes with a gentle click.

I stand frozen for a moment, watching her disappear behind the door before glancing down at my grey sweatpants hanging low on my hips, no shirt. I move toward her bed, pulling back the covers. The sheets beneath are a deep burgundy silk, so different from the worn cotton ones on mine. They look expensive, luxurious.

The mattress dips slightly as I slide between the sheets. They smell faintly of her—vanilla and something uniquely Bebe. They're cool against my bare skin, impossibly smooth. I prop myself up against her pillows, waiting. The bathroom door opens with a soft click, and she emerges in the dim light.

My breath catches. The silky pajamas cling to her curves, the shorts revealing long, toned legs that seem to go on forever despite her petite frame. Her tank top dips low, exposing delicate collarbones and the subtle swell of her breasts. But it's her hair that captivates me most—it cascades in flowing waves over her shoulders and down her back.

She stands there briefly, observing me with those extraordinary eyes, a slight smile playing at the corners of her mouth. She's breathtaking without even trying.

She slips beneath the covers beside me, her body radiating warmth as she settles against my side. I lift my arm instinctively, and she nestles into the space I've created, her head finding its place on my chest as if it belongs there.

"Is this okay?" she asks softly, her breath warm against my skin.

"More than okay," I manage, my voice rougher than intended.

My hand extends to the small lamp, fingers reaching the switch and plunging the room into darkness. Only the faint moonlight filtering through her curtains remains, casting silver shadows across her face. The silence between us feels natural, comfortable—like we've done this a hundred times before.

Bebe shifts against me, burrowing closer. Her arm rests on my bare chest, one leg tangling with mine beneath the silken sheets.

I trace lazy patterns on her shoulder with my fingertips, savoring this moment of quiet intimacy. Her breathing has slowed, and I wonder if she's drifting toward sleep. But something gnaws at me. A conversation we need to have—I need to have—words that need to be said.

"I'm sorry about today," I whisper into the darkness. "With my dad. I shouldn't have let Wes introduce you as my girlfriend without warning, and I definitely shouldn't have let my dad send you away."

She stirs against me, tilting her face toward mine, though I can barely make out her features in the faint light.

"It's okay," she murmurs. "I understand."

"That doesn't make it right," I say. "You deserved better than being dismissed like that."

She props herself up on one elbow; her face now hovering above mine, those mismatched eyes somehow visible even in the darkness. "Luke, really. I get it. Family dynamics are... complicated."

"There's something you should know," I confess. "Our father pays for this house. We get monthly allowances too. He thinks we're living here alone, just the three of us. If he knew we were renting out a room for extra cash..."

Bebe's laugh is unexpected—a light, musical sound that breaks the tension.

"So your father doesn't know you're renting out a room in the house he pays for?"

"No," I admit, bracing for her judgment. "That's why Wes introduced you as my girlfriend."

"Actually," she says, her voice taking on a playful tone as she traces her finger along my collarbone. "It was kind of fun pretending to be your girlfriend."

I can feel her smile against my chest as she settles back down, her hair spilling across my skin.

"We should do it again sometime," she adds softly. "I think I was pretty convincing."

I chuckle, trying to sound casual despite the way my heart races at her suggestion. "Yeah, you were great. Very believable."

But my laugh feels hollow, even to my own ears. Because the truth is, I don't want to pretend. I want this—her in my arms, her breath against my skin, her laughter in my ears—to be real.

"Bebe," I whisper, my fingers tangling gently in her hair. The words hover on my lips, dangerous and thrilling. *Should I ask her? Make this official? Tell her that I want her to be my girlfriend?*

Chapter Thirteen

BEBE

HIS HEARTBEAT THRUMS beneath my ear like a secret Morse code I can't quite decipher. His warmth seeps into my bones, making me forget, just for tonight, that I'm not meant to have this.

"Bebe," Luke whispers, my name carrying a slight question.

I respond with a silent hum against his chest, feeling the vibration travel through both our bodies. My wordless question mirrors his, waiting for whatever weighs on his mind.

His chest expands with a deep breath, and he swallows hard. The tension in his muscles tells me he's gathering courage for something significant. My heart races, anticipating words that might change everything between us.

Be his girlfriend, perhaps? The thought sends equal waves of longing and dread through me. *How cruel would it be to say yes, knowing what waits for me in nine months?*

"Are you going to Wes's football game tomorrow?" he

finally asks, his voice carefully casual, as if he's just remembered this mundane detail.

The question—the shift in his voice is subtle—a slight retreat, like someone stepping back from the edge of a cliff at the last moment. Whatever he truly wanted to ask has been tucked away, replaced by something safer. *And that might be best for the both of us.*

"The game?" I ask, trying to hide my disappointment. "I hadn't thought about it."

His fingers continue their lazy path through my hair; his breathing has become measured, controlled. "You should come. He's remarkable on the field, and the whole stadium experience is fun if you've never been."

Another first experience he wants to share with me.

"I'd love to," I say softly.

Luke's body relaxes beneath me, the tension melting away. His lips press gently against the top of my head, lingering there. The tender gesture makes my heart flutter traitorously in my chest.

We fall into comfortable silence, my palm resting over his steady heartbeat. The rhythm of his breathing gradually slows, deepens.

My eyelids grow heavy as sleep tugs at the edges of my consciousness. The last thing I remember is the gentle rise and fall of his chest beneath my cheek, lulling me into the most peaceful sleep I've had in a long time.

When consciousness begins to seep back in, I'm aware of warmth enveloping me from behind. Luke's body is curved around mine, his chest pressed against my back, his arm draped over my waist, holding me close. Our legs are tangled together beneath the sheets.

The early morning light filters through the curtains, painting the room in a soft golden glow. I blink slowly, savoring this moment of peace before reality intrudes. I've never woken up in someone's arms before. The intimacy of it —this quiet vulnerability—feels right.

He stirs behind me, his breathing pattern changing as consciousness finds him too. His lips press against my bare shoulder, soft and warm.

"Good morning," he murmurs, his voice deliciously deep and raspy with sleep.

He stretches languidly, his body extending like a cat, muscles flexing against me before he settles back into position, his arm returning to my waist.

"Good morning," I whisper, turning to face him.

For a long moment, we simply stare at each other. His eyes, bluer than ever in the morning light, study my face with unhurried appreciation. His hair is tousled, sticking up in places, and there's a faint stubble along his jaw. He looks softer somehow, more vulnerable.

His thumb reaches to trace the line of my chin, feather-light, before moving to outline my lower lip.

His gaze drops to my lips, and I hold my breath as he shifts closer, the space between us slowly disappearing. My heart pounds so loudly I'm certain he can hear it. His nose touches mine, and I let my eyes flutter closed, anticipating the press of his lips against mine. *My first kiss...*

"I sure hope everyone's decent in here!" Wes's voice booms as my bedroom door swings open. "Or at least my brother is."

Luke jerks back. I clutch the sheets to my chest instinctively, though we're both clothed.

"Rise and shine, lovebirds!" Wes leans against the

doorframe, a spatula in one hand and a knowing smirk on his face.

"Well, well, well. What do we have here?" Chase squeezes into the doorway, eyes dancing with amusement as he takes in the scene—Luke's bare chest, our guilty expressions.

"Ever heard of knocking?" Luke growls, running a hand through his already disheveled hair.

"Where's the fun in that?" Wes winks at me, twirling the spatula between his fingers. "You weren't in your room, so we figured you might be here. Anyway, we made breakfast. Pancakes, bacon, the works."

"I've already had a third helping," Chase says, pushing off the doorframe. "Don't take too long or there won't be any left."

"Luke's face gets all scrunchy when he's embarrassed. It's adorable." Wes wiggles his eyebrows. "Like right now."

"Out!" Luke throws a pillow that Wes easily dodges as he pulls the door shut, his laughter echoing in the hallway.

When we're alone again, Luke turns to me with an apologetic smile, the tension from our almost-kiss lingering between us. Our eyes meet, and suddenly we both burst into laughter—the kind that bubbles unexpectedly and releases all the awkwardness in the room.

"Are you hungry?" he asks when our amusement subsides, his hand finding mine atop the sheets. "Wes's pancakes are actually pretty amazing."

I nod, suddenly aware of the emptiness in my stomach. "Starving."

He squeezes my hand and pulls me gently from the bed. I pad across the cool hardwood to my closet, where I slip my feet into my pink fuzzy house shoes with little cat faces on them—

a silly impulse purchase I'd made during my first week of "normal" college life.

As we leave my bedroom, his hand finds mine, his fingers intertwining with mine naturally. We make our way downstairs, and the rich aroma of maple syrup and sizzling bacon grows stronger.

A mountain of golden pancakes, crispy bacon, and fresh fruit covers the table, filling the air with the sweet scent of warm buttermilk and meaty bacon.

"Orange juice?" Luke asks, his thumb brushing against the back of my hand.

"Yes, please," I reply, reluctantly letting his fingers slip from mine as he moves toward the refrigerator.

I slide into the chair across from Chase, who passes me the plate of pancakes.

"These look mouthwatering," I say, selecting two thick, golden and fluffy discs and placing them on my plate then drizzling maple syrup on top. The first bite is heavenly— buttery perfection. "Oh my God, Wes. These are amazing. Thank you both for breakfast."

"Chase did the bacon," Wes says, mouth full of pancake. "Perfect crispy-to-chewy ratio."

Luke returns with a tall glass of orange juice, setting it beside my plate.

"Bebe's coming to your game tonight," he announces to Wes, settling into the chair beside me. His knee presses against mine under the table.

Wes's face lights up instantly. He pushes his chair back with such enthusiasm it nearly topples over.

"That's perfect!" he exclaims, practically bouncing to his feet. "I have something for you."

He strides to the kitchen counter, where a shopping bag sits unnoticed until now. With a dramatic flourish, he pulls out a folded piece of fabric. The navy blue and silver fabric unfurls as Wes shakes it out, revealing a Dalton Dragons football jersey. He holds it up with pride, the bold white number 12 emblazoned across the front and back. Above the number, "SULLIVAN" arches in crisp lettering.

"For you," he says, extending it toward me. "Had to search through the entire rack at the team store. Sullivan jerseys sell out faster than any other player." He winks. "Luckily, they had one small left in stock. The universe wanted you to have it."

I take the jersey, running my fingers over the smooth material and stitched numbers. Something warm spreads through my chest at the thought of wearing their family name across my back. Being included—belonging, even if only symbolically.

"Thank you; this is really thoughtful." I hold it against my chest, smiling at him. "I'll wear it tonight."

"You better," he says, ruffling my hair before returning to his seat. "Can't have my new biggest fan showing up without proper gear."

Luke's fingers locate my fingers below the table, squeezing gently.

"I bet Bebe doesn't even know what to expect at a college football game," Chase says, spearing a piece of bacon with his fork. "It's nothing like watching it on TV."

"You're right," I admit, taking another bite of pancake. "I have no idea what I'm in for."

Chase's eyes light up as he leans forward. "The best part is definitely the student section. It's absolute chaos—everyone packed together, jumping and screaming until they lose their voices. When the team scores, the whole place erupts, and you're hugging complete strangers like they're your best friends."

"Don't forget the chants," Luke adds, his thumb tracing circles on my palm under the table. "There's this one where our side of the stadium shouts 'DALTON' and the other side responds with 'DRAGONS' and it gets louder and faster until everyone's just screaming."

"And the wave!" Chase jumps up, nearly knocking over his orange juice in excitement. "When it picks up momentum and goes around the stadium three or four times, man, there's nothing like it."

"What about you, Wes?" I ask. "What's your favorite part as a player?"

His expression shifts, a mischievous glint appearing in his eyes as he leans forward, elbows on the table.

"The reward after," he says with a slow smile. "But only if we win." He pauses dramatically. "The afterparty."

Chase laughs. "Of course, that's your answer."

"Hey, you haven't experienced college football until you've been to a victory party at the team house," Wes defends. "The entire team, cheerleaders, and half the student body crammed in there celebrating. The music is so loud the neighbors threaten to call the cops every twenty minutes. The energy is..." he kisses his fingertips like a chef, "perfection."

"The last one got a little out of hand," Luke says, his tone cautionary as he glances at me. "Someone jumped off the roof into the pool."

"Yeah, that was me," Wes admits proudly.

Chapter Fourteen

BEBE

"Holy shit," I whisper, frozen at the top of the entrance ramp as the full scale of the stadium unfolds before me. Endless rows of seats cascade down toward an impossibly green field where figures in uniforms dart back and forth. The roar of the crowd physically pushes against my chest, a living, breathing entity of collective excitement. "This is a lot bigger than I expected for a college team."

Luke's hand finds the small of my back, steady against the jersey I'm wearing. "Pretty impressive, right? Dalton U takes its football seriously."

I take in the massive video screens at each end of the stadium, the elaborate light displays, the sea of painted faces and team colors stretching in every direction. "This looks professional."

Chase appears on my other side, balancing a tower of food —loaded nachos, hot dogs, and what appears to be a fried something-or-other in a paper container. "They sell out every home game," he adds, nodding toward the packed stands. "There are thirty thousand people here today."

"Look, there's Wes!" Luke points to the field where players are warming up. He points to a figure in a navy jersey with the number 12 on the back. "He's doing drills with the offense."

I follow his finger, squinting until I spot him among the identical uniforms. When I finally see him, I wave with excessive enthusiasm, jumping to make myself more visible. Wes must notice because he raises his hand in our direction before a coach calls him back to the drill.

"Oh my God, he saw me!" I exclaim, feeling ridiculously pleased, as if he's a celebrity and not my roommate.

Luke laughs. "Come on, our seats are in the student section."

As we navigate through the throng of bodies, Luke suddenly stops, patting his pockets. "Damn, we forgot straws and napkins. Those nachos are going to be a disaster without them."

"I can go back," Chase offers, still balancing his tower of concessions.

"No, you two go ahead. I'll meet you at our seats," Luke says, already turning back toward the concession area. "Save my spot!"

I watch him disappear into the crowd, his blond hair visible for a few moments before the sea of bodies swallows him completely. Chase nudges me forward with his elbow, careful not to upset his food tower.

"This way," he guides, leading me down the concrete steps toward the field. "We're right behind the home team bench."

We've barely settled into our seats when a deep voice calls out.

"Chase!"

Chase's head whips around, eyes widening in surprise. Mr. Sullivan stands at the end of our row, impeccably dressed in a navy blazer with a Dalton U pin on the lapel; looking more like he's attending a business meeting than a football game.

"Dad?" Chase shifts uncomfortably, placing the food on the seat beside him. "We didn't expect to see you here."

Mr. Sullivan's gaze slides from Chase to me, recognition flickering in his eyes. "Bebe, pleasure to see you again," he says flatly, then looks back at his son. "It's Wes's final year. Scouts will be out in full force. I'm already talking to prospective agents."

Mr. Sullivan's eyes drop to my torso, lingering on my jersey. "Number twelve," he observes, his tone suddenly cooler. "Wearing Wes's jersey, I see."

The way he says it makes me feel like I've broken some unspoken rule. My fingers instinctively reach for the hem, tugging it down as if I could somehow hide it from his scrutiny.

"He gave it to me," I explain, my voice smaller than I intended. "As a gift. For my first college game."

Mr. Sullivan's lips press into a thin line. "Is that so?" His gaze sweeps over me again, more calculating this time. "Interesting choice. Most girlfriends wear their boyfriend's number, not his brother's."

Chase shifts beside me, clearing his throat. "Dad—"

"No matter," Mr. Sullivan interrupts, waving dismissively. "I'm sure Luke understands. The quarterback always gets the attention, doesn't he?"

My cheeks burn as Mr. Sullivan watches me closely. Before

I can respond, Luke appears, napkins and straws clutched in his hand.

"Dad," he says, surprise evident in his voice. "I didn't know you'd be here."

"Lucas." Mr. Sullivan nods curtly. "Just telling your girlfriend how unusual it is to see her wearing Wes's number."

Luke's eyes flick to me, noticing my rigid posture and the way my fingers have curled into fists at my sides. He slides into the seat beside me, his arm brushing mine in silent support.

"It's just team spirit, Dad," Luke says easily. "Wes is the star quarterback. We're here to support him."

Mr. Sullivan's gaze hardens. "Is that what you tell yourself? When your girlfriend parades around in another man's jersey—your brother's, no less?"

"It's harmless," Luke defends.

Something dangerous unfurls inside me—the part of me that Gabriel cultivated, The Bee with her lethal instincts. My blood is boiling beneath my skin, anger flooding my system like venom. The Bee stirs, evaluating Mr. Sullivan as a target—noting the vulnerable points at his throat, the precise angle needed to incapacitate.

I dig my fingernails into my palms, forcing myself to remain seated. *Breathe. Focus.* This isn't a situation that requires my other skills. Still, it takes everything in me not to show this man exactly what happens when someone tries to intimidate me.

Mr. Sullivan straightens his already perfect tie. "I should join the boosters in the box. Have fun watching the game, boys." His eyes slide to me, cold and dismissive. "Nice meeting you again."

He turns and walks away, each step radiating authority as he disappears up the concrete stairs.

I exhale slowly, uncurling my fingers. That was close—dangerously close. If he'd stayed another minute, I might have shown him exactly who he was dealing with.

"I'm sorry about that, Bebe," Luke says quietly. When I turn to him, his face is a mask of embarrassment and concern.

"Why does he hate me?" I ask, my voice barely audible over the crowd's noise. "I haven't done anything to him, or to you."

Luke's blue eyes met mine with sudden intensity. "No, Bebe, it's not—"

"He's an asshole," Chase cuts in bluntly, leaning forward so I can hear him clearly. "Don't take it personally. That's how he is with everyone." He snorts, unwrapping a hot dog with more force than necessary. "Dad likes to control everything and everyone around him. Especially who we date." He takes an aggressive bite, speaking around the food. "He's had Wes's future mapped out since birth, same with Luke and me."

The stadium erupts in cheers as the teams begin filing onto the field for introductions, but I barely notice.

"You know what's really rich?" Luke says, his voice taking on an edge I've never heard before. "He hasn't been to a single one of Wes's games until today. Four years of college football, and suddenly he shows up for the last season because the NFL scouts are watching."

"Dad didn't want him playing football at all," Chase explains. "Wes was supposed to take over the family business. He had it all planned out."

I turn to Luke, surprised. "But I thought you were the one going into the business?"

"I am now. Dad fought it for years. I was supposed to play baseball for Dalton U. Wes was the firstborn, so naturally, he was the heir to the family business. But he's always been about football. Since we were kids, it was all he cared about."

"So you stepped up instead?" I ask.

"Someone had to," Luke shrugs. "Better me than Chase. Chase has always been interested in law and that was something dad could get behind."

If Luke stepped into the leader role out of obligation, it makes me wonder what he would have done if he had been given a choice. Continue baseball, maybe?

Chase leans in, balancing nachos. "Dad was furious when Wes got the scholarship and didn't need to draw from our families' trust to pay for schooling. Threatened to cut him off completely."

"So what changed?" I ask, genuinely curious.

"Money," Luke says flatly. "NFL money. Wes is better than he thought and will get drafted. Suddenly, dad sees dollar signs."

Chase snorts. "Funny how principles vanish when there's enough cash involved."

As I sit here listening to them talk about their controlling father, I realize it's not much different in my world with my brother. Gabriel is mapping out my entire life, deciding my husband, my future, even which people I kill.

"It must be hard," I say softly, "having your path chosen for you."

Luke's hand finds mine, his fingers intertwining with my own. The gesture feels both protective and seeking comfort.

"You have no idea," he murmurs.

But I do. I understand better than he might imagine. The

weight of family expectations crushing your own desires, molding you into someone you never asked to be.

The crowd suddenly erupts around us as the announcer's voice booms through the stadium. "And now, your Dalton Dragons quarterback, number twelve, Wes SULLIVAN!"

Wes runs onto the field, helmet raised high, and the roar becomes deafening. Luke and Chase leap to their feet, pulling me up with them. I let myself be swept away in the collective excitement, screaming Wes's name until my throat burned.

Chapter Fifteen

LUKE

"SUL-LI-VAN! SUL-LI-VAN!" The chant reverberates through the team house, the walls practically pulsing with the collective energy of hundreds of students packed together in celebration. The floor beneath my feet vibrates from the thundering bass of music blasting through speakers positioned in every corner of the living room.

Bebe and I are pressed against the far wall, clutching red cups, watching in awe as the crowd parts like the Red Sea. Wes and his teammates enter through the front door, freshly showered after their game, hair still damp, faces flushed with triumph.

"That's our quarterback!" someone shouts, and the crowd erupts again.

Wes's face splits into his familiar cocky grin as he raises his arms above his head, basking in the adoration. The rest of the team files in behind him. Each player greeted with their own wave of cheers, though none quite matching the quarterback's welcome. His eyes scan the room until they find us.

He weaves through the throng, fist-bumping knuckles and accepting back-slaps until he reaches us, that victorious smile never leaving his face.

"So?" he asks Bebe, leaning in close to be heard over the music. "What did you think of your first college football game?"

Her mismatched eyes light up with genuine excitement. "It was incredible! I've never experienced anything like it." She bounces on her toes, looking more carefree than I've ever seen her. "And you were amazing out there. That last-minute touchdown—I couldn't believe it!"

"She's not exaggerating," I tell my brother, nudging his shoulder. "Bebe was on her feet the whole time, screaming louder than anyone in our section."

She laughs, the sound barely audible over the music but impossibly sweet. "My throat is still raw."

"Worth it, though, right?" His grin widens as he leans closer to her.

Before she can answer, Chase appears with four shots balanced between his fingers. "Tequila," he announces, distributing the small glasses.

Wes takes his shot with a flourish, raising it high. "To crushing State! First win of many this season!"

"To Wes!" I add, lifting my glass alongside Chase's.

We all clink our shots together, the sound lost in the party's chaos. I knock mine back, the familiar burn racing down my throat. My eyes find Bebe as she brings the small glass to her lips.

She takes a tentative sip, her nose immediately wrinkling,

eyes squinting as she fights against the alcohol's bite. Instead of throwing it back like the rest of us, she continues with tiny sips. Her face scrunches up adorably as she struggles through the shot, looking like she's being tortured in the most endearing way possible. Her determination to finish it despite clearly hating the taste makes something warm unfurl in my chest.

"You can just set it down," I whisper close to her ear, trying not to laugh.

She shakes her head stubbornly, taking another miniature sip. "I want the full college experience," she insists.

I laugh as she finally finishes the shot with a dramatic shudder, her eyes watering. She hands me the empty glass with a triumphant smile.

A group of rowdy offensive linemen descend on Wes. "Sullivan! Keg stand time!" they chant, already hoisting him by his arms. He barely has time to hand his glass to Chase before they're carrying him away.

I watch her eyes follow him, a small smile playing on her lips. The bass drops on a new song, and the crowd erupts in cheers of recognition. The energy in the room shifts instantly, bodies pressing closer together as people move toward the makeshift dance floor.

"Come on," I say, taking her empty shot glass and setting it on a nearby table. My fingers find hers, intertwining naturally. "Let's dance."

Her eyes widen slightly. "Oh, I don't—I mean, I've never actually—"

"Another first?" I ask, and she nods. "There's no right way to do it. Just feel the music."

I guide Bebe through the crush of bodies, feeling her

hesitation as we reach the edge of the dance floor. The music pulses around us, a rhythmic heartbeat that vibrates through the floorboards. When we find a small pocket of space, I turn to face her, noticing the uncertainty on her face.

I place my hands on her hips, my fingers pressing lightly against the denim of her shorts. I begin to sway, guiding her body to match the rhythm of mine. She's stiff at first, her movements mechanical as she tries to follow my lead.

Her eyes dart around nervously, watching the other dancers—some grinding provocatively, others jumping with wild abandon, everyone lost in their own world of music and movement. I can see her analyzing, maybe wanting to copy what she sees, but her confidence is faltering.

"Hey," I say, tilting her chin up with my finger until her eyes meet mine. "Don't worry about them."

I pull her closer. The hesitation in her body melts away as she leans into my touch. Something shifts in her expression—a silent decision made behind those extraordinary eyes.

She meets my gaze with newfound intensity, her pupils dilating slightly in the dim light. With the next heartbeat, it's as if someone flipped a switch inside her. Gone is the uncertain girl from seconds ago, replaced by a woman who suddenly owns every inch of the space around her.

Her palms slide up the ridges of my abs through my t-shirt, coming to rest against my chest, fingers splaying against the fabric. The touch is gentle but deliberate and possessive, as if she's claiming me with her touch. I'm sure she can feel my heart hammering beneath her fingertips. She moves her hips, finding the rhythm of the bass as naturally as breathing.

"There you go," I murmur, though I'm not sure she even hears me over the music.

She turns in my arms, her back pressing against my chest, head tilting to rest against my shoulder. Her hands reach behind to find my neck, fingers threading through my hair as she grinds against me.

Chase materializes beside us, balancing three drinks despite the crush of bodies. His eyebrows rise appreciatively as he takes in Bebe's newfound confidence on the dance floor.

"Thought you might be thirsty," he shouts over the music, extending a cup toward her. "It's just beer."

She takes the cup with a grateful smile, her hips still swaying to the beat as she brings it to her lips. She winces at the bitter taste but takes another sip anyway, determined in a way I've come to recognize. Her movements slow a bit, becoming more languid as she leans back against me.

I watch her carefully, noting the slight flush spreading across her cheeks, the way her eyelids have grown heavier in the last few minutes. Between the tequila shot, the two beers we had when we arrived, and now this beer, I should keep an eye on her alcohol intake. She's tiny—can't weigh more than a hundred-twenty pounds soaking wet—and I doubt she's built up any tolerance before tonight. The last thing I want is for her first college party to end with her head over a toilet bowl.

"Having fun?" I ask, my lips close to her ear so she can hear me over the thundering bass.

She nods enthusiastically.

Chase leans in closer, a knowing grin spreading across his face. "Look at our sweet, innocent Bebe—she's buzzing right now."

She giggles, her head tilting in acknowledgment as she turns back to face me again. The flush on her cheeks deepens, her eyes slightly unfocused but sparkling with joy. "Maybe a little," she admits.

As she moves, I catch one of Dalton U's offensive linemen, Trent—I think—staring at her from across the dance floor. As she dances, he fixes his predatory gaze on her ass, darting his tongue out to wet his lips. Something protective and primal stirs in my chest.

Before I can react, Chase must have noticed, too. He slides behind Bebe, effectively creating a barrier between her and Trent's leering eyes. He places his hands lightly on her waist, creating a Sullivan sandwich with her safe between us.

"Can't let the wolves get your girl," Chase says near my ear, nodding subtly toward Trent, who's now scowling at our formation.

I'm flooded with gratitude as Chase's protective instinct mirrors my own. We're still in the early stages of whatever Bebe and I are building, but already my brothers treat her as someone who matters—someone worth shielding from the predatory stares of drunk football players.

The music shifts to something with a heavier beat, and her movements become more fluid, her body responding to the rhythm. She raises her arms above her head, swaying between Chase and me with uninhibited joy.

Wes appears through the crowd, red cup in hand. He watches us for a moment, his expression shifting from amusement to something warmer as he takes in our formation around Bebe.

"Damn, little roomie!" he yells over the music, nodding appreciatively. "You've been holding out on us! Those are some serious moves you've got there!"

Her face lights up at the compliment. She leans forward

slightly and grabs Wes's forearm to steady herself. "I think I might be a little tipsy," she confesses, her voice carrying a slight singsong quality.

He grins, his eyes crinkling at the corners as he leans in close to Bebe. "Well then, make sure Luke takes good care of you tonight," he says, his voice playful but with an undercurrent of genuine concern. He throws me a meaningful look before turning back to her with an exaggerated wink. "He's always been the responsible one."

She nods solemnly, as if he's entrusted her with a sacred mission rather than just suggesting I look after her.

"I will," she promises.

Wes squeezes her shoulder affectionately before disappearing back into the crowd, immediately swallowed by a group of adoring fans chanting his name. Chase follows him, shooting me a knowing smile over his shoulder.

She turns back to me, her body swaying gently to the rhythm. I place my hands on her hips again to steady her, and she melts against me, her arms wrapping around my neck. The music transitions to something slower, more sensual.

As we sway together, her body warm against mine, I'm struck by how quickly Bebe has become essential to my life. Just weeks ago, I didn't know she existed. Now, I can't imagine my days without her mismatched eyes greeting me across the breakfast table, her laughter filling the spaces that I didn't even realize were empty. The realization hits me with startling clarity as I hold her against me: *I'm falling for her.* Not just attracted to her, not just enjoying her company—I'm falling completely, irrevocably in love with Bebe.

Everything about her amazes me. The way she approaches each new experience with wonder, as if the most ordinary things—bowling, football games, even this chaotic college party—are magical discoveries. How she fits so perfectly in my arms, like she was designed specifically to be held by me.

She looks up at me now; her eyes reflecting the pulsing lights, lips slightly parted, and I'm overcome with the desire to kiss her. But I won't—not here, not when she's had alcohol and might not remember it tomorrow. I want her to remember every second when it happens.

"You're staring," she murmurs as she reaches up to touch my face.

"Just thinking about how glad I am that you answered our roommate ad," I say, tucking a strand of hair behind her ear.

Her smile softens. "After a few more songs, do you want to get out of here?"

Chapter Sixteen

LUKE

DESIRE AND ALCOHOL make a dangerous combination—especially when the kitchen is dark and we're finally alone.

"I need something sweet," Bebe announces as she flicks on the stove light and heads for the pantry. The rideshare driver had given us knowing looks in the rearview mirror the entire drive home. Her pressed against my side, head on my shoulder, my fingers drawing lazy circles on her thigh.

I hang back, leaning against the archway, watching her search through shelves with single-minded determination.

"Aha!" She emerges victorious, clutching a bag of s'more-sized marshmallows and a jar of Nutella. "Perfect." She giggles, looking impossibly cute, those extraordinary eyes bright with alcohol-induced happiness.

"Drunchies, huh?" I can't help but smile as she hops up to sit on the kitchen island, legs swinging like a child's.

"Drunk munchies," she elaborates, popping a marshmallow in her mouth. "I learned a new slang term today," she says with a proud little smile, unscrewing the Nutella jar. She dips a marshmallow inside, coating half of it before putting it in her mouth with a satisfied hum.

I can't resist her magnetic pull any longer. She looks up as I approach, her eyes following my movement. The kitchen feels smaller suddenly, the air between us charged with something electric. I step between her dangling legs, my hands finding her bare thighs. Her skin is impossibly soft beneath my palms as I slide them upward, stopping at the hem of her shorts.

"Want one?" she asks, her voice soft, holding a marshmallow between her fingers.

I part my jaw open, and she tosses it gently into my mouth with surprising accuracy. The sweetness explodes on my tongue. As I chew, I can't take my eyes off her—the way her hair falls around her shoulders, how her lips curve into a perfect smile, the slight flush across her cheeks. *I've never wanted to kiss someone so badly in my life.* All I can think about is how much sweeter her lips must taste. How perfectly they would fit against mine.

"What are you thinking about?" she asks, tilting her head.

"About how bad I want to kiss you right now," I confess, the words slipping out before I can second-guess myself.

Her eyes widen slightly, lips parting before a blush spreads across her cheeks. Her fingers curl into the fabric of my shirt as if to draw me closer.

"I'd like that," she whispers, her gaze dropping to my mouth. "Very much."

I hesitate, my conscience battling with desire. "You've been drinking, Bebe. I want you to remember our first kiss."

"I'm not drunk," she protests, straightening her posture as if to prove her sobriety. "Just... happy."

I raise an eyebrow skeptically. "Bebe—"

"I can prove it." She narrows her eyes at me, accepting the challenge. "Z, Y, X, W, V, U, T..." she begins confidently, her voice clear and letters precise as she works her way backward through the alphabet. "S, R, Q, P, O, N, M, L, K..." She continues, gaining confidence with each letter.

I smile, impressed, and press my finger to her lips, stopping her recitation. "Okay, I'm convinced. You're not drunk."

Her eyes sparkle with triumph as I cup her face in my hands. My thumbs trace the delicate line of her cheekbones as I lean in slowly, giving her time to pull away if she wants. But she doesn't—instead, she meets me halfway, her breath catching as our lips finally touch.

The first contact is gentle, exploratory, but the spark is immediate. Her lips are impossibly soft against mine, tasting of marshmallows and hazelnut-cocoa. I deepen the kiss, and she responds eagerly, her hands sliding up my chest to wrap around my neck, pulling me closer.

Her lips are pliant and yield to my every move, enticing me to explore deeper. So, when my tongue traces the seam, she opens for me without hesitation. The first slide of her tongue against mine sends electricity racing down my spine. She tastes sweeter than I'd imagined—and the little sound she makes in the back of her throat drives me wild.

Her legs wrap around my waist, ankles locking behind me as she presses herself closer. I run my hands down to her hips, fingers digging into the soft flesh as I pull her against me.

My hands travel upward, one sliding beneath the jersey to

find the warm skin of her back while the other moves to cup her breast through the fabric. She fits perfectly in my palm. I squeeze gently, my thumb brushing over where I can feel her nipple hardening below the layers.

"Luke," she breathes my name like a prayer.

Her fingers find the hem of my t-shirt, tugging upward with impatient little pulls. I pull back just enough to help her, raising my arms as she strips it off, tossing it carelessly to the kitchen floor. The cool air hits my bare chest for a moment before her warm hands are exploring the newly exposed skin.

Bebe stares at me with darkened eyes before reaching for the bottom of her jersey. In one fluid motion, she pulls it over her head and tosses it aside. My breath catches at the sight of her in nothing but a delicate white lace bra and those tiny denim shorts.

"You're beautiful," I whisper, taking in the contrast of the pristine lace against her golden skin.

She blushes under my gaze but doesn't shy away. Instead, she reaches for me, pulling me back between her legs.

Our lips crash together again, the kiss deeper and more urgent than before. My hand slides up her smooth back, fingers finding the clasp of her bra. With a quick twist, it comes undone; the straps loosen around her shoulders. She shrugs, allowing the delicate lace to fall forward, revealing herself to me.

I break the kiss to look, unable to contain the low, appreciative sound that escapes my throat. Her breasts are perfect—high and full, with dusky rose nipples. How she looks—half-naked in my kitchen, perched on the counter where we eat breakfast every morning, is almost too much to process.

"God, Bebe," I whisper, voice rough with desire. "You're incredibly sexy."

Our eyes lock as my hands move to the waistband of her shorts. I hold her gaze, silently asking permission as my fingers find the button. Her breath catches, but she nods, her lips parting in anticipation. I pop the button with deliberate slowness, then drag the zipper down. The rasp of the zipper sounds impossibly loud in the quiet kitchen as I drag it tooth by tooth.

My fingers slip beneath, grazing the soft skin of her lower abdomen. I tug them down her thighs, helping her wiggle free of the denim until they join the growing pile of clothes on the kitchen floor. Her matching white lace panties are the only barrier left between us, a small damp patch visible at their center.

I trace the delicate lace edge with my fingertip, watching her shiver at the featherlight touch. When I finally slide my hand beneath the fabric, I find her slick with arousal. My middle finger traces her pussy lips before carefully pressing inside. *Fuck, she's tight.* Her breathing quickens as I press forward.

"Is this okay?" I whisper, carefully observing her face.

She nods, her bottom lip caught between her teeth. "Yes," she breathes.

I move with deliberate slowness, watching her face for any sign of discomfort, but find only pleasure blooming in her expression. Her eyes flutter closed, lips parting on a sigh that sounds like surrender. I carefully add a second finger. The sound she makes—a soft, surprised moan—sends heat rushing through me.

I work my fingers deeper, curling them to find the spot

inside her that makes her gasp. My thumb finds her clit, swollen and sensitive, and traces gentle circles around it. The effect is instantaneous—her back arches, pushing her breasts forward.

"Oh!" The sound is half-surprise, half-pleasure, her hips instinctively rocking against my hand.

I increase the pressure, watching in awe as her body responds to my touch. Her breathing grows ragged, small whimpers escaping with each exhale. Seeing her like this—head thrown back, lips parted, skin flushed with arousal—is the most beautiful thing I've ever seen.

Her eyes fly open suddenly, meeting mine with a mixture of wonder and alarm. "Luke," she gasps, fingers digging into my shoulders. "Something's—I think something's happening to me."

Her thighs begin to tremble around my waist, her inner walls tightening around my fingers.

"Let go, baby," I whisper in her ear, pressing my lips to her temple. "I've got you."

The realization hits me like a thunderbolt—I'm witnessing her first orgasm, guiding her through this intimate moment. Something possessive and primal unfurls in my chest as I watch her climb toward release. Not just her first, but if I have any say in it, I'll be her *only*. The thought catches me off guard, this sudden certainty that I want to be the last man who ever touches her this way.

Her body tenses, then shudders as she comes apart against my hand.

"Luke," she gasps, her voice breaking on my name. "Oh my god."

I watch her face intently in fascination, memorizing every

detail of her expression—the way her pupils dilate, how her lips part on each ragged breath. I keep my fingers moving, drawing out her climax until she collapses against my chest, trembling and breathless.

I've been with other women before, shared intimate moments, but never felt this consuming need to claim someone as mine. This isn't just desire—it's something deeper, more profound. I want mornings and evenings and everything in between with her. *I want a future.*

Chapter Seventeen

BEBE

I'D BEEN TRAINED to kill in sixteen different ways, but no one ever taught me how to survive pleasure—prepare me for the utter surrender of my first orgasm.

Luke's fingers are still inside me as I come down from what could only be described as a near-death experience—the most exquisite kind. My body trembles with aftershocks, each sending ripples of sensation through my core. I collapse against his chest, unable to hold myself upright any longer, my breath coming in ragged gasps against his neck.

"Are you okay?" he whispers.

I nod wordlessly, still trying to comprehend what had just happened to me. How had I lived eighteen years without knowing my body could do *that*?

"That was..." I struggle to find the words, my brain fuzzy and disconnected from my mouth. "I don't even know how to describe it."

He carefully withdraws his fingers, the movement sending

one final shudder through me. His eyes—those impossibly blue eyes—study my face with such tenderness it makes my chest ache.

Luke's eyes are dark with desire as he presses his forehead against mine, his breathing as ragged as my own. "You're incredible," he murmurs, his voice rough. "The way you respond to my touch..."

I laugh softly, feeling strangely vulnerable yet powerful all at once.

And that kiss—my God. But it wasn't just a kiss. It was a feeling—of being seen, chosen, and maybe even a little loved. I know I'll never forget that moment. I'd never want to.

My legs remain wrapped around his waist, my bare chest pressed against his, our heartbeats gradually slowing to match rhythms. I can't stop a smile from spreading across my face.

There's a distinct hardness against me where our bodies meet. I glance down between us, forehead still touching his, and notice the prominent bulge straining against the denim of his jeans. Heat rushes through me again—a different kind this time, mixed with curiosity and determination.

"My turn," I whisper, trailing my fingers down his chest, feeling the defined muscles tense beneath my touch. I explore the ridges of his abs, following the thin trail of hair that disappears beneath his waistband. My hand moves to the button of his jeans.

"Bebe," Luke says softly, his hand covering mine. "You don't have to do anything. Tonight can just be about you."

I look up, meeting his gaze. The tenderness there nearly undoes me, but I see something else too—desire barely restrained.

"I want to," I tell him, my voice steady. "I want to make you feel good, too."

His eyes darken as he searches my face, looking for any hesitation. Finding none, he nods slightly, removing his hand from mine.

I unfasten his jeans and drag down the zipper. The sound fills the quiet kitchen as I push the denim down his hips, his boxer briefs following. My breath catches in my throat as he springs free.

I've seen anatomical drawings in biology textbooks and glimpsed images on the internet, but nothing prepared me for the reality of Luke standing before me. He's long and thick, the skin flushed a deep pink, with prominent veins running along the shaft. The head is smoother, almost velvety-looking, with a small bead of moisture at the tip.

He remains perfectly still, his breathing shallow as he watches me. When my fingertips finally make contact, we both gasp—me at the surprising contrast of textures, him most likely at the sensation.

He's impossibly hard, yet the skin is soft, like steel wrapped in silk. And he's warm—so much warmer than I expected, pulsing with life beneath my touch. He inhales sharply as my fingers explore his length, learning the feel of him.

"Is this okay?" I ask, mimicking his earlier question to me.

"Mmmmm," he manages.

I tighten my grip on him, testing the firmness without squeezing too hard. My fingers wrap around his girth, and I'm surprised to discover my hand doesn't completely encircle him —there's a noticeable gap where my thumb and index finger fail to meet.

"How is this ever supposed to fit inside me?" I wonder, my eyes widening as I consider the logistics.

Luke's breath catches, and I realize I've spoken my thoughts aloud.

"We'd go slow," he says softly, his voice deep and reassuring. "Your body will adjust." He brushes my hair back from my face. "There's no rush, Bebe. Not for anything."

The tenderness in his tone makes my heart flutter. I continue my exploration, fascinated by the way he responds to my touch—and now I understand what he meant when he said that to me—the subtle flex of his abdomen, the slight catch in his breathing when I run my thumb over the sensitive head.

"Show me how," I whisper, looking up at him through my lashes. "Show me what feels good for you."

"Like this," he murmurs, his larger hand enveloping mine completely. He tightens my grip slightly, showing me the perfect pressure—firm but not too tight. "Start slow, from base to tip."

I follow his guidance, mesmerized by how his breathing changes with each stroke. His hand remains over mine for several passes, establishing a rhythm before gradually releasing control to me.

"That's perfect," he encourages as I continue on my own.

I experiment with different pressures and speeds, cataloging his reactions with fascination. When I twist my wrist a little on the upstroke, his breath hitches sharply, his stomach muscles contracting. I repeat the motion, delighting in the low groan it pulls from his throat.

"God, Bebe," he breathes, his eyes heavy-lidded as they lock with mine. His hands find my thighs, fingers digging into my flesh with enough pressure to anchor himself. His hips twitch forward, seeking more of the sensation I'm creating.

The intimacy of the moment overwhelms me—how we're connected through just my hand, how his pleasure is literally in my palm. With each stroke, more of the clear fluid appears at his tip, and I'm fascinated by it.

I run my fingertip over the glistening droplets, spreading the moisture around the head. The slickness makes my movements smoother, and his reaction is immediate—a sharp intake of breath, his eyes briefly closing before finding mine again with renewed intensity.

The raw vulnerability in his expression sends a thrill through me. *I, Bebe Laurent, trained assassin, can reduce this beautiful man to trembling need with my hand.* It's a different power than I'm used to—one that gives rather than takes.

Luke leans forward suddenly, capturing my lips in a hungry kiss. I continue stroking him, maintaining the rhythm, while my free hand slides up to tangle in his hair. The soft strands feel like silk between my fingers as I tug gently, drawing a deep groan from his throat that vibrates against my lips.

His kiss deepens, growing more desperate as my strokes become more confident.

"Bebe," he whispers on my lips, "I'm getting close."

I increase my pace, maintaining the pressure he showed me. His breathing grows ragged, his kisses more frantic. I can feel him swelling even larger in my hand.

"Bebe, I'm..." His voice catches as his body tenses. With a swift movement, Luke's hand covers mine, guiding me through the last strokes before sliding his fully over the head of his cock. His other hand braces against the counter beside my hip as he shudders, his release spilling in his hand rather than onto mine. His eyes never leave me as he comes, letting me witness every moment of his vulnerability.

I'm transfixed by the raw emotion on his face—the parted lips, furrowed brow, and the intensity in those blue eyes. It's beautiful, watching him come apart this way, knowing I caused it.

For a moment, we stay frozen like this—me perched on the counter; him standing between my legs, both of us breathing heavily in the quiet kitchen.

He presses a gentle kiss on my forehead before stepping back.

"Just a second," he murmurs, moving to the kitchen sink.

He washes his hands thoroughly, his broad back to me, the muscles shifting beneath his skin with each movement. With his clean hands, he pulls up his boxer-briefs, tucking himself back inside—leaving his jeans unzipped and hanging off his hips.

When he returns, he positions himself between my legs. His breathing has steadied now, but his eyes still hold an intimate intensity that makes my stomach flutter. He cups my face in his hands, his thumbs gently stroking my cheeks.

"That was amazing," he whispers, his voice tender with emotion. "You're amazing."

I lean into his touch, savoring the warmth of his palms against my skin.

Our lips meet again, but this time the kiss is unhurried and gentle. No desperate passion, just a soft, sweet connection. His fingers thread through my hair as he pulls me closer, his bare chest warm against mine.

I melt into him, my arms wrapping around his neck. Every brush of his lips feels like a promise, every sigh a secret language between us. This isn't just physical attraction—it's something I've never experienced before, something I wasn't trained to recognize or defend against.

The sudden click of a key in the front door lock shatters our moment.

Our eyes fly open simultaneously, panic mirrored in both our expressions. We freeze for a heartbeat—my naked chest, his unbuttoned jeans, clothes scattered across the kitchen floor —before springing into action.

"Shit." Luke snatches the jersey off the floor and thrusts it into my hands. He positions himself strategically in front of me, his broad shoulders and back creating a protective barrier between my exposed body and the doorway.

The kitchen lights turn on, and it's suddenly too bright.

"Whoa, sorry guys!" Chase's voice carries from the other side of Luke. "Looks like we're interrupting something."

"Or we're just in time," Wes drawls, his tone playful and suggestive as he leans against the archway, making no move to leave.

A laugh bubbles from my throat, surprising even me. I should be mortified—half-naked in the kitchen, caught in such a compromising position—but instead, I find myself giggling. Perhaps it's the lingering effects of alcohol, the absurdity of the situation, or simply the delicious secret of what Luke and I just shared.

I swiftly pull the jersey over my head, grateful for his broad shoulders shielding me from his brothers' view. The fabric slides down, covering my exposed skin just as Luke clears his throat.

"I thought you guys would be at the party for a few more

hours," he says, his voice impressively steady despite our predicament. "What happened?"

"Cops showed up. Someone called in a noise complaint, and when they arrived, they found underage freshmen everywhere," Chase says. "Party over."

"The neighbors are getting soft," Wes grumbles. "Last year they'd let us go until at least 1 AM before calling it in. This year they barely gave us two hours."

I peer around Luke's protective frame, tapping him lightly on the lower back. When he glances over his shoulder, I point downward s at my denim shorts still crumpled on the kitchen floor, just visible beyond his feet.

Luke's eyes follow my gesture. He subtly shifts his stance and quickly leans down to grab my shorts, handing them to me as he rises back up.

"So the whole team scattered?" Luke asks, buying time as I put them on.

"Some went to Riley's place," Wes says. "But I wasn't feeling it."

I tug the zipper up on my shorts, trying to smooth my hair with my free hand. Now fully dressed—well, minus one important undergarment—I tap Luke's shoulder to signal I'm decent.

Luke steps aside. "We were about to head upstairs," he says casually, reaching back to take my hand.

"I bet you were," Wes smirks, making no attempt to hide his knowing gaze as it travels between us.

Luke ignores the comment. His fingers intertwine with mine as he helps me slide off the counter, my feet landing softly on the cool tile.

We move toward the doorway. Wes steps aside to let us pass, dramatically bowing like a butler at a fancy hotel.

"Bebe," Chase's voice stops me. I turn to find him standing by the counter, dangling my white lace bra from his index finger.

"Forgetting something?" he asks, his expression a perfect blend of amusement and mischief.

Heat floods my face instantly. I can feel the blush spreading down my neck, surely turning my skin the same shade as a strawberry.

"Thanks," I manage to squeak out, reaching back to snatch the bra from his finger. "Goodnight!" I call over my shoulder, practically dragging Luke toward the stairs. Behind us, Wes and Chase's laughter follows. They certainly know how to ruin a moment.

Chapter Eighteen

BEBE

"These are going to be slightly undercooked and weirdly shaped, just so you know," I say, flipping another pancake onto the growing stack, the mouthwatering aroma of bacon sizzling in the pan fills the kitchen. Chase stands beside me at the stove, expertly cracking eggs into a bowl with one hand while whisking with the other.

"Where did you learn to cook like this?" I ask, genuinely impressed by his technique.

He grins, not looking up from his task. "Mom taught all of us the basics, but I was the only one who actually paid attention. Luke can manage not to burn toast, and Wes—well, Wes makes a mean protein shake. He does well at pancakes, too."

I laugh, pouring more batter into the pan. There's something soothing about this domestic scene—standing side by side in the morning light, preparing food with someone. It feels normal in a way my life rarely does.

"Something smells yummy," Luke's voice comes from the archway. I turn to see him and Wes entering the kitchen, both freshly showered after their morning run.

Luke's hair is still damp, a few droplets clinging to the strands as he crosses the space to press a kiss to my temple. The casual intimacy of the gesture makes my heart flutter.

Wes inhales deeply, his nostrils flaring dramatically as he leans against the counter. "Well, at least the kitchen smells like bacon today instead of sex."

I nearly dropped the spatula, my cheeks instantly burning with embarrassment.

"We didn't have sex in the kitchen," Luke protests, his voice low but firm as he moves closer to me. "Not that it's any of your business."

Chase snorts, cracking another egg. "You would have if we hadn't walked in when we did. If we'd been even ten minutes later coming home..."

Heat rushes to my face, but I refuse to be embarrassed. In one swift motion, I grab the dish towel hanging from the oven handle and snap it toward Chase, catching him on the hip.

"Ow!" he yelps, rubbing the spot where the towel connected with exaggerated pain. "That's assault with a kitchen weapon! Oh, it's on now."

He grabs a towel from the drawer and twists it into a tight coil, his eyes gleaming with mischief.

I squeal and dart behind Luke, using his body as a human shield.

"Oh no you don't," Wes laughs, reaching for another dish towel from the drawer for himself. "You can't hide behind your boyfriend after starting this war. That's against the rules."

I peek around Luke's shoulder, expecting him to defend me, but he shakes his head with a mischievous grin.

"He's right, you know," Luke says, stepping aside to expose me fully. "You fired the first shot."

Wes tosses a rolled-up towel to Luke, who catches it effortlessly and gives it an experimental snap that cracks through the air like a whip. *The betrayal!*

"Three against one?" I back up slowly, eyeing the kitchen doorway and calculating my escape chances. "That hardly seems fair."

"All's fair in love and towel wars," Chase declares, advancing with his weapon raised.

I grab a wooden spoon from the counter, holding it out like a sword. "Stay back! I'm armed!"

The brothers exchange amused glances.

Wes darts forward, his towel snapping against my thigh with a sharp sting that makes me yelp. I swing my wooden spoon wildly, connecting with nothing but air as Chase circles to my left, his towel making a whistling sound as it cuts through the kitchen.

"Get her!" Wes calls, and suddenly Luke is behind me, his strong arms wrapping around my waist, lifting me slightly off the ground.

"Traitor!" I squeal, kicking my legs as he holds me in place. "I trusted you!"

Luke's laughter rumbles through his chest against my back. "Consider this payback for stealing all the blankets last night."

Chase's towel connects with my exposed calf, the sting making me squirm in Luke's arms. Wes follows as another snap catches my arm.

"Not fair!" I protest through my laughter, still trying to wriggle free.

Now, am I really trying to fight them? No. If I wanted to, I could end this war I started in thirty seconds, hogtying the three of them using the same towels they're snapping me with... but it's playful—fun.

I hook my foot around Luke's ankle, throwing him off balance so his grip loosens. I twist in his arms, breaking free enough to land a solid smack with my wooden spoon against Luke's shoulder. It wasn't as hard as I could have done it. He gasps in mock outrage as I dance away, brandishing my kitchen weapon triumphantly.

"Oh, you're in trouble now," Luke warns, advancing with his towel raised.

I back up against the counter, cornered by all three Sullivan brothers with their weapons poised. But the smell of something burning reaches my nose just as Chase's eyes widen in alarm.

"The bacon!" he shouts, throwing his towel on the counter and rushing to the stove where smoke rises from the forgotten pan. He quickly moves it off the heat, waving away the smoke with frantic motions. "Truce, truce!"

The tension dissolves into laughter as we all lower our weapons. Chase shakes his head, examining the charred bacon with a sigh.

"Saved most of it," he announces, transferring it to a paper towel-lined plate. "Let's eat before everything's ruined."

I'm still giggling, an unspoken ceasefire settling over the kitchen. As I catch my breath, a strange feeling washes over me —a lightness I've never experienced before. *This playful chaos, this mock battle with no real stakes, no real danger... is this what normal siblings do? Is this what I missed growing up with Gabriel and my brothers?*

I abandon my wooden spoon and carry my plate to the table, where Luke pulls me onto his lap instead of letting me take my own chair. His arms wrap around my waist as I settle against him, my back pressed to his chest. He brushes my hair aside and places a soft kiss on the side of my neck, sending pleasant shivers down my spine.

"So what's on your agenda today?" he murmurs against my skin between bites of pancake.

I can't contain my excitement as I twist to face him. "I signed up for some clubs! Three of them—Anime Club, Board Games, and Stargazing." I bounce slightly on his lap, my enthusiasm bubbling over. "The Stargazing Club meets tonight on the cliffs. I've never really looked at constellations before."

Wes nearly chokes on his orange juice, coughing as he tries to suppress his laughter.

"Oh, Bebe," he says, wiping his mouth. "Stargazing Club isn't for looking at stars."

My forehead wrinkles in confusion. "What do you mean? The flyer had these pictures of constellations and a telescope..."

Wes laughs, leaning back in his chair. "The Stargazing Club is just what freshmen call the spot where everyone goes to hook up. It's not a university-sanctioned club. It's an excuse to get someone alone in the dark."

"Yeah," Chase adds, shoveling a forkful of pancake into his mouth. "Nobody's actually looking at stars."

My face falls, genuine disappointment washing over me. "Really?"

Chase shrugs. "Trust me, I've been to those cliffs plenty of times. The only stars people are seeing are the ones behind their eyelids."

I slump against Luke's chest, a pout forming on my lips. "That's disappointing. I was looking forward to learning about constellations."

Luke's arms tighten around me, his chin resting on my shoulder. "I'm sorry, Bebe. But hey, I could take you stargazing sometime. I know a spot in the foothills where the light pollution is minimal," he says. "We could bring a blanket, some hot chocolate. I've heard of an app that shows all the constellations when you point your phone at the sky."

His lips brush against my ear as he whispers, "And maybe we could do a little making out under them, too."

Wes makes an exaggerated gagging noise, clutching his neck dramatically. "Please, I'm trying to eat here."

Chase joins in, pretending to stick his finger down his throat. "Seriously, you two are worse than a Hallmark movie."

I laugh, leaning back against Luke's chest. Despite their teasing, I can see the genuine affection in both brothers' eyes.

"Speaking of better plans," Chase says, "a bunch of us are heading to Serenity Beach today. The weather's supposed to hit eighty. You should come, Bebe. A lot of the people in our social circle will be there. You want to make some friends, yeah?"

Luke reaches around me, plucking a crispy piece of bacon from my plate. He holds it to my lips, his eyes encouraging. "It'll be fun," he says as I take a bite. "What do you say? Beach day?"

The salty crunch gives me a moment to consider as I chew thoughtfully. "I'd love to go," I admit, swallowing. "To be honest, it's been harder to make friends than I expected. I've tried talking to girls in my classes, but everyone already seems to have their groups formed."

Wes leans forward, elbows on the table. "That's because you're a guy's girl, not a girl's girl."

"A what?" I furrow my brow, genuinely confused.

Luke's arm tightens around my waist. "He means you're the type of girl who naturally gets along better with guys," he explains, his breath warm against my ear. "Like how you clicked with us right away."

"Exactly," Wes nods, gesturing with his fork. "You don't play games or get caught up in drama. You just... fit in."

"It's not just that," Chase adds, setting down his fork with a thoughtful expression. "Many of the girls at Dalton U are..." he pauses, searching for the right words, "well, they're mean girls—totally fake. They put on this perfect sorority persona but talk about each other behind their backs constantly." He shrugs. "Or they're the opposite—so focused on their GPA and résumé-building that they don't want friends, just study partners and networking connections."

I twist slightly on Luke's lap to better see his face. "Well, I'm grateful I found you guys." My voice softens as unexpected emotion wells up in my throat. "Thank you. For everything. For being such amazing friends and roommates. For including me in your lives." I glance down suddenly shy. "For teaching me about normal stuff that everyone else seems to know already—like Stargazing Club."

When I look up, all three brothers are watching me.

"Hey," Wes says, his usual playful tone replaced with something gentler. "That's what roommates are for."

Luke's lips press against my hair. "You don't need to thank

us." He gives me a gentle squeeze. "Now finish your breakfast so we can get changed into our swimsuits and grab our beach gear. If we leave in the next hour, we might find a good parking spot before the tourists show up."

I take another bite of my pancakes, savoring the sweetness as excitement bubbles through me. Another first—a real beach day with friends. Not the private, roped-off sections of the Mediterranean coastline where Gabriel conducted business meetings, but a public beach with regular people having fun.

Chapter Nineteen

LUKE

THE WHEELS CRUNCH on the gravelly lot as Wes pulls the Jeep in next to Brandon's lifted truck at the beach parking lot. A chorus of whoops and hollers erupts from a cluster of people lounging against their cars. His crew, about eight people sprawled across tailgates and coolers, raising their drinks in greeting.

"The Sullivans have arrived!" someone shouts. "About damn time!"

I catch Bebe's expression in the side mirror—a mix of amusement and uncertainty as she takes in the rowdy welcome. She's wearing oversized sunglasses and one of my baseball caps, her hair spilling out in waves beneath it.

"Ready for this?" I ask her as Wes kills the engine.

She nods, her smile genuine, if a little nervous. "They seem... energetic."

Chase laughs from the backseat. "That's one word for them."

Chase hops out first, immediately high-fiving his way through the crowd. Wes follows, slipping his sunglasses on with a coolness that makes three sophomore girls giggle from their perch on a nearby tailgate.

I help Bebe out of the back, keeping my hand at the small of her back as we navigate through the throng of familiar faces. Everyone wants to say hi, to slap my back or bump fists. I introduce her to each person, some of whom she's already met, watching how she smiles politely but stays close to my side.

"Let's get set up," I suggest, popping the Jeep's trunk.

We grab our gear from the Jeep—coolers, towels, umbrellas, and a portable speaker. Wes shoulders most of the heavy stuff, showing off as usual, while Chase grabs the volleyball and cooler. I take the beach umbrella and my backpack, letting Bebe carry just her tote bag as we follow Brandon down the wooden walkway that cuts through the dunes.

The beach stretches before us, already dotted with colorful umbrellas and sunbathers. He leads us to a relatively empty patch of sand near a volleyball net that's been set up.

As we set up our little camp, Bebe carefully unfolds her towel—a bright blue one that I recognize as mine—and smooths it meticulously on the sand. She settles onto it cross-legged, looking small but content in her oversized t-shirt and denim shorts.

"Alright, let's get this volleyball game started!" Brandon calls out.

Wes strips off his tank top, tossing it onto his towel with a flourish that draws appreciative glances from nearby sunbathers.

"You coming, Luke?" Chase calls, already jogging toward the net.

"In a minute," I reply, kneeling beside Bebe. "Are you good here?"

She nods. "Go play. I'll watch."

I'm about to stand when I notice her expression change. Her smile fades, eyes fixed on something behind me. Following her gaze, I turn to see a group of girls approaching —including Alexa and Ashley from the bowling alley—they peel off their cover-ups to reveal bikinis underneath. Ashley, in particular, makes a show of it, slowly pulling her sundress over her head to reveal a barely there red bikini.

Turning back to Bebe, I notice her shrink slightly, tugging at the hem of her oversized t-shirt. It hits me suddenly—she's comparing herself to them. *Is she self-conscious?*

"Hey," I say, reaching for her hand as an idea comes to me. "Come play with us."

Her eyes widen. "What? No, I'll watch."

I pull her to her feet, not taking no for an answer. "Trust me, you'll have fun."

I turn toward the volleyball net where my brothers are already warming up.

"Hey, Chase!" I shout across the sand. "We've got one more!"

I reach for the hem of my t-shirt and pull it over my head in one smooth motion, tossing it back toward our towels. The sun feels good on my skin, and I catch Bebe's gaze traveling across my chest and abs. Her eyes linger, and she bites her lower lip, a small smile playing at the corners of her mouth.

"Your turn," I say softly, stepping closer to her. My fingers find the hem of her shirt, and I pause, searching her eyes for permission. She gives a tiny nod, and I slowly lift the fabric, revealing inch by inch of her smooth skin until the shirt clears her head completely. My breath catches in my throat as I take her in. The white bikini top she's wearing underneath is simple but stunning against her sun-kissed skin. It's not flashy or over-the-top like the other girls' bikinis, but it looks perfect on her.

"Let's get those shorts off too," I murmur, my fingers moving to the button at her waist. She hesitates for a second before nodding, her eyes never leaving mine as I pop the button open and ease down the zipper. I watch transfixed as she shimmies the denim down her hips and steps out gracefully.

The matching white bikini bottoms tie at each hip with delicate bows that make my fingers itch to tug them loose. The contrast against her golden skin is mesmerizing, and the way the fabric hugs her curves makes my mouth go dry.

"Damn," I whisper, unable to help myself.

A shy smile plays across her lips, but there's a new confidence in the way she stands before me now, no longer hunched or hiding. *She's breathtaking, and she knows I think so.*

Her fingers intertwine with mine, warm and small, against my palm. The sand is warm between our toes as we walk, and I'm acutely aware of every head turning in our direction. Brandon nearly misses a pass, his attention diverted. Wes's eyebrows shoot up to his hairline as he looks over at us approaching the net. I can sense eyes following us—following her—from all directions. I don't blame any of them for looking. The way Bebe's hips sway with each step, how the sunlight catches the curves of her body—she's magnetic. Even

Ashley and her friends have stopped their preening to stare with thinly veiled envy.

Pride swells in my chest as I wrap my arm around her waist, drawing her closer to my side. My hand rests possessively on her hip, thumb brushing against the tie of her bikini bottom. The message is clear to everyone watching: *she's with me.* We haven't put a label on what we are yet, but at this moment, I don't care—I want everyone to know she's off limits.

"Sullivan brothers and Bebe versus Brandon's crew!" Chase announces, clapping his hands to get everyone's attention.

Wes immediately motions to us, his game face already on. "Alright, huddle up, team." We gather in a circle. "Luke, I want you to take the back left. Make sure you're ready to cover any gaps there. I'll cover the middle and keep things steady. Chase, you're our strongest server, so—"

"Wait," Bebe interrupts, looking between us with genuine confusion. "Is this really necessary? Don't you just hit the ball over the net and try not to let it touch the ground?"

I can't help but laugh at the serious look on Wes's face as he strategizes like we're in the Olympics. "Bebe, just let Wes have his fun with this. Strategy meetings are his thing."

"Oh," she says, nodding earnestly. "Sorry." She straightens her posture and focuses intently on Wes. "How would you like me? What position do you want me in?"

Chase and I lock eyes immediately, both of us fighting to keep straight faces. Wes freezes, his mouth hanging open. The silence stretches for a beat too long, and I watch the confusion bloom across her face, followed by the slow dawn of realization as her cheeks flush crimson.

"For the game," she clarifies quickly, her voice an octave higher than usual. "I meant for volleyball!"

Wes recovers first, clearing his throat. "Right, of course. For volleyball." He gives her a wink, making her blush deepen. "I think you should start on the right side. Less traffic there for a beginner."

"Got it. Right side." She nods firmly, clearly trying to move past her unintentional innuendo.

Forty minutes and several intense volleys later, I'm still catching my breath as Wes spikes the final point, sending sand flying as Brandon dives unsuccessfully to save it. The ball hits the sand, and Chase lets out a whoop of victory.

"Game point! Sullivans win!" Wes shouts, raising his arms triumphantly.

I wipe sweat from my forehead, surveying our makeshift court with pride. What began as a casual game turned into a surprisingly competitive match, largely thanks to our secret weapon. Bebe may have started tentatively, but by the second set, she was leaping for the ball with unexpected athleticism, her coordination improving with each play. The look of pure joy on her face when she landed her first spike—sending the ball rocketing between Brandon and his teammate—is something I won't forget.

Brandon jogs over to our side of the net, his expression a mix of disbelief and admiration as he extends his hand to Bebe.

"Damn, girl! Where'd you learn to hit like that?"

Her face lights up as she shakes his hand. "I've never played before. But I've watched a lot of Olympic volleyball on TV."

"Never played?" His jaw drops. "Could've fooled me. That spike in the third set was brutal."

"Beginner's luck," she says with a shy smile, tucking a strand of hair behind her ear.

Jason steps forward, offering her a fist bump. "Luck, my ass. You've got natural talent."

"Seriously," Brandon agrees, nodding appreciatively. "You can hang with us anytime. We're always looking for players who actually want to get in the game."

He glances pointedly toward where Ashley's group is lounging under umbrellas, taking selfies.

"Unlike some people," he continues, lowering his voice conspiratorially, "who are too worried about breaking a nail or getting sand in their hair to have fun."

Bebe follows his gaze, her expression unreadable as she watches the girls giggling over their phones.

"Thanks," she says finally, turning back to Brandon with a genuine smile. "I'd like that."

See... a guy's girl.

"Well, we're heading out," Brandon announces, checking his phone. "The rest of the crew's meeting us at Cody's for drinks later if you guys want to swing by."

"Maybe," I say, though I'm not planning on it. I'm enjoying this day too much to cut it short.

My brothers are already helping gather his stuff. I join them, grabbing the cooler while Brandon folds up the portable volleyball net.

"I'll help you guys carry this," I tell Brandon, nodding toward the parking lot. "Bebe, I'll be right back."

She waves from where she's sitting on our beach towel, looking content.

The trek back to the parking lot is a workout itself, the sand shifting under our feet as we haul Brandon's gear up the wooden walkway. We load everything into his truck, exchanging shoulder slaps and promises to catch up later.

"Your girl's something else," Brandon says quietly as the others load the last cooler. "I've never seen someone pick up volleyball that fast."

"Yeah," I reply, unable to keep the pride from my voice. "She's full of surprises."

When I return to our spot on the beach, our towels are empty. For a brief moment, a flash of worry crosses my mind until I spot her standing at the water's edge. She's facing away from me, her slender figure silhouetted against the sparkling ocean. The white of her bikini stands out against her skin as she cautiously inches forward, letting the waves wash over her feet.

I pause, taking in the sight of her. Her arms are slightly outstretched for balance, head tilted back as if drinking in the sun. She doesn't just steal my breath—she makes it beg to stay gone.

I pull my phone from my pocket and frame her on the screen. The lighting is perfect—golden afternoon sun catching her hair, the foam of a retreating wave swirling around her ankles. I snap the photo just as a larger wave rushes in, making her laugh and dance backward a step.

I stare at the image I've captured. It's perfect—her profile lit by sunlight, joy radiating from her expression, the wonder of someone experiencing something for the first time and savoring every sensation.

Chapter Twenty

BEBE

I STARE out into the depths of the Pacific Ocean, and the vastness of it takes my breath away. I've seen oceans before, but never like this—never with this sense of freedom, of belonging. A wave rushes forward to greet my toes, then retreats in a foamy swirl, leaving tiny bubbles that pop against my skin. I dig my feet deeper into the wet sand, feeling it shift and mold around my toes. The water is cooler than I expected, but refreshing against my sun-warmed skin.

I close my eyes and breathe in the salt air, letting the rhythmic sound of the waves wash over me. Each time the ocean washes over my toes, I feel a little more connected to this moment, to this place.

Strong arms encircle my waist from behind, and I instantly recognize Luke's touch. His chest presses against my back, warm and solid. I lean into him instinctively, letting my body melt against his.

"What are you thinking about?" he murmurs, his breath tickling my ear.

"How perfect today is," I answer honestly. "How I want to remember every detail."

I turn my head up to him, taking in his sun-kissed face, the way his eyes crinkle at the corners when he smiles. The sun catches golden highlights in his hair, making him look ethereal against the backdrop of endless blue. His lips find mine in a gentle kiss that tastes of salt and sunshine.

I break the kiss and glance down the shore where the girls from earlier are still lounging. Their perfectly tall bodies gleam with expensive tanning oil.

I bite my lip, suddenly aware of my body pressed against his—my shorter frame, smaller breasts. Growing up, I never had other girls to compare myself with, never had those sleepovers where teenagers try on clothes and talk about their insecurities while assuring others that they're gorgeous or giggling about which boys had crushes on them.

The women in my brothers' world are all stunning in that intimidating, untouchable way—models, actresses, the wives and girlfriends of powerful men. Next to them, I always felt invisible. Next to these college girls, I feel... unfinished somehow.

"What's going on in that head of yours?" Luke asks, his thumb tracing my cheekbone.

"Just... thinking about those girls," I admit softly. "They're beautiful."

He follows my gaze, then turns my face back to his. "They're not you," he says simply, as if that explains everything. And somehow, it does. The way he looks at me—

like I'm the only person on this entire beach—makes all those insecurities seem suddenly insignificant.

"Come swimming with me." His hand tugs gently at mine, pulling me deeper until the cool water laps at my waist, making me gasp at the sensation. "Can you swim?" he asks, eyes searching mine.

"Yes," I nod. "I mean, I've been in pools before. Never the ocean."

"I've got you," he promises, tugging me a few steps further where the water reaches just below my ribs. The gentle current pushes against us, and I feel the sand shifting beneath my toes with each passing wave.

I move toward him instinctively and wrap my arms around his neck so I can jump up, my legs encircling his waist. Luke's hands slide down to support me, his palms cupping my ass underwater, holding me securely against him.

The intimacy of our position sends a thrill through me. Suspended in the water like this, our bodies pressed together, I feel weightless and protected all at once. The world narrows down to just us—the gentle rise and fall of the waves, the warm pressure of his hands on my skin, the rhythm of his breathing matching mine.

"I love watching you experience things," he says, his voice low and intimate. "The way your eyes light up when you discover something new... it's beautiful." He adjusts his grip, one hand moving to the small of my back to keep me close. "I'm glad you had fun today," he continues, his eyes never leaving mine. "Seeing you smile—it was honestly the best part of my day."

Something shifts inside me at his words, a swell of emotion so powerful it catches me off guard. Before I can stop it, a single tear escapes, trailing down my cheek to mingle with the surrounding saltwater.

Luke's brow furrows with concern. "Hey," he says softly, brushing the wetness from my skin with his thumb. "I just said I like seeing you smile. Why are you crying?"

I shake my head, unable to find the right words immediately. The vastness of what I'm feeling seems impossible to capture. "You're part of the reason," I finally manage, my voice barely audible above the crashing of the waves. "For my happiness, for my smiles."

His eyes soften, his gaze traveling across my face with such tenderness it makes my heart ache. "Come here," he whispers, pulling me closer.

His lips find mine, and this time, the kiss deepens immediately. His tongue traces the seam of my lips, seeking entry, and I open to him without hesitation. The salt of the ocean mingles with the taste that is uniquely Luke as our tongues slide against each other, exploring, discovering. The water laps around us, creating a gentle rhythm that our bodies naturally follow.

The world dissolves. The laughter from the beach, the calls of seagulls overhead, the distant music from someone's portable speaker—it all fades away. The buoyancy of the ocean makes me feel weightless in his arms, like we're floating together in our own private universe. Every sensation is heightened—the press of his chest against mine, the gentle scrape of his stubble against my chin, the way his hands grip me more tightly as the kiss intensifies. Everything else disappears, leaving only Luke and me suspended in this perfect bubble of connection.

I've never felt so wanted, so desired, so... seen. The

chemistry between us is electric, undeniable. His body against mine feels right in a way I can't explain but instinctively understand.

He begins to sway in the water, our bodies moving together with the gentle push and pull of the waves. His strong hands grip my waist as he spins us slowly, water splashing around us in a glittering cascade. The unexpected motion pulls a laugh from deep in my chest—a sound of pure, unbridled joy that surprises even me.

"I love that sound," he says, his voice husky.

Suddenly feeling playful, I loosen my hold on him, letting my arms slip from around his neck as I lean backward. The water cradles me, supporting my weight as I arch my back and let my head dip into the cool embrace of the ocean. My hair fans out around me like dark seaweed, floating in the gentle current.

The sun beats down on my upturned face, warm and golden against my closed eyelids. I spread my arms wide, fingertips skimming the surface of the water. This feeling— this perfect balance between floating and being held—is intoxicating.

When I open my eyes and tilt my chin to look at him, my breath catches. The intensity in his gaze steals the air from my lungs. He's not looking at the horizon or the beach or anything else—just me. His eyes trace a slow path from my face down my body, lingering on the curve of my throat, the rise and fall of my chest where the bikini barely contains me. There's something reverent in his expression, like he's committing every detail to memory.

I feel beautiful under his gaze. Powerful. Wanted.

I pull myself upright in one fluid motion, water cascading

off my body as I return to him. My arms find their place around his neck once more, my chest pressing firmly against his as the wet fabric of my bikini does little to separate us. Droplets cling to his eyelashes as I capture his mouth with mine, no longer gentle or exploring, but demanding and fierce. He responds immediately, one hand tangling in my wet hair while the other presses against my lower back, eliminating any space between us.

The kiss deepens, becoming something more urgent, more vital. His tongue slides against mine as I press myself impossibly closer. The cool water contrasts with the heat building between us, creating a delicious tension that makes me shiver despite the warmth of the day.

"Jesus, get a room!" Wes's voice cuts through our bubble, followed immediately by a massive splash of cold water hitting us from the side.

I break away from Luke with a startled gasp, turning to find Wes grinning mischievously, his hand still dripping from the splash he'd sent our way. Chase wades in behind him, dragging something bright yellow through the water.

Luke shakes his head, water droplets flying from his hair. "Seriously? There's an entire ocean, and you two choose this exact spot?"

Chase laughs. "What can I say? It's prime real estate. Best view of the lifeguard tower."

"What's that?" I ask, pointing to the yellow board Chase's dragging behind him.

"This?" He lifts it out of the water. "It's a boogie board. Never seen one?"

"No, I haven't," I say, taking a step toward him, my interest genuinely piqued. "Does it float? Or do you sit on it?"

His eyebrows shoot up in surprise. "You've seriously never seen anyone boogie boarding before?"

I shake my head, reaching out to touch the smooth yellow surface. "Can you show me how it works?"

"Sure thing, beach rookie," Chase says with a grin. He moves a few feet away where the waves are breaking with more force. "You basically wait for a good wave, then hop on your stomach like this—"

He demonstrates, positioning the board in front of him and launching himself forward as a wave rolls in. The ocean carries him effortlessly toward shore, his body perfectly balanced on the small board as he rides the wave all the way in until it dissipates near the sand.

"That looks fun!" I call out, clapping my hands together with genuine excitement.

Chase jogs back to us, water streaming down his body. "Want to try it?"

"Can I?" I ask, already reaching for the board. The plastic feels smooth under my fingers.

He hands it over to me. "The trick is timing. Wait until you feel the wave starting to pick up, then push off with your feet."

Luke stands behind me, his hands gently positioning my fingers on the sides of the board. "Hold it like this," he instructs, his voice close to my ear. "And keep your weight centered."

I nod eagerly, wading deeper into the water with the board clutched against my chest. The waves seem bigger from this angle, rolling toward me with foamy white crests. I feel a flutter of nervousness in my stomach, but excitement quickly overpowers it.

"Wait for it," Chase calls from my left. "Not this one... the next one looks good!"

I see it coming—a swell larger than the others, building momentum as it approaches. I position the board in front of me just as Chase showed me, my heart hammering against my ribs.

"Now!" Wes shouts.

I kick my feet against the sandy bottom and thrust my body forward as the wave begins to crest. For a terrifying second, I feel myself wobble, certain I'm going to flip over. But then something magical happens—the wave catches me, and suddenly I'm gliding forward, propelled by the water. The sensation is exhilarating, a perfect balance between control and surrender as I speed toward the shore.

"Go, Bebe!" Wes's voice carries over the rush of water.

"Yeah! Look at her go!" Chase hollers, clapping wildly.

Luke's distinctive whistle pierces the air as I ride the wave to where it peters out in the shallow water.

I leap up from the surf, clutching the boogie board against my ribs, adrenaline still coursing through my veins. My heart pounds with excitement as I jog back toward where the three brothers wait.

"That was incredible!" I exclaim, breathless from the rush.

Luke catches me as I reach him, his strong arms sliding around my waist. The pride in his eyes makes my chest swell as he pulls me close.

"You're a natural," he murmurs, his lips grazing my ear. His hands drift lower, fingers splaying possessively across my wet skin. "And by the way," his voice drops to a husky whisper that only I can hear, "your ass looks amazing in that bikini.

When we get home later, I'm going to untie those little bows on your hips."

My breath catches in my throat; a delicious shiver runs down my spine. Heat blooms deep in my belly at his words, at the promise in his voice. I inhale sharply, my fingers instinctively tightening around the boogie board. My heart races with anticipation, thoughts of the beach and waves suddenly far from my mind.

I rise on my tiptoes and capture his lips with mine, my free hand sliding around his neck to pull him closer. The kiss is deep and deliberate. My body pressed against his as the water continues to lap around our waists. When I finally break away, my lips brush against the shell of his ear.

"Let's go home," I whisper, my voice low and husky. "Now."

His sharp intake of breath tells me everything I need to know. His fingers tighten momentarily on my hips before he steps back, eyes dark with desire.

"Wes, Chase," he calls out as he takes the boogie board from my hands, giving it back to Chase. "We're ready to go."

Wes glances between us. "Already? The sun's still up."

"I'm getting sunburned," I lie, though the flush spreading across my chest and face probably makes it convincing.

Chase snorts, clearly not buying it. "Yeah, I bet that's the reason."

Chapter Twenty-One

LUKE

As I take Bebe's hand and pull her through the garage entrance to the house, Chase shouts something about grabbing the cooler and towels from the Jeep. But the door slams behind us, cutting off Chase's requests mid-sentence.

"Come on," I murmur, tugging her upstairs and to my bedroom. The urgency between us is palpable, electric. Each brush of her fingers against mine sends sparks racing up my arm.

The door barely closes before her lips find mine, hungry and insistent. I pin her against the wall, my hands sliding down her sides to grip her hips. She tastes of salt and sunshine, her skin warm beneath my palms.

"Shower," I whisper against her mouth.

She nods, already pulling at the hem of my t-shirt. I lift my arms, letting her tug it over my head. Her fingers trace the contours of my chest, leaving goosebumps in their wake.

I lead her to the bathroom, flicking on the light. The room

fills with a soft glow as I reach into the walk-in shower stall to turn the water on. It hisses to life, steam quickly billowing into the small space.

I turn back to Bebe, who's standing in the center of the room, watching me with wide eyes that somehow manage to look innocent and hungry at the same time. The white bikini is the only barrier between us now, stark against her sun-kissed skin.

"Let me," I whisper, stepping closer. My fingers find the bikini tie between her shoulder blades, lingering there for a moment before pulling. The top loosens, falling away from her body to land silently on the tile floor.

Her breasts are perfect—full and round, with dusky nipples. I cup one in my palm, feeling its weight, its softness. When I roll her nipple between my thumb and forefinger, she gasps, her head falling back slightly as her eyes flutter closed.

"Beautiful," I murmur, mesmerized by her reaction. My hands drift downward, tracing the gentle curve of her waist, the flare of her hips. I find the delicate bows at each hip that hold her bikini bottoms in place, my fingers curling around the thin strings.

Her hands move to my forearms, gripping them. There's something desperate in her grip, something needy that makes my heart race faster. Her eyes lock with mine, dark with desire, silently pleading.

I tug one string slowly, watching it unravel. Then the other side, the fabric loosens until it falls away completely, pooling around her ankles. My breath catches in my throat as I take in the sight of her—the neat strip of dark hair, just as she'd described.

"You're perfect," I whisper, unable to look away.

She steps closer, her naked body pressing against mine as her fingers find the drawstring of my board shorts. With deliberate slowness, she pulls the knot free; her knuckles brushing against my stomach. The shorts loosen instantly, hanging precariously on my hips.

Bebe's gaze drops downward. Her lips part, her breathing quickens as she hooks her thumbs into the fabric and slides my shorts down. They fall to the floor with a soft rustle, leaving me completely exposed, my cock hard and jutting between us.

"Luke," she breathes.

Her eyes linger on me, wide with wonder. I can't wait any longer. My hands cup her face as I capture her lips with mine, the kiss deep and demanding. She responds immediately, matching my intensity as I guide her backward toward the shower. The steam surrounds us as we step inside, the warm water cascading over our bodies.

I press her against the cool tile wall, our lips never breaking contact. Her hands find my hips, fingers digging into my skin as I explore her mouth with my tongue. Water streams between us, washing away the sand and salt.

My hand slides down her stomach, finding the slick warmth between her thighs. She's already wet for me—not just from the shower. I trace gentle circles around her clit, applying just enough pressure to make her gasp against my lips. The sound is intoxicating, spurring me on.

She breaks the kiss, her head falling back against the tile as her eyes close in pleasure. I watch her face—the parted lips, the flush spreading across her cheeks, the water droplets clinging to her eyelashes. I continue my ministrations, learning what makes her body respond, what makes her breath catch. Her reactions guide me, tell me where to touch, how to touch. I drop my lips to the curve of her neck, the pulse point, where I suck gently, tasting the sweetness of her skin mingled with shower water. She moans, a sound so primal and needy it makes my cock twitch against her thigh.

"More," she whispers, her voice barely audible over the running water.

I slide my middle finger along her pussy before slowly pushing inside her. She's impossibly tight, her inner walls gripping my finger as I curl it upward, searching for that spot that will drive her wild. When I find it, her entire body jolts, a gasp tearing from her throat.

"There?" I murmur against her neck.

"Yes," she breathes, her hips rocking against my hand. "God, yes."

I add a second finger, stretching her gently as I establish a rhythm. Her breathing becomes erratic, little whimpers escaping with each exhale. I pull back just enough to watch her face, to see pleasure overtake her features. Her eyes flutter open, meeting mine with an intensity that steals my breath. There's something incredibly intimate about holding her gaze while my fingers work inside her.

"That's it," I encourage, feeling her inner walls beginning to flutter around my fingers. "Let go for me, baby."

She doesn't look away, her expression open and vulnerable as she surrenders completely to the sensation. Her walls clench around my fingers, rhythmic pulses that match the sharp cry escaping her lips. She trembles against me, her entire body shuddering with release as warm wetness floods my hand. I keep my fingers moving, drawing out her pleasure until she grabs my wrist, oversensitive.

"Oh my God," she pants, her chest heaving as she catches

her breath. A languid smile spreads across her face, her eyes half-lidded with satisfaction.

I bring my fingers to my lips, tasting her essence with a groan of appreciation. Her eyes darken as she watches, something shifting in her expression—the satisfied smile transforming into something more predatory, more determined.

Without warning, she places her palms against my chest and pushes, sending me backward until my shoulders hit the opposite shower wall. The cool tiles contrast with my heated skin as she holds my gaze, slowly sinking to her knees before me.

The sight of her kneeling, water cascading on her perfect naked body while she looks up at me through her lashes with those innocent yet hungry eyes, nearly undoes me. My breath catches as her delicate fingers encircle my length, the contrast of her small hand against my size making me throb with anticipation. She strokes experimentally, finding a rhythm that has me fighting to keep my eyes open, desperate to watch but overwhelmed by sensation as my hips involuntarily buck forward.

"Is this okay?" she asks, her voice husky with want, eyes never leaving mine.

"God, yes," I rasp out, one hand bracing against the shower wall for support.

When her lips part and she leans forward, the first touch of her warm mouth against my tip sends electricity up my spine.

I can tell she's inexperienced—there's a tentative quality to her movements, a careful exploration as she tries to find her rhythm. Her technique lacks the practiced precision of women who've done this countless times, but God, what she lacks in experience she more than makes up for with enthusiasm. Her eyes never leave mine, watching my reactions intently, adjusting based on the sounds I make, the way my muscles tense.

She takes me deeper, and she gags slightly, then immediately tries again with renewed determination. Something primal stirs in my chest. This isn't just physical— she's giving herself to me completely, learning me, wanting to please me. The combination of her eagerness and the sight of her looking up through those wet lashes makes this more intense than anything I've experienced before.

"That's perfect," I encourage, my voice strained as I thread my fingers gently through her wet hair.

The sensation is overwhelming—soft, warm, perfect. A groan tears from my throat as she slides her full—pouty lips down my shaft, taking me deeper than I expected. Her tongue swirls around the head with each retreat, a maddening pattern that has me fighting for control.

"Fuuuuck," I breathe, my head reclining back against the tile.

She hums in response, the vibration sending shockwaves of pleasure through my body.

She hollows her cheeks, creating an exquisite suction that pulls a strangled moan from deep in my chest. I watch in awe as she takes me impossibly deeper with each bob of her head until I'm at the back of her throat. Then somehow she goes further, her lips reaching all the way to the base where they press against my skin.

"Jesus Christ," I gasp.

No woman has ever taken all of me before. The sight of

her—this beautiful girl—swallowing my entire length like she was made for it shatters my control. When she pulls off for air —sucking in a deep breath—her lips are swollen, chest heaving, and a thin strand of saliva connects her mouth to my cock.

This image—her perfect face, lips parted, open and panting, my cock resting against her cheek. She looks absolutely debauched. Like something from my deepest fantasies. And it pushes me over the edge. I try to pull back, but she holds my hips, keeping me close as the first pulse erupts. Hot streams of cum paint across her cheek, her parted lips, even catching in her eyelashes. She doesn't flinch or turn away—instead—she closes her eyes and tilts her face upward, accepting every rope as my release covers her beautiful face. The sight is so erotic, so raw, that I can barely process it. My body shudders with aftershocks as the last pulses coat her lips, which she licks instinctively.

"Come here," I whisper hoarsely, helping her to her feet.

She rises gracefully, water streaming down her cum-splattered face. I reach for the washcloth, dunking it under the warm spray. With gentle strokes, I clean her face, wiping her cheeks, her eyelids, her parted lips. The tenderness of the moment contrasts with the raw passion of seconds before.

Her eyes slowly open as I finish, looking at me with something like reverence in their depths. There's no disgust, no regret—only a soft wonder, and I don't know how one person can make me feel so much at once.

"Thank you," she whispers, leaning into my touch as I wipe the last traces from her chin.

I cup her face in my hands, overwhelmed by the trust she's showing me. "I'm so happy we found each other."

I pull her against me, our wet bodies pressed together under the stream of warm water. The tenderness I feel overwhelms me as I lean to place a gentle kiss on her forehead, lingering there as our breathing gradually slows to normal.

I can't believe this is real—that she's real. Just weeks ago, I was living my normal, predictable life, and then she appeared, quite literally on my doorstep. Now I can't imagine my world without her in it. We've connected on every level I've never experienced with anyone else. Not just physically, though, that chemistry is undeniable, and we haven't even had actual sex yet, but emotionally, intellectually. She fits into my world as if she were always meant to be here.

Chapter Twenty-Two

LUKE

"Markers," I call out, going down the list on my phone. "Four of them, two semi-auto and two pump action."

Wes tosses the paintball guns into the large duffel bag. "Got 'em."

"Masks," I continue, watching Chase collect the protective face shields from the storage shelf in the garage.

"All here," he confirms, examining each one before carefully placing them in the bag. "Mine's got a scratch on the right lens, but it's still usable."

"Air tanks?" I look up from my phone.

Wes pats the side pocket of the duffel. "CO2 tanks, all filled yesterday. We're good for at least three hours of play."

"Hoppers and pods?"

Chase holds up the plastic containers. "Got enough pods for about two thousand rounds. Should be enough unless Wes goes full Rambo again."

"It was one time," Wes protests, grabbing the hoppers from his hands. "And we still won."

I sigh, checking off the remaining items on my list. "Chest protectors?"

"Right here," Chase says, holding the padded vests. "Though I don't think Luke needs one. He's got natural padding with all those muscles from the gym."

"Jealousy doesn't look good on you, little brother," I say, flexing an arm dramatically.

The door to the house inside the garage swings open, and Bebe appears in the doorway, silhouetted by the late morning light. Her cinnamon hair is pulled back in a messy bun, loose tendrils framing her face. She's wearing a simple white t-shirt and leggings, but somehow makes it look like runway fashion.

"There you are," she says, her mismatched eyes finding mine immediately. She crosses the garage in quick steps, rising on her tiptoes to press her lips against mine. The kiss is brief but electric, sending that familiar jolt through my system that hasn't diminished at all in the week since our beach day.

I can't help but smile against her mouth, my hand automatically finding her waist. She pulls back, her eyes taking in the equipment scattered around us. "What are you guys doing?" she asks, running her finger along the barrel of one of the paintball markers.

"Going to the paintball range," Chase answers, zipping up the duffel bag with a decisive tug. "Ambrose Battlefield just opened a new course last weekend. We've got a reservation at noon. It's a tradition—first Saturday of every month." He glances at Bebe. "Team Sullivan versus whoever's unlucky enough to get matched against us."

"That sounds fun," she says as weighs a marker in her hands, her fingers finding the proper grip position.

Wes raises an eyebrow, watching her handle the marker. "You want to come with us?" he asks, a mischievous grin spreading across his face. "That is, if it's okay with your *boyfriend*." He nods toward me, emphasizing the word "boyfriend" with exaggerated significance.

Her eyes flick to mine, a slight flush coloring her cheeks. We haven't had the "what are we" conversation yet, despite spending every night together since the beach.

"I don't want to intrude on guy time," she says, carefully placing the marker back on the workbench.

"You wouldn't be," I insist, stepping closer to her. "We'd love to have you join us."

"We could use a fourth," Chase adds. "Otherwise, they'll assign some solo stranger to our team."

I have the thought of introducing Bebe to another first experience to try, and I've come to love watching her discover new things.

Her face lights up with sudden excitement. She bounces on her toes, actually jumping in place, her enthusiasm bubbling over. I notice she's wearing those pink fuzzy cat slippers she loves so much. The ones that somehow make her look both adorable and sexy at the same time.

"Okay! I'll go change," she exclaims, practically vibrating with excitement.

She gives me a quick kiss on the cheek before darting out of the garage, her slippers making soft padding sounds against the concrete floor.

As soon as the door closes behind her, Chase lets out a low whistle. "Man, you are so whipped."

"Look at his face," Wes chuckles, nudging Chase with his elbow. "He gets all dopey-eyed whenever she's around."

I roll my eyes, trying to appear unaffected. "Shut up."

"Boyfriend," Chase mimics in a singsong voice. "You haven't made it official yet? What are you waiting for?"

"Yeah," Wes adds, crossing his arms. "You sleep in her room every night. We can hear you two, by the way. The walls aren't that thick."

"It's... complicated."

"What's complicated?" Wes scoffs. "You like her. She likes you. Boom. Relationship."

I sigh, leaning against the workbench. "I'm worried about dad." I run a hand through my hair. "She's not... you know. She's not in the Keeper Society. And you know how he feels about outsiders. He has said nothing about it yet, but I know it's coming. The lecture—he's done it to all of us before when we've had a regular girl around for a period of time."

Chase is the first to speak. "Maybe we could bring her in? I mean, if things are serious between you two..."

"Are you kidding?" Wes interrupts, lowering his voice even though we're alone. "Bebe's great and all, but do you really think she'd understand what we're involved in?" His voice drops even lower. "This isn't like joining a fraternity or a book club. I mean, think about it—secret meetings, oaths of silence, generations of family obligations. If someone outside heard about it without context, they'd run for the hills. The Keepers aren't something you can explain over dinner."

"I know that," I reply, frustration edging into my voice.

"Look," Chase interjects, "I like Bebe. We both do. If you're serious about her, it might be worth considering talking to dad about."

"Even if he did," Wes picks back up, "think about how it would sound to her. 'Hey Bebe, by the way, my family is part of a secret society tied to Dalton U that's existed for centuries, influencing the town and events all over the country from the shadows.' Not to mention the stupid robes and initiation."

"And that's just the beginning," I say, pushing off from the workbench. "How do I explain the monthly meetings? The family obligations? How the women in it are practically supposed to act like housewives from the 50s, bear children—especially boys to continue the legacy and pass on the brotherhood—and have dinner on the table by five."

Chase tosses a paintball hopper from hand to hand, considering. "The alternative is to keep it from her forever."

I hate that they're right. The secrecy that surrounds The Keepers has always made relationships complicated. I've seen it happen before—members trying to bring outsiders in, only for those relationships to implode when the truth comes out. Most women can't handle it.

Before I can formulate a response, the door swings open again and Bebe reappears. My words die in my throat at the sight of her. She's changed into a bright pink tank top that hugs her curves perfectly and reveals a tantalizing strip of midriff. Her white shorts are impossibly tiny, exposing long, toned legs that disappear into pristine white tennis shoes. She's clearly dressed for comfort, but compared to our battle-ready attire of faded long-sleeve shirts and dark cargo pants, she looks woefully unprepared.

Wes's eyes widen as he takes in her outfit. "Is that what you're wearing?" he asks, gesturing toward her ensemble.

She glances down at herself, confusion crossing her

features. "What's wrong with it?" She tugs self-consciously at the hem of her tank top.

I step forward, taking her hands in mine. "The paintballs will destroy those clothes," I explain gently. "They're filled with dye that stains fabric—sometimes permanently. And when they hit bare skin..." I trail off, wincing. "Let's just say you'll have colorful bruises for days..."

She considers my explanation for a moment, then shrugs with surprising nonchalance. "I'll be fine," she says, her tone dismissive as she brushes off the warning.

I open my mouth to protest further—to explain about welts and bruises and how much those tiny shorts will leave her exposed—but Chase cuts me off.

"If she insists," he says with a casual wave, already hefting the duffel bag over his shoulder. "Her choice, man."

I look to Wes for support, but he just gives me a subtle head shake and a look that clearly says let her learn the hard way. He tilts his head toward the Jeep.

"Fine," I sigh. "But at least take my long-sleeved shirt."

Bebe rolls her eyes but accepts the navy shirt I pull from my gym bag, tying it around her waist instead of putting it on. "Happy?"

Wes laughs, jingling his keys. "Let's roll before we lose our reservation."

We pile into the Jeep, equipment stowed in the back. Bebe claims shotgun before Chase can, earning a playful glare from him as he climbs into the back with me. She's practically bouncing in her seat as Wes backs out of the driveway.

Chapter Twenty-Three

LUKE

"SEE that flag in the center there?" I point to the red pennant fluttering on a pole in the middle of the field from the platform of the viewing deck that overlooks the paintball course. "That's the objective. Each team starts from one of the four corners." I gesture to the quadrants marked with colored banners. "When the horn sounds, everyone races to capture the flag and bring it back to their starting zone without getting hit. If you get hit—you're eliminated."

Bebe follows my finger, her eyes scanning the elaborate battlefield with its wooden barriers, overturned vehicles, and artificial trenches. The course is impressive—nearly two acres of tactical terrain designed to test even experienced players.

"Okay," she says with a casual shrug, adjusting the protective mask in her hands. "Grab the flag without getting shot and return it to the starting point."

I can't help but chuckle at her nonchalance. Sweet, innocent Bebe has no idea what she's in for. The game seems simple in theory, but the reality involves strategy, teamwork, and quick reflexes—skills that take time to develop.

"Yeah, that's basically it," I reply, watching her examine the pink rental marker we picked up at the front desk.

Wes stands beside us, adjusting his tactical vest. He gives her an appreciative once-over, grinning as she straps on her own protective gear.

"Damn, Bebe," he says with a low whistle. "You look like a cute little Lara Croft with that getup."

She tilts her head, brow furrowing beneath her half-secured mask. "Who's Lara Croft?"

The three of us exchange glances before breaking into laughter. Chase doubles over, while Wes looks genuinely offended that she doesn't know his reference.

"Tomb Raider?" he tries again. "Video game character? Hot archaeologist with dual pistols?" When Bebe's expression remains blank, he shakes his head in mock disappointment. "Add having a gaming marathon to our growing list of to-dos. Your education is severely lacking."

The sudden blare of an air horn cuts echoes across the field. The referee's voice crackles over the loudspeaker: "One minute to starting positions! Teams to your corners!"

My instincts kick in as we hurry down the platform stairs toward our assigned spots. The electronic scoreboard begins counting down from sixty seconds. We use the remaining time to check our markers and adjust our masks.

I turn to Bebe. "Stay close to me," I tell her, resting a hand on her shoulder. "The first game could be overwhelming, so just follow my lead."

Her lips curl into a confident smile. "No," she says softly, adjusting her mask. "*You*—stay close to *me*."

I blink at her, momentarily confused by her words. Before I can respond, the final countdown blares through the speakers.

Three... two... one...

The horn blasts and the starting gate swings open. Instead of huddling behind me as expected, Bebe launches forward in a blur of movement.

"Cover me!" she shouts over her shoulder, already sprinting toward the center field.

Wes, Chase, and I exchange bewildered glances before Wes snaps into action. "You heard her! Move!"

We fan out behind her, markers raised. Bebe drops into a perfect combat roll, somersaulting behind a wooden barricade as paintballs whiz overhead. Without pausing, she pops up in a shooter's stance—feet shoulder-width apart, marker braced against her shoulder, elbows tucked—and fires three rapid shots.

"What the—" Chase mutters beside me as three opposing team members crumple to the ground, bright pink splatters marking their chest protectors. Her shots are precise—center mass.

I watch in awe as she continues firing, each pull of the trigger resulting in another opponent marked with paint. Her movements are fluid, graceful, almost choreographed, as she darts from cover to cover. She isn't just playing—she's dominating the field with military precision.

"Holy shit," Wes breathes beside me. "Where did she learn to—"

"Less talking, more shooting!" I snap, finally breaking from my stupor. My brothers and I spread out, adding our own firepower to Bebe's assault. Chase takes the left flank

183

while Wes provides covering fire from behind an overturned barrel. I push forward, trying to keep pace with her as she methodically clears a path toward the central flag.

The opposing teams regroup, focusing their fire on the petite girl who's decimating their ranks. Paintballs whiz past Bebe's head, but she senses them coming, ducking and weaving with uncanny timing.

I'm so distracted watching her that I don't notice the player flanking me until it's almost too late. A flash of movement in my peripheral vision is my only warning.

Suddenly, Bebe materializes beside me, her small hands gripping my shoulders with surprising strength. She spins me around and slams me against the nearest barrier, pressing me flat as a paintball whizzes past where my head had been seconds before. In one fluid motion, she circles me, raises her marker, and fires a single shot. I hear a groan and turn to see an opponent clutching his chest where a bright pink splatter blooms across his vest.

"Watch your ass, Sullivan," she says, her voice light but commanding. Her eyes sparkle with adrenaline behind her mask, lips curved in a playful smile that makes my heart race faster than the surrounding firefight. "I might not be there to save it next time."

She taps my chest protector twice with her finger. "Cover the left flank," she directs, nodding toward a cluster of barrels. "I'll circle around and go for the flag. Wait for my signal."

With that, she's gone, disappearing behind a stack of wooden crates. I stare after her, momentarily stunned by this unexpected side of Bebe—confident, commanding, deadly accurate.

She reappears at the edge of a trench, catching my eye. She

taps her ear twice, then points forward with two fingers. The gesture is so crisp, so military, I respond instinctively.

I signal to Chase and Wes, who both nod in understanding. When she raises her hand and drops it sharply, we burst from our positions simultaneously, covering fire in three directions.

"Go! Go! Go!" I shout as we sprint across open ground.

Chase slides in beside me behind a concrete barrier, breathing hard. "Who the hell is this girl?" he pants, gesturing toward Bebe as she executes a perfect tactical roll to avoid incoming fire.

"I honestly have no idea," I reply, unable to keep the admiration from my voice. "But I really, really like her."

Wes appears on my other side, dropping to his knee to reload. "Whoever she is, she's—" His words cut off as he spots an opponent attempting to outmaneuver us. He takes a deep breath, steadies his aim, and fires many shots in quick succession. "Got him!" he shouts as his target drops dramatically, throwing his hands up in surrender, blue paint splattered across his chest protector.

"Path clear!" Wes calls to Bebe, who's crouched behind a barrier about fifteen feet from the flagpole.

She nods once before sprinting toward the pole. Her movements are a blur of pink and white as she reaches the base and begins to climb. Her small frame moves with incredible agility, scaling the metal pole as if she's done it a thousand times.

"Cover her!" I shout, laying down suppressive fire toward two opponents trying to line up shots on Bebe's ascending form.

My brothers fan out, creating a triangle of protection

around the pole. Paintballs whiz past our heads, splattering against barriers and the ground around us. One grazes my shoulder, barely missing me.

She reaches the top in seconds, snatching the red pennant with one hand while maintaining her grip with the other. After securing the flag, she slides down the pole, landing in a crouching position.

"Chase!" Bebe calls out, sprinting toward us with the flag clutched tightly in her hand. "Take it home!"

He breaks from our formation, positioning himself to receive the handoff. She tosses the pennant to him; her aim is perfect despite the surrounding chaos.

"I've got you covered!" I shout, stepping between Chase and the remaining opponents. I fire a rapid succession of shots, forcing them to duck behind cover as he races toward our starting zone, the flag fluttering behind him like a victory banner.

Wes slips in beside me, his marker trained on two players attempting to flank our position. "Bebe, nine o'clock!" he warns.

Without hesitation, she swivels and fires three precise shots. Pink splatters bloom across an opponent's mask and chest protector, dropping him instantly.

"Go, go, go!" I urge Chase, who's sprinting toward our corner. The distance closes—twenty yards, fifteen, ten...

I continue engaging in suppressive fire, my heart pounding as he dives across the threshold of our starting zone, flag clutched to his chest. He reaches the mark and the horn sounds, its piercing blast echoing over the battlefield. We won!

"Yes!" I shout, pumping my fist in the air as our team name flashes on the scoreboard. Around us, players from the opposing teams pull off their masks, expressions of disbelief and frustration clear on their paint-splattered faces.

Wes lets out a wild whoop, rushing toward Chase to clap him on the back. I turn to find Bebe, my heart still racing with adrenaline and something else—pride, amazement, desire.

She's standing in a small clearing, her marker held casually at her side, surveying the battlefield like a general after a successful mission. Most of the opposing team members are covered in pink splatters—her signature color leaving its mark across the field.

"That was incredible!" Chase shouts, jogging back to us, flag still in hand. "We've never cleared a course that fast!"

Wes runs over to us, grinning wildly as he throws his arms around Chase. I reach them in three quick strides, and we form a huddle of adrenaline and victory. Without hesitation, we pull Bebe into our circle, arms interlocking around shoulders as we jump and shout like children.

"Team Sullivan dominates again!" Wes roars.

The four of us break apart, breathless and laughing. She reaches up, pulling off her mask. Her hair tumbles free, damp with sweat and clinging to her flushed cheeks. Those mismatched eyes shine with exhilaration, more alive than I've ever seen them.

Something primal and possessive surges through me. I rip my mask off and close the distance between us. My hands find her waist, lifting her effortlessly into the air. She responds instantly, her legs wrapping around my waist. Her arms loop around my neck, and I capture her mouth with mine.

The kiss is different from our others—hungry, public, claiming. The taste of salt and victory mingle between us as her fingers thread through my hair. Around us, Wes and Chase whoop and holler, but I barely register their voices. All I can focus on is the warmth of her body pressed against mine, the softness of her lips, the way she smiles against my mouth like she's never been happier.

When we finally break apart, her eyes are shining with something wild and jubilant. Her cheeks are flushed, hair dampened with sweat at her temples, and I've never seen anything more beautiful.

"That," I breathe, still holding her against me, "was incredible."

She laughs, the sound light and carefree. "I told you I have three brothers," she says with a wink as I set her back on her feet.

"Wait a minute..." The realization crashes over me like a wave. "You've played paintball before, haven't you?" I study her face, seeing the mischief dancing in her mismatched eyes.

Wes strides over, yanking off his mask. "You never told us you were good at this," he accuses, though his grin betrays his admiration.

"Good? She's a fucking paintball assassin!" Chase beams.

Bebe shrugs, casually examining her pink marker. "You guys never asked, just assumed I hadn't." Her voice carries an innocent lilt. "I wanted to surprise you."

Chase slings an arm around Wes's shoulders. "Consider us surprised. And slightly terrified."

I shake my head in wonder, taking in this new facet of Bebe. The tactical precision, the combat rolls, the way she commanded the field—this wasn't just someone who'd played a few casual games. This was expertise, honed through practice and training. Like a soldier. Or something else entirely.

"Where did you learn to move like that?" I ask, voice lower now. "Those were tactical maneuvers."

A shadow flickers across her expression—so brief I almost miss it—before her smile returns, perhaps a touch too bright.

"I told you, my brothers are competitive. I played all the time growing up. Along with laser tag and video games." She busies herself with adjusting the strap of her marker, avoiding my eyes. "The oldest was into military stuff."

There's truth there, but not the whole truth. I can feel it. The way she handled herself on that field was beyond sibling rivalry.

Wes claps his hands together. "I don't know about you guys, but I worked up an appetite. Let's hit Smokey's BBQ going home."

Chase nods enthusiastically. "I could demolish a full rack of ribs right now."

Bebe's expression brightens at the change of subject. "BBQ sounds amazing," she agrees, already turning toward the exit.

I catch up to her in two strides, draping my arm around her shoulders and pulling her close against my side. As we walk to the parking lot, I think about how she might just be tough enough and open-minded to be initiated into The Keepers. If I want this to work with her—she'll have to do it.

I'm falling in love with her.

Chapter Twenty-Four

BEBE

I'M REALIZING that happiness has a face—Luke's.

I step out of the shower and wrap a towel around myself. The water drips down my legs onto the tile floor as I wipe condensation from the mirror. My reflection emerges through the fog—flushed cheeks, bright eyes, and the ghost of a smile I can't suppress. I don't mean to smile; it just happens, like muscle memory or breathing whenever I think of him. It feels good seeing myself like this—alive, exhilarated, normal.

For once, I wasn't Bebe Laurent, The Killer Bee with sixteen ways to end a life. I was just a girl showing off at paintball, impressing her—*boyfriend?*—and his brothers with skills that, for once, didn't need to be hidden. The rush of dominating the course without having to conceal my abilities —it was freeing.

I run my fingers through my damp hair, working out the tangles before reaching for my brush. As I pull it through, I can't help but remember Luke's face when I took down those first opponents—that mixture of shock, admiration, and something else. Pride, maybe. Or desire.

The smile on my lips widens as I recall the way he lifted me after our victory, how his kiss tasted of sweat and triumph.

Part of me was afraid he would want a different Bebe, one like Ashley on the beach, who preferred to sit on the sidelines, tanning, wearing a triangular bikini that barely covers anything, and taking selfies rather than breaking a nail playing volleyball. *But he likes me.*

I set the brush down and secure my towel more tightly before opening the bathroom door, a cloud of steam following me into the bedroom.

My breath catches in my throat.

Luke stands beside my bed, water droplets glistening on his broad shoulders, hair darkened by his own shower. The navy towel slung low around his hips reveals the defined V-shape disappearing beneath the fabric. His skin is still flushed from the hot water, muscles relaxed yet sculpted in the soft glow of my bedside lamp.

Our eyes lock across the room, and the electricity between us is immediate and overwhelming.

"Hi," I whisper, suddenly shy despite the intimacy we've already shared.

He crosses the space in two long strides, one hand coming up to cup my cheek while the other settles at my waist. His lips meet mine with gentle pressure. The kiss is unhurried—an uncharted road leading me to a place I had only dared to imagine. His hand slides from my hips to the small of my back, drawing me closer until our bodies press together.

When he pulls away, his blue eyes search mine with such tenderness it makes my heart ache. There's a question in his gaze—a silent request that needs no words. I understand completely what he wants, what we both want.

My fingers find the edge of my towel where it's tucked above my breasts. Without breaking eye contact, I loosen the fabric and let it fall to the floor in a soft heap around my feet. The cool air kisses my bare skin, raising goosebumps across my body.

Luke's breath catches audibly. His gaze remains fixed on my face for several heartbeats before slowly, reverently trailing down, appreciating every curve, every freckle, every inch of skin revealed to him. The admiration in his eyes makes me feel beautiful, powerful, cherished.

"Your body is amazing," he whispers, his voice rough.

His hands find my waist, guiding me backward toward the bed. When my legs touch the mattress, I sit, then recline, my hair fanning out across the pillow as I look up at him with a mixture of vulnerability and desire. He reaches for his own towel, tugging at the knot until it falls away. My breath hitches at the sight of him fully naked, arousal evident with his growing cock.

He stands before me like something carved from marble, a masterpiece of masculine perfection. His broad shoulders taper to a narrow waist, every muscle defined yet proportionate. The golden light from my bedside lamp casts shadows that accentuates the ridges of his abs, the curve of his pectoral muscles, the powerful lines of his thighs.

My gaze travels lower, to where his erection stands against his stomach. He's magnificent—thick and long, the head flushed a little, a single vein running prominently along the underside.

"Luke," I whisper, my voice barely audible even in the

quiet room. I reach for him, fingers trembling slightly as they make contact with the warm skin of his hip.

He lowers himself onto the bed, his weight causing the mattress to dip as he positions himself between my thighs. His hands slide up from my ankles to my knees, gently pushing outward.

"I want to taste you," he whispers, his breath warm against my inner thigh, pressing soft kisses there.

My heart hammers against my ribs as I nod, unable to form words. His eyes hold mine for one more moment before he lowers his head.

The first touch of his tongue sends a jolt through my entire body. "Oh!" I gasp.

It's warm, wet, impossibly soft yet insistent. My hands fly to his head, fingers threading through his damp hair as he explores me. Each stroke sends waves of pleasure rippling through me, building upon one another like concentric circles in water.

He shifts his approach, focusing on the sensitive bundle of nerves at my center. His tongue traces deliberate patterns—circles, quick flicks that make my hips buck involuntarily. I'm lost in sensation, my breathing ragged, small whimpers escaping my lips with each expert stroke.

When he looks up, our gazes lock over the landscape of my body. His blue eyes intense with desire as his mouth continues its relentless attention. The image of him between my thighs, watching my reactions while pleasuring me, is so erotic that something inside me snaps.

A wave of pleasure crashes over me. My back arches off the bed, my fingers clutching his hair as I cry out his name. The orgasm pulses through me in endless waves, each one making me shudder and gasp.

When the tremors finally subside, I stare at him in wonder, my chest heaving with ragged breaths. "That was..." I can't find words to describe the intensity of what just happened.

He rises slowly, wiping his mouth with the back of his hand, his eyes never leaving mine.

He crawls up my body with the predatory grace of a jungle cat. He captures my lips in a searing kiss that tastes faintly of me. I melt into him, my hands sliding down his back, feeling the muscles flex beneath my fingertips.

Luke shifts his weight, positioning himself perfectly between my legs as they fall open for him. The heat of him presses against my center, hard and insistent, but he doesn't push forward. Instead, his mouth begins a slow, deliberate journey down my body.

His lips trace the column of my throat, lingering at the pulse point where my heartbeat races beneath his tongue. He continues lower, pressing open-mouthed kisses along my collarbone, taking his time as if memorizing the taste of my skin. When he reaches my breast, he pauses, his breath hot against my sensitized flesh before taking my nipple into his mouth.

The sensation is electric—warm, wet suction that sends currents of pleasure straight to my core. I arch into him, a soft moan escaping my lips as his tongue circles the hardened peak. His hand finds my other breast, thumb circling in perfect synchronization.

I thread my fingers through his hair, holding him against me as pleasure radiates outward from every point of contact.

When he releases my nipple, the cool air makes it tighten further.

He raises his head, his expression suddenly serious as his eyes search mine. "Are you on anything?" he asks softly, his meaning clear.

I nod. "Yes, implant."

Luke's eyes hold mine, a vulnerable sincerity in his gaze. "I'm clean," he murmurs, his thumb tracing my cheekbone. "I've never not used a condom. But with you, I'd like to feel you—all of you—if that's okay."

My heart flutters at the intimacy of his request. I shake my head yes, unable to find words as emotion wells in my throat. The trust between us feels monumental, almost sacred .

"I want that too," I finally manage, reaching up to trace his jawline.

The realization crashes over me—I'm about to have sex for the first time. Not just with anyone, but with Luke Sullivan, this beautiful man who makes my heart race with a single glance. With him, it doesn't feel like losing something. It feels like choosing—him, this, us.

Looking at Luke, his blue eyes filled with tenderness and desire, I can't bring myself to care about what comes after. I'm falling for him—deeply. The realization should terrify me, but in this moment, it feels like the most natural thing in the world. As if my heart had been waiting for him all along.

I push away the whisper of Alessandro's name in my mind; the clock is counting down my freedom. Nine months suddenly seems both infinite and fleeting all at once. The shadow of my arranged marriage tries to creep in, but I refuse to let it steal this moment.

No. Not now. Not tonight.
Tonight belongs to Luke and me alone.

Chapter Twenty-Five

BEBE

HE POSITIONS himself between my legs, his weight shifting as he sits back on his heels. His hand wraps around his length, giving himself several slow, deliberate strokes. My breath catches at the sight of him touching himself while his eyes remain locked on mine, sending a fresh wave of heat coursing through my body. The muscles in his forearm flex with each movement.

"You're beautiful," I whisper, the words escaping before I can catch them.

Luke's lips curve into a smile that's both tender and hungry. His hand continues its languid pace. "I want you to see how much I want you," his voice is deep and husky. "How just looking at you makes me ache. How every part of me is desperate to be connected to you."

His words make me tremble with anticipation. The raw honesty in his voice, the vulnerability in his expression—it's overwhelming in the most beautiful way.

He leans forward, bracing himself above me with one muscular arm while his other hand guides himself to my entrance. The blunt pressure sends anticipatory shivers through me. His eyes never leave mine as he begins to push forward, slowly and carefully. There's resistance at first, my body tensing instinctively against the unfamiliar intrusion. The pressure is both foreign and exquisite as my body stretches to accommodate him.

"Breathe, baby," he murmurs, his thumb tracing soothing circles on my hip as he waits for my body to adjust. "If it's too much, we can stop anytime you want."

He lowers his head, capturing my lips in a tender kiss. His mouth moves against mine with such exquisite gentleness that I find myself melting beneath him. The tension in my muscles begins to dissolve as I lose myself in the kiss, my body responding to his wordless reassurance. His tongue traces the seam of my lips, and I open for him, the distraction working as I feel myself yielding.

I'm so caught up in the kiss that I barely register the increased pressure until he suddenly stops. His forehead presses against mine, our breaths mingling in the small space between us. I can feel him trembling with restraint.

"This part might hurt," he whispers, his voice strained. "I'll go slow."

He withdraws slightly before pushing forward again with careful movements. The rhythm is gentle but persistent—back and forth, each time pressing a little deeper. The barrier gives way suddenly with a sharp pinch that makes me gasp against his mouth.

"I'm sorry," he murmurs, holding perfectly still as I adjust to the unfamiliar sensation.

The brief sting fades almost immediately, replaced by a fullness that borders on uncomfortable yet somehow perfect.

"You okay?" he whispers against my lips.

"Yes," I breathe, surprised by how quickly the discomfort transformed into something else entirely. "It feels... good."

The sensation is indescribable—being filled, stretched, completed in a way I never imagined. He begins to roll his hips in slow, shallow thrusts, each one easier than the last. The initial burn gives way to pleasure that builds with every careful stroke. The fullness shifts from strange to sublime, awakening nerve endings I never knew existed.

My hands find his hips, fingers digging into taut muscle as I tentatively lift my pelvis to meet his movements. The synchronicity of our movements feels instinctive, as if my body already knows the dance.

"That's it," he encourages, his voice husky with desire. He pulls one of my thighs higher around his waist. "You feel so good, Bebe."

His words wash over me like a physical caress, building my confidence. I arch my back slightly, changing the angle of our connection, and I'm rewarded with a deeper sensation that pulls a gasp from my throat. I experiment with rhythm, finding a natural counterpoint to his thrusts that seems to amplify the pleasure for both of us.

"Perfect," he whispers, his eyes never leaving mine.

I watch in fascination as pleasure transforms his features—the slight furrow of his brow, the flush spreading across his cheekbones, the way his lips part with each measured breath. There's something profoundly intimate about witnessing his vulnerability, knowing I'm the cause of it.

He shifts his weight to one forearm, his other hand sliding

between our bodies to find where we're joined. His thumb circles my sensitive bundle of nerves, precise and knowing. An electric sensation shoots through me, building upon the pleasure already mounting with each thrust. The dual stimulation is overwhelming—his hardness filling me completely while his thumb works its magic.

"Luke," I gasp. The sound seems to trigger something primal in him; he groans deeply, the vibration rumbling through his chest into mine.

His thrusts deepen, hitting a spot inside me that makes stars explode behind my eyes, but I refuse to look away—our eyes locked on each other's faces.

I'm suddenly seized with an intense need to maintain this connection. I want him to see me—truly see me—as pleasure builds to a peak. His eyes are midnight blue now, pupils blown wide with desire, yet focused entirely on me.

The tension coils tighter in my core, a gathering storm about to break. I clutch his shoulders, fingernails leaving crescent marks on his skin as waves of sensation crash through me. Still, I don't look away. I want him to witness everything—every tremor, every gasp, every moment of my surrender.

When it happens, it's like nothing I've experienced until now—more intense, more all-consuming than the pleasure he's given me with his hands or mouth. I fracture into a thousand pieces beneath him, my entire body tensing as waves of ecstasy crash over me. Still, I hold his gaze.

His eyes darken as he watches me come undone. His rhythm falters, becomes erratic. A deep groan tears from his throat as his head drops to my shoulder, his body tightening above me. He pulses inside me, the warm flood of his release filling me completely. The sensation is strangely intimate—his essence becoming part of me.

He continues with gentle, shallow movements, prolonging our pleasure until finally collapsing against me, his weight a comforting anchor. Our hearts thunder together, his breath hot against my neck. For several moments, we remained perfectly still, connected in the most primal way.

When he finally lifts his head, his eyes are filled with something that makes my breath catch—tenderness, wonder, and something deeper I'm afraid to name. He brushes damp strands of hair from my forehead.

"I didn't know it could be that good. You're all I ever wanted," he whispers, lowering his lips to mine.

This kiss is different—deep, soul-reaching. More intimate somehow than what we just shared with our bodies. Tears prick behind my eyelids at the sweetness of it. His lips brush mine with such gentleness, such care, as if sealing a promise between us.

I feel the words forming in my throat, three simple words that suddenly seem too enormous to contain. *I love you.* They hover there, desperate to be spoken, pushing against my lips like a physical force. My heart pounds with the truth of them.

But I swallow them back.

What am I doing? This beautiful moment suddenly crashes around me as reality intrudes. Exactly what I didn't want to happen. This—what Luke and I are building—has an expiration date I've known about from the beginning.

My chest tightens with the realization of my selfishness. I've been living in this fantasy, taking what I want without considering the consequences. Without considering what this means to him.

The tenderness in his eyes as he gazes at me isn't casual. The way he touched me, the care he took with my body—this wasn't just sex to him. I can see it in the softness of his expression, feel it in the gentle stroke of his thumb across my cheekbone.

I'm being reckless with his heart.

Luke gently eases himself from my body, the separation leaving me feeling oddly bereft. He shifts to lie beside me, one arm draped across my waist.

"Are you okay?" he asks softly, his voice tinged with concern. His eyes search mine intently. "Did I hurt you at all?"

I shake my head, touched by his consideration. "No, I'm fine." I shift position, turning onto my side to face him properly, our bodies mirroring each other.

The movement causes a slight twinge between my legs—not painful, just a reminder of what we've shared. Our faces are close enough that I can count each individual eyelash, feel the warmth of his breath against my cheek.

Something flickers across his expression—a flash of vulnerability that appears and disappears quickly. His lips part as if he's about to speak, then press together again. His eyes drop momentarily before returning to mine, holding something back.

My stomach tightens with sudden anxiety. Was it not what he expected? Not good enough? I was a virgin—maybe I disappointed him. Maybe he's comparing me to others he's been with. Or worse, maybe he regrets crossing this line with me.

"What is it?" I whisper, unable to keep the worry from my voice. I reach out, my fingers tracing the line of his jaw.

"I was just thinking..." he says, a smile slowly spreading across his face.

"Thinking what?" I encourage him, my fingers resting against his jaw.

He captures my hand, bringing it to his lips to press a gentle kiss against my palm. The gesture is so tender it makes my heart ache.

"I was thinking that I'd like it if you were officially my girlfriend," he says, never breaking eye contact.

A smile tugs at my lips despite the warning bells clanging in my head. "I thought I already was," I tease, trying to keep my tone light even as my pulse races.

He smiles, but then his expression shifts into something more serious as his hand slides to my hip, warm and steady against my skin.

"I'm serious, Bebe," he says, his voice dropping lower. "I've never felt this way about anyone before. Not even close. When I'm with you, everything just... makes sense." He pauses, his thumb tracing circles on my hip. "I think about you all the time. I want you to be mine. Exclusively."

The sincerity in his voice makes my chest ache. This is the moment I should pull away. I should tell him no, that this can't be anything serious. That it's a college fling with a deadline.

But looking into those earnest blue eyes, I can't form the words. I can't push him away. Everything in me rebels against the idea of denying what's blooming between us, even though I know I should.

"Luke," I whisper, my voice catching.

He waits, patient and vulnerable, his heart exposed for me to either cherish or shatter. The weight of my secret hangs between us—the arranged marriage, my family, the blood on my hands. I should tell him everything now, before we go any further.

Instead, I find myself reaching for him, my fingers threading through his hair as I pull him closer.

"I would love nothing more than to be your girlfriend," I tell him, the words tumbling out before I can stop them.

His face lights up with such pure joy. He captures my lips in a kiss that feels like a promise, his arms wrapping around me and pulling me against his chest. I melt into him, pushing away the voice of reason screaming in the back of my mind.

As his arms encircle me, holding me against the steady rhythm of his heartbeat, guilt and happiness war within my chest. I've just committed the ultimate selfishness—claiming something I know I'll have to surrender.

Chapter Twenty-Six

LUKE

"Earth to Luke," Wes says, glancing at me in the rearview mirror. "You with us, bro?"

"Yeah, sorry. Just thinking."

My brothers and I are on route to our parents' house for a family meeting—Keeper business. Dad calls these meetings every week, usually when there's some important matter to discuss regarding the society. I stare out the Jeep as Wes drives, watching the familiar landscape blur past. Chase sits in the passenger seat, scrolling through his phone, as always.

"About Bebe?" Chase asks, not looking up from his phone.

I nod, though he can't see it. It's been four days since we made things official, since she'd given me the precious gift of her virginity, and while it was perfect and I should be on cloud nine, something feels off. The memory of that night—her body against mine, her agreeing to be my girlfriend—still sends warmth through me, but it's quickly followed by unease.

"Something's wrong. She's just... different now," I admit, rubbing the back of my neck. "Ever since we put a label on us, it's like she's pulling away. The other night I reached for her hand while we were watching a movie, and she flinched—actually flinched. And she doesn't cuddle with me anymore, you know, like she'll let me hold her, but there's no reciprocation—she doesn't hold me back."

She's different now. The change is subtle, but unmistakable. Her smile doesn't quite reach her eyes anymore. When I kiss her, there's a moment's hesitation before she responds. At breakfast this morning, she barely looked me in the eye, pushing food around her plate before claiming she needed to study. I didn't know you could miss someone sitting three feet away from you. She stopped looking at me like I was hers. It was like she'd become a ghost of the person I fell for, and I'm not sure how to bring her back.

"Have you talked to her about it?" Chase asks, finally taking his eyes off his phone.

"I'm afraid to bring it up. What if she says it was a mistake? What if she wants to end things?"

Wes catches my eye in the mirror. "Look, she's never had a boyfriend before, right? She's probably adjusting. Give her some time to get used to being in a relationship."

"He's right," Chase chimes in. "Maybe putting a label on it freaked her out."

"What do you mean?" I ask.

He shrugs. "Some people like keeping things casual. No expectations, no pressure. Once you call someone your boyfriend or girlfriend, everything changes."

I stare out the Jeep again, watching the trees flash by. "But she said yes," I finish, running a hand through my hair. "She seemed happy about it."

"Women," Wes says with a sigh. "The eternal mystery."

Something doesn't add up. There's something else going on. I don't know what it is, but I want it to go back to how it was before. Before the label when things felt simple and natural between us.

"Maybe she regrets sleeping with me," I breathe, the thought's been haunting me finally escaping into the open air of the car.

Wes's eyes flick to the rearview mirror again, his brow furrowed. "What makes you think that?"

I stare at my hands, suddenly finding my cuticles fascinating. "Her virginity... What if I rushed her? What if she wasn't ready?"

"Nah, man," Wes says, shaking his head as he changes lanes. "Trust me, you didn't rush her. You two have been all over each other."

Chase snorts, putting his phone down again. "You're so lucky, dude. Bebe is fucking hot. And if she's as good in bed as she is at everything else—"

I shoot him a glare so intense that his words die in his throat.

"What?" he asks, turning to look at me. "I was just saying—"

"Don't," I cut him off, my voice tight. "Just don't talk about her like that." I lean back against the seat, crossing my arms. "She's not some conquest to brag about. She's..." I trail off, not even sure how to explain what she means to me.

"Sorry," Chase mumbles after a moment. "I meant

nothing by it. It was a compliment." He clears his throat. "Was she reluctant that night?" he asks, turning in his seat to face me.

"No," I answer honestly. "But afterward, that's when things changed."

The memory of her body trembling beneath mine, the trust in her eyes as she gave herself to me completely—it makes my chest ache now, knowing something's wrong.

"Or maybe," I continue, the words feeling like gravel in my throat, "she's comparing herself to others. Thinking she didn't measure up somehow."

Wes snorts. "Women do that."

Chase sighs. "First times are complicated. Especially for girls. I was once with a virgin, and she wouldn't even look at me for three days after. It was awkward as fuck seeing her in class."

"It's a normal reaction," Wes suggests, turning onto our parents' street. "Remember Kelly from sophomore year? After we hooked up, she got all weird and distant too. And my buddy Ryan said his high school girlfriend cried for hours after their first time. Not because it hurt, but because she felt like something fundamental had changed in her. Like she'd crossed some invisible line she couldn't uncross."

Chase nods thoughtfully. "There's probably a lot of emotional stuff we don't understand. I mean, think about it— girls attach all this meaning to losing their virginity. It's a huge milestone for them. Society puts all this pressure on it being perfect."

"And then reality hits," Wes says. "It's awkward, maybe a little painful, definitely not like the movies. They feel disappointed or embarrassed."

"Then they get all in their heads and wonder—" Chase starts.

"If they gave it to the right person," I finish quietly.

"Or they worry the guy will see them differently," Wes adds. "Like now that he's gotten what he wanted, he'll lose interest."

"Which is exactly what half the guys in high school did," Chase says with a grimace. "No wonder they're paranoid."

I consider their words. Could that be it? Is Bebe processing her first time? I've been with virgins before, but none that fit what my brothers are talking about. They'd been my first girlfriend in high school, which I was a virgin too, so that was awkward all the way around. Or casual hookups— women that wanted to lose their virginity and maybe sought me or my brothers out trying to do it.

We pull into the driveway of our childhood home, the sprawling secluded colonial tucked away in the suburbs, looking exactly as it has for the past twenty years, nestled among old trees. Its weathered charm and whitewashed walls were simplistic, with a wide green front lawn in front of a circular driveway; a three-car garage to the left side. To the right is a wrought-iron side gate leading to the backyard, half-hidden in ivy.

My phone buzzes in my pocket, and pull it out to see Bebe's name on the screen.

> Going to the city tonight. Don't wait up. I'll be back late. Have fun with your family.

"Everything okay?" Chase asks.

"Bebe's going to see her brothers. She'll be home late."

I pocket my phone with a sigh as we head up the stone

pathway to the front door. The familiar scent of mom's lasagna hits me as soon as we step inside—her specialty for family meetings. The house smells like it always has: herbs, garlic, and lemon-scented furniture polish.

"Boys!" Mom calls from the kitchen. She appears in the doorway, wiping her hands on a floral apron, her pearl necklace gleaming against her cashmere sweater. This is a perfect picture of domestic bliss. She was bred and raised in Keeper society and, for lack of a better word, 'trained' how to be the ideal housewife. "Dinner's almost ready."

She embraces each of us in turn, her perfume cloud enveloping me as she pats my cheek. "You look tired, Lucas. Are you getting enough sleep?"

Before I can answer, heavy footsteps sound on the stairs. Dad appears, dressed in his usual meeting attire—dark slacks and a button-down shirt, his Keeper ring on his right hand.

"Good, you're here," he says, nodding at us collectively before checking his watch. "Let's get settled in the living room. We have matters to discuss before dinner."

We follow him into the sunken formal living room with its leather furniture and bookshelves, settling into our usual spots on the oversized leather couches. Wes sprawls in the corner seat, Chase takes the armchair, and I sit on the opposite end from Wes. The room feels smaller now that we've all grown, but the décor hasn't changed in decades—leather-bound books, family photos, crystal decanters on the mahogany bar. The setting for countless Keeper meetings through the years.

Dad settles into his leather chair, the unofficial throne. He surveys us with a calculating gaze.

"Wes," he begins, leaning forward. "The scouts at

Saturday's game—what did they say? I saw three NFL representatives in the stands."

Wes straightens instantly. "The Raiders want me to come out to Vegas after graduation for a private workout. The Dolphins guy talked about my 'exceptional field vision' and the Patriots scout said I have first-round potential if I keep performing at this level."

Dad nods, a rare smile touching his lips. "Good. Very good. The connections will be valuable regardless of which team drafts you. I've already spoken with Mitchell about representation. He's the best sports agent in the business—he has contacts throughout the league."

"I was thinking of interviewing a few agents myself," Wes begins, but dad waves his hand dismissively.

"No need. Mitchell is one of us." Dad shifts his attention. "Chase, how are the LSAT preparations coming along? Harvard is still your top choice?"

He nods, setting his phone face-down on the armrest. "Yes, sir. My practice test score came back last week—175."

Dad nods approvingly. "Excellent. The Harvard Alumni Association has several high-ranking Keepers. I'll make some calls."

He shifts uncomfortably. "Actually, I've been thinking about Georgetown, too. Their international law program—"

"Harvard," Dad interrupts firmly. "The connections there are invaluable."

His gaze sweeps past me as if I'm invisible, landing on the mantle clock. He doesn't bother asking about my business classes or my internship plans. He never does. I'm not his first choice to take over the company.

"Now, to Keeper business," Dad says, leaning forward.

"The quarterly dues have increased by five percent. The Council cited infrastructure upgrades at the old winery. The increase will come out of your monthly allowances, as usual," he continues, his tone making it clear this isn't up for discussion. "I expect you boys to manage your finances accordingly."

Marc shifts on the couch, his casual demeanor slipping. "Dad, come on. My training supplements alone—"

"Are a choice you make," Dad cuts him off. "Perhaps if you partied less and spent more time studying Keeper archives like you're supposed to, you'd pass your societal tests and I'll be more willing to reinstate your original allowances."

Wes and Chase exchange glances before looking at me. At least we have Bebe's rent money to fall back on.

"The annual Solstice Ceremony is being moved to the Seattle compound this year," Dad continues. "Security concerns at the usual location here in Ambrose. All members are expected to attend." He adjusts his Keeper ring, twisting it around his finger. "The Council believes we need to present a united front in these uncertain times."

"Uncertain times?" Chase asks.

Dad's expression darkens. "That's another matter. As you know, the L.A. Chapter has been dealing with The Killer Bee situation... targeting our members."

Mom enters the doorway, her smile faltering as she senses the tension.

"Richard, should I delay dinner?" she asks quietly.

Dad waves her away without looking. "Give us fifteen minutes, Caroline."

When she's gone, he lowers his voice. "I have been working with their Chapter to devise a plan. They are setting a trap for The Bee. Tonight," Dad continues, leaning forward with intensity. "Archibald Wilson will be at home, positioned as bait. A carefully orchestrated ambush."

"And you think The Bee will show up?" Wes asks, skepticism clear in his voice.

"They've leaked false information through channels they believe the killer monitors. I don't know what that information is—but they think it's exactly the bait this assassin can't resist." Dad's eyes gleam with satisfaction. "He'll have a panic button, which was my idea," he says, pleased with himself. "It will alarm mercenaries, paid security, that will be set up in a van a few houses down."

"When The Killer Bee arrives expecting to find a vulnerable target, a team will be waiting," Chase concludes.

Dad nods. "Once they capture him, they'll alert the authorities."

My stomach tightens. Something about this feels wrong, though I can't place why, other than it's stupid to aggravate this Bee and might end up in more people being killed.

Chapter Twenty-Seven

BEBE

I TOLD Luke I was going to visit my brothers, but it's a half-truth. Tonight, Gabriel has summoned me for Bee business.

Archibald Wilson lives in an upscale neighborhood with manicured lawns and security systems that would intimidate amateur intruders. But I'm not an amateur.

I scan the perimeter once more before moving toward the back entrance. Something feels off. I've done this plenty of times, but tonight my instincts are screaming at me to turn around. I push the feeling aside. I've never hesitated before. This is just another job, another name on Gabriel's list of people who deserve punishment.

Maybe I feel this way because of Luke. My chest tightens thinking about him—how I've been pulling away, how confusion clouds his blue eyes whenever I react to his touch. I didn't mean to become distant. It's just that putting a label on things made everything too real, too painful, knowing I'll have to leave him eventually. I hate myself for it, yet I can't take it back either.

"Focus," I whisper to myself, crouching beside a perfectly trimmed hedge. This is a job.

The lock on the back door is child's play. My pick slides in and with three practiced movements. I hear the telltale click and ease the door open, careful not to make a sound as I slip inside.

Disabling the security system takes me forty-four seconds. Seventeen slower than usual. I'm definitely feeling off tonight.

The house is quiet. Too quiet. No television hum, no distant sounds of water running, nothing but silence. I move like a shadow through the kitchen, my soft-soled boots making no sound on the marble floors.

My heartbeat quickens as I navigate through the dark house. I pause at the bottom of the stairs, listening intently. Nothing. I ascend slowly, testing each step before putting my full weight down. At the top of the stairs, I pause again.

The hallway stretches before me, shadows playing across expensive artwork. I hesitate at each doorway, listening, sensing. Nothing. I draw the syringe with the honey toxin from my pocket, removing the protective cap with practiced fingers.

The master bedroom door stands slightly ajar. I peer through the crack, spotting a figure in the king-sized bed. My target.

I slip through the partially open door, my movements fluid and silent as I approach the bed. The figure lies still, blankets pulled up to his chest, breathing steadily. Moonlight spills through the curtains, illuminating his face—Archibald

Wilson, mid-fifties, gray at the temples, exactly like the photo in his file.

When I stand directly over him, his eyes suddenly fly open. Instead of fear or shock, his lips curve into a calm, knowing smile. The expression freezes me in place—no target has ever smiled at me before. They've screamed, begged, fought, but never smiled.

My gaze drops instinctively to his right hand resting atop the blanket. My blood turns to ice. Clutched in his fingers is a small black fob with a single red button in the center. A panic button.

"Hello, Bee," he says, his voice steady and confident.

Shit. I've been set up.

I lunge forward with the syringe, aiming for his neck, but he's faster than I expected. His free hand catches my wrist in a crushing grip while his thumb presses the button. A soft beep echoes through the room.

I twist my arm, trying to break his hold, but stumble backward when he releases me unexpectedly. My back hits the wall as I calculate how much time I have. Thirty seconds? A minute?

I hear the crackle of radio static downstairs, followed by footsteps pounding up the hardwood stairs. Backup has arrived.

"You're not going anywhere," Archibald sneers, advancing toward me.

I need an exit—fast. The bedroom windows might be my only chance. I dart sideways, yanking the heavy curtains open to reveal double-paned glass overlooking a steep drop to the garden below. Before I can assess if the jump is survivable, strong fingers dig into my waist, dragging me backward.

Pure instinct takes over. I drive my elbow back with precision, connecting solidly with Archibald's solar plexus. The satisfying whoosh of air leaving his lungs tells me I've hit my mark. He doubles over, loosening his grip just enough for me to pivot and deliver a powerful front kick to his chest. His body flies backward, slamming against the wall with enough force to crack the plaster.

The bedroom door crashes open. Three men in tactical gear flood in—all built like linebackers, faces set with grim determination. Their coordinated movement speaks of professional training. Not the police though, private security —mercenaries.

The first man lunges toward me with frightening speed, but I'm already moving. I drop to the floor as his meaty fist whistles over my head, then sweep my leg in a wide arc that catches his ankles. He crashes down with a surprised grunt.

The second mercenary doesn't wait, charging at me with a tactical baton raised high. I spring to my feet, catching his descending arm and using his momentum to flip him over my shoulder. His body slams into an antique dresser, wood splintering under the impact.

Pain explodes across my back as the third man lands a solid kick. I stumble forward but transform the movement into a controlled roll, coming up in a fighting stance. My size works against me as they regroup, surrounding me in a triangle formation.

"It's just a girl," one mutters, blood trickling from his nose. "Take her down!"

They attack simultaneously. I duck the first punch but catch a baton strike across my ribs, stealing my breath.

Ignoring the sharp pain, I drive my fist into the nearest attacker's throat. He drops to his knees, gasping.

A punch connects with my jaw, snapping my head back with stunning force. Lights flash behind my eyes, but the pain sharpens my focus. Time slows as I center myself, drawing on years of training.

I launch into a fluid series of strikes—elbow to solar plexus, knee to groin, palm heel to nose. The mercenary staggers backward, blood streaming down his face. I snatch his baton mid-fall and pivot toward the second man. The weapon connects with his temple. He drops instantly.

The third mercenary, the one I'd struck in the throat, has recovered and fumbling for his gun. I'm on him before his fingers find the holster. My leg whips out in a crescent kick, catching his jaw hard enough to snap his head sideways. The sound of vertebrae breaking echoes in the quiet room.

Three bodies lie motionless around me. I stand in the center, chest heaving, tasting blood where my lip split. I scan the space, spotting Archibald huddled in the far corner. His earlier confidence has evaporated, replaced by terror as he takes in the carnage.

My syringe. Where is it?

I spot it glinting under the bed, knocked aside during the struggle. Diving for it, my fingers close around the plastic just as Archibald makes his move. He bolts toward the door, terror giving him unexpected speed. In three fluid strides, I'm on him, arm snaking around his throat in a practiced hold. He struggles, clawing at my forearm, but I've done this too many times. My grip is perfect—tight enough to control, loose enough to keep him conscious.

"Please," he gasps, voice barely audible.

The syringe hovers near his neck. For a heartbeat, I hesitate. Then the image of Gabriel's cold eyes flashes in my mind, and I plunge the needle home. The honey toxin enters his bloodstream with mechanical efficiency. His body goes rigid, then slacks as the paralytic takes effect.

We both collapse to the floor. His weight dragging me with him, and I don't have the strength to break my fall. The impact jars my already bruised ribs. Archibald's eyes remain open, fixed on mine with silent accusation as the toxin works through his system. His breathing grows shallows before it stops.

I roll away from him, my back against the wall, chest heaving. I stare at the dead man's face, his eyes solidified in his final moment of terror. The three mercenaries remain still around me. My hands tremble as the adrenaline begins to fade, leaving behind a hollow emptiness that threatens to swallow me whole.

Something inside me breaks. A dam I've carefully constructed over years of training suddenly ruptures, and emotion floods through the cracks. I curl into myself, back pressed against the wall, and for the first time since I was a child, I cry.

Not delicate tears, but gut-wrenching sobs that tear through my chest. Four men were dead by my hand in less than five minutes. Four lives extinguished because Gabriel pointed and I obeyed. Like a trained animal. Like a weapon without will.

I think of Luke—his gentle hands, his kind eyes, the way he looks at me like I'm something precious instead of something deadly. I think of the life we could have if I were normal. If I weren't The Killer Bee.

"I don't want this anymore," I whisper to the empty room, to the dead men who can't hear me. "I never wanted this."

The sound of a floorboard creaking downstairs freezes me mid-sob. More follow—deliberate, unhurried. Someone else is in the house.

I force myself to move despite my body's protests. Every muscle screams as I drag myself upright, wiping tears from my face with bloodied knuckles. I need to disappear before whoever is coming makes it upstairs.

Slipping quietly out of the bedroom, I swiftly move to the next room, careful to stay concealed in the shadow cast by the ajar door. My eyes have adjusted to the dim light, allowing me to see clearly, but I'm taken aback when I spot the figure standing on the landing. My mouth falls open in shock as I recognize him—Mr. Sullivan, Luke's father, with his familiar stern expression and neatly combed hair.

He moves with quiet confidence, dressed in a suit that's out of place for a midnight raid. "Oh my God," he breathes, looking around the master bedroom where the four bodies lie before running out of the room and back downstairs.

My mind races frantically. *What is he doing here? How is he connected to this trap? Does Luke already know who I am?*

Chapter Twenty-Eight

BEBE

"What the hell, Gabriel?" I slam my hands on his desk, making his coffee cup rattle. Blood still cakes under my fingernails despite my attempts to scrub it off. "It was a fucking trap!"

His expression remains impassive as he stands from his seat. "Every mission carries risk—"

"Don't give me that bullshit!" My voice rises dangerously. "They were waiting for me. They knew I was coming!"

He circles his desk slowly. "Tell me exactly what happened."

"What happened? I killed four men tonight. One target, three mercenaries. They had a panic button. They called me by name—Bee." I'm shaking with rage now. "And you want to know the best part? My boyfriend's father was there!"

I freeze, realizing my mistake.

"Boyfriend?" his voice drops to a dangerous whisper. "What boyfriend?"

"Luke Sullivan." I cross my arms defensively. "I want the truth, Gabe. What exactly did I walk into? You vetted the Sullivan's and you don't make mistakes. You must have known something."

He sinks back into his chair. His fingers steeple beneath his chin as he studies me.

"The Sullivans are Keepers," he says calmly. "A secret society of brotherhood dating back centuries. They present themselves as pillars of the community—but they're much more than that. They've infiltrated every level of society—business, politics, law enforcement."

I stare at him in disbelief. "A secret society? Are you serious?"

"Deadly serious." He opens a drawer and removes a thick file folder. "The Sullivans are prominent members. Wesley Sullivan Sr.—your *boyfriend's* father—sits on their governing council."

He slides several candid photographs across the desk. One shows Mr. Sullivan shaking hands with men in dark suits; another captures him entering an ornate building with Chase, Wes, and Luke following behind, all dressed in floor-length robes—hoods over their heads.

"Our intel found that the L.A. Chapter of The Keepers have been using its legitimate businesses as fronts for drug distribution," he continues. "They've been moving a new synthetic opioid through the city. Thirty-seven deaths in the last six months alone."

My mind reels. "Luke wouldn't be involved in something like that."

"Perhaps not knowingly," he concedes. "Our evidence points to the L.A. Chapter, whereas The Sullivans are part of

Headquarters. But the family business? The Sullivans? All part of their network, and Mr. Sullivan appears to be helping them, especially after your admission that he was there tonight." Gabriel's expression darkens. "The L.A. Chapter has corrupted their purpose. Not just any drugs. Designer compounds ten times more potent than fentanyl. Most of your last targets have all been linked to the distribution and deaths of innocent people."

I shake my head, trying to process everything. "If The Keepers are so dangerous, why not shut them down? You have evidence, connections. Why send me in to kill individual members?"

His jaw tightens. He looks suddenly tired, the lines around his eyes more pronounced than usual.

"It's not that simple, Bebe. This is bigger than me." He stands and moves to the window, looking out at the city lights. "The Keepers have Chapters in every major city across the country. Their roots run deeper than you can imagine— judges, police commissioners, senators. They protect their own." Gabriel turns, his expression hardening. "I thought if The Bee eliminated a few key players, it would send a message. Scare them into retreating."

"Well, that worked out brilliantly," I snap. "They set a trap. They're not retreating—they're hunting me now."

"A miscalculation," he admits, the closest he'll ever come to an apology.

I run my fingers through my tangled hair, trying to make sense of everything. "So what now? What should I do?"

"The Killer Bee is done—for now. We need to reassess, regroup."

Relief washes through me. No more missions means no more blood on my hands, at least for a while.

"Continue your classes, your normal day-to-day," he pauses, his eyes hardening. "But you need to end things with the Sullivan boy. Immediately."

My heart drops. "What?"

"Breakup with him." His tone is clinical, as if discussing nothing more consequential than a business transaction. "It was purely a coincidence that you were hunting for a place to live at the same time the boys put an ad out. I encouraged you to proceed with an application, hoping if anything, you could be my eyes and ears if this turns into a full-on drug war. You can continue living in the house—we need to keep an eye on the Sullivans. Just keep your distance emotionally. You've allowed yourself to become attached, and that's risky."

A hollow laugh escapes my lips. "So I'm supposed to... what? Tell him it's over with no explanation? That these past weeks meant nothing?"

"Yes." His voice is firm. "This isn't a negotiation, Bebe. The Keepers are dangerous if the Sullivans or Luke himself are involved or not. And need I remind you that you're already promised to Alessandro? In less than eight months, you'll be married. What did you think was going to happen with this boy?"

His words land like physical blows. The truth I've been avoiding crashes down around me.

"You're leading him on," Gabriel continues, his tone softening slightly. "It's a complication that needs to end. For both your sakes."

I stare at my brother, hating him at this moment, yet unable to argue against the cold logic of his words. *He's right.* I know he is. I've been selfish, pretending I could have something real with Luke when my future was already decided.

"I'll end it." The words taste bitter as they leave my mouth.

I turn and walk out of his office before he can say anything else, before he can see the tears threatening to spill. The penthouse feels suffocating as I make my way to my old bedroom, each step heavier than the last.

Once inside, I peel off my Bee jumpsuit, the black fabric sticking to places where blood has dried. I catch my reflection in the full-length mirror and barely recognize myself. Angry purple bruises bloom across my ribs where the baton struck. My jaw sports an ugly red mark that will darken by morning. My lip is split, and small bruises dot my arms and legs, a constellation of violence mapped onto my skin.

I wince as I probe the tender area along my rib cage. Nothing feels broken, but the pain radiates with each breath.

The sudden movement of my cellphone startles me. I glance at the nightstand where it vibrates insistently, Luke's name lighting up the screen. My heart twists painfully in my chest as I hesitate before answering.

"Hello?" My voice sounds strange even to my own ears.

"Bebe!" Luke's voice floods with relief. "I've been calling you for hours. I was getting worried."

I sink onto the edge of the bed, wincing as the movement jars my bruised ribs. "I'm sorry. There was a... family crisis. My brother had an emergency, and I got completely distracted." The lie comes easily.

"Is everything okay?" His concern makes my chest ache worse than the bruises.

"It's fine now." I press my fingertips against my swelling jaw, wondering how I'll hide it when I see him. "Nothing serious."

"When are you coming home?"

The way he says 'home' makes something twist painfully inside me. The house with the Sullivan brothers has become more of a home than here.

I close my eyes, picturing his worried face. "In the morning. I'll stay here tonight."

"Tomorrow? Can't you come back tonight? I can come get you."

"No," I say too quickly. "I mean, it's late and... I should be here for Gabe."

"Okay," he says after a moment, his voice soft with resignation. "I get it. Family comes first."

Tears threaten to spill, my ribs throb with every breath, and the bruise on my jaw pulses with pain. There's no way I could face him like this—my body a canvas of violence, my face battered. The questions would be impossible to answer.

"Are you sure you're alright?" he asks again when I say nothing. "You sound... different."

"I'm fine," I lie, wincing as I shift positions. "Just tired."

"I miss you," he blurts. "The house feels empty without you here."

Something breaks inside me. The tears I've been holding back spill down my cheeks, hot and unstoppable.

My heart is already breaking at the thought of what I'll have to do when I see him tomorrow. End it. Break his heart. Walk away from the only genuine happiness I've ever known.

I'll have to watch his face crumble, see confusion replace

affection. I'll have to stand firm as he asks why, as he searches my face for answers I can't give him.

How do you dismantle love with words? How do you convince someone that what felt real wasn't?

"I miss you too," I whisper, my voice cracking on the last word. I press my palm against my mouth, trying to stifle a sob.

"Are you crying?"

"No," I lie, swallowing hard. "I should go. I'll see you tomorrow. Goodnight Luke."

"Bebe, wait—"

I end the call before I lose the last shred of composure holding me together. The phone slips from my trembling fingers, landing softly on the plush bedspread. A raw, guttural sound escapes my throat—half sob, half scream—as I curl my battered body around itself. I draw my knees to my chest, ignoring the sharp protest from my bruised ribs, and surrender to the tears that have been threatening all night.

They come in violent waves, racking my body until I can barely breathe. I press my face into the pillow to muffle the sounds, terrified that Gabriel might hear this weakness. My tears soak through the expensive cotton pillowcase as I bury my face in it.

I cry for the men I killed tonight. For the person I might have been if I'd been born into a different family. For the future with Luke that I've been pretending could somehow have.

My body shudders with each sob until exhaustion finally claims me, dragging me into merciful darkness.

Chapter Twenty-Nine

LUKE

THREE NIGHTS and she hasn't come home.

I check my phone for the hundredth time today, scrolling through our text history. The messages from Bebe are frustratingly vague.

> Still with family. Don't worry about me.

> I get that, but it's been a few days... What's going on?

> Please, Luke, give me some space. I'll be back soon.

> I miss you.

> Bebe? Don't you miss me too?

> Please don't keep calling. I'll come back when I can.

Each more distant than the last. I've left voicemails that go unanswered, sent texts that receive only these cryptic replies. It's like she's vanished, leaving digital breadcrumbs to prove she still exists.

"Still nothing?" Wes asks, leaning against my door frame. His expression carries genuine concern beneath his usual casual demeanor.

I shake my head, tossing my phone onto the bed. "She hasn't been to any classes either," I say. "Professor Wright asked about her today. Said she missed two lectures."

Chase joins us, leaning against the doorframe. "You think something happened with her brothers? The ones in the city?"

"'Family emergency' is what she said, but I don't know what to think." I run my hand through my hair. "Maybe we should go to her brother's place," I suggest, standing. "I know she mentioned they're in Los Angeles, maybe we can use Keeper resources to—"

The sound of the front door opening cuts me off mid-sentence. I freeze for a split second, then bolt from my bed, nearly colliding with Wes and Chase in the doorway. The three of us crowd the landing, peering down.

Bebe stands in the entryway. My heart hammers against my ribs as relief floods through me. *She's here. She's safe. She's home.*

But as she begins climbing the stairs, the comfort curdles into dread. Something's different. Her usual fluid grace is replaced by a careful, measured ascent. When she looks up, those mismatched eyes find mine immediately. My relief at seeing her evaporates as I take in her appearance—dark circles under her eyes, her normally vibrant face pale. But it's her expression that turns my blood cold—distant, closed off, like she's looking at a stranger instead of her boyfriend.

Her face is carefully composed, expressionless. There's a faint yellowish discoloration along her jawline—makeup not quite concealing what appears to be a healing bruise. And her lip looks like it's healing from a cut—a red line remains visible where the skin has knitted back together.

My feet move automatically, propelling me down the steps toward her. Marc and Jake follow, their footsteps thundering behind me as we descend as one.

"What happened to you?" I ask, my voice barely containing the rage building inside.

She flinches, taking a half-step back as her hand flies up between us, palm facing outward like a traffic cop halting vehicles.

"Don't," she says, her voice brittle.

We freeze on the stairs, the three of us suspended in motion.

My brothers exchange a glance before backing away, retreating toward their rooms without a word.

She continues up the stairs at a careful, measured pace, brushing past me without meeting my eyes, heading straight for her bedroom.

I follow behind her, my concern battling with rising frustration. "Three days, Bebe. Three days you've been gone, and I have no idea why."

She enters her room, and I step in after her, closing the door with a soft click that somehow sounds final in the tense silence.

She moves to her dresser, back turned to me, and begins

mechanically removing her earrings. The distance between us feels insurmountable despite being only a few feet apart.

I wait for her to say something—*anything*—to explain her disappearance, the bruise, her lip, the distance in her eyes.

My eyes track her movements, noting how she favors her left side slightly. The yellowish mark on her jaw draws my attention again, partially concealed beneath a foundation that doesn't quite match her skin tone. And the only reason I notice the difference is because Bebe doesn't wear makeup.

The quiet stretches between us, thick and suffocating. I should demand answers, should let my worry and frustration pour out in a torrent of questions. Seeing her like this—this shell of the vibrant girl I know—leaves me speechless.

I reach out, fingers moving toward her face. "What happened to you?" I finally ask.

She slaps my hand away with surprising force, her eyes suddenly fierce. "Don't."

The sharp sting of rejection hits harder than her physical rebuff. I pull my arm back, curling my fingers into a fist at my side.

"Enough," I say. "Where have you been, Bebe? Really?"

She turns to face me fully. "I told you. With my brothers."

"And this?" I gesture toward her jaw, the bruise she's so carefully tried to hide. "What happened?"

"I can't talk about it."

"Can't or won't?" I press.

"It's family stuff, Luke." Her voice carries a warning edge I've never heard before. "Leave it alone."

"Family stuff?" I repeat incredulously. "Bebe, you're my girlfriend. Why can't you talk to me about family stuff? You disappear for three days, come back looking like you've been in a bar fight, and all you can say is 'family stuff'?"

She flinches at my raised voice but stands her ground. "Yes. Family stuff. And why should I tell you anything?" she challenges, her eyes suddenly flashing with an emotion I can't quite place. "Do you tell me everything about *your* family, Luke?"

The question hits me like a sucker punch. Images of Keeper meetings flash through my mind—dad's stern face in the dimly lit room, the ancient oaths—robes. The trap my father helped set for the famous Killer Bee... I can't tell her I'm in a secret society.

I open my mouth, but no words come out.

"That's what I thought," she whispers, the fight suddenly draining from her. She sits on the edge of her bed, wincing slightly. "I've noticed, you know. When your father calls and the three of you disappear for those mysterious family discussions. How you all come back different—tense, preoccupied." Her eyes meet mine. "But I never pushed. Never demanded explanations. Because I understand that some family matters are private."

The irony of her words isn't lost on me. I've been keeping a family secret from her since the day we met.

"You're right," I admit, the words heavy on my tongue. "I haven't been completely honest with you."

The realization hits me with sudden clarity. Maybe this is what we need—honesty between us. If I open up about The Keepers, perhaps she'll feel safe enough to share whatever's haunting her.

I take a deep breath. "Bebe, there's something I have to tell you about my family—"

"I can't do this anymore," she interrupts.

My confession dies on my lips as the world tilts beneath me. My lungs constrict, refusing to draw breath as her words register. I search her face for any sign this is a joke, a misunderstanding—anything but what it seems. But her expression remains resolute, those mismatched eyes I've come to love now cold and distant. "What?"

"Us," she says, gesturing between us with a trembling hand. "This relationship. I can't do it."

"Because of whatever happened these past three days?" I ask, struggling to process the sudden shift.

She shakes her head, still avoiding my gaze. "No. Because that's not why I'm here." Her fingers twist together in her lap. "I came to Dalton U to go to school, to be normal, before..." She pauses like she's rethinking her words. "I shouldn't have let things go this far between us."

"Let things go this far?" I repeat, disbelief coloring my words. "You make it sound like some mistake."

"Maybe it was." Her voice is flat, emotionless, but her hands tremble, betraying her.

"You don't mean that," I whisper, my voice barely audible even in the quiet room.

"I do." Bebe stands. "I should never have let things get this far. I came here for college, not to develop feelings. Which is what I did. I fell in love with you, Luke, but I can't..."

Her voice breaks, a sob catching in her throat as tears fill her mismatched eyes. She presses a finger to her lips, trying to hold back the emotion that's suddenly overwhelming her.

I stand frozen, her words echoing in my mind. *I fell in love with you, Luke.* The declaration I've been waiting to hear, delivered in the same breath as a breakup. My heart pounds against my ribs as I struggle to make sense of the contradiction.

Did she just tell me she loves me? In the middle of breaking up with me?

Something doesn't add up.

She stiffens. "It's over."

I hear what she's saying, but I see the truth. The slight quiver of her bottom lip. The way she can't quite meet my eyes. The tension in her shoulders like she's physically restraining herself from reaching for me.

She's breaking up with me, but she doesn't want to.

I move deliberately, closing the distance between us. Before she can protest, I wrap my arms around her waist, pulling her gently against me. She feels smaller somehow, more fragile than before she disappeared.

"Don't," she whispers, shaking her head. Her hands come up to my chest, palms flat against my shirt, creating a barrier, but there's no force behind it. Her fingers curl slightly into the fabric, neither pushing me away nor pulling me closer.

"I love you," I say, my voice clear and steady despite the storm raging inside me. "I'm in love with you, Bebe."

"You can't," she whispers. Her resistance crumbles instantly. A small, broken sound escapes her throat as she collapses against me, her cheek finding its place against my chest. Her fingers uncurl from their defensive position, instead wrapping around my waist, clinging to me like I'm a lifeline in a tempest. I know she can feel my heart hammering beneath her ear—the physical proof of my declaration.

"I'm not going anywhere," I murmur into her hair, breathing in her familiar scent. "Whatever this is, whatever you're going through, we'll face it together. When you're ready to talk, I'll be here. I'm not giving up on us."

She trembles against me, her shoulders shaking with silent sobs. I hold her carefully, mindful of whatever injuries she's hiding beneath her clothes. My palm traces gentle circles on her back as the dampness of her tears soaks through my shirt.

We stand like this for what feels like hours, my arms holding her as if I could shield her from whatever demons are chasing her. When her sobs finally quiet, she doesn't pull away. Instead, she presses closer, her fingers clutching my shirt like she's afraid I'll disappear if she lets go.

I think about how I should be hurt and heartbroken—and I am. The pain of her attempted breakup still echoes through me. But something deeper, more instinctive, tells me to hold on. Whatever drove her to push me away isn't what she truly wants. It's obvious she's going through something profound, something that terrifies her, and it breaks my heart to see someone I love suffering this way.

"You don't have to tell me everything right now," I whisper against her hair. "But please just tell me—no one touched you—you weren't—" I'm unable to say the word.

She pulls back slightly, those extraordinary eyes finally meeting mine. The vulnerability there steals my breath—I've never seen her look so raw, so exposed.

"No—I promise," she says. And I find some relief in knowing her injuries weren't the result of a sexual assault. "I can't tell you about my family. What happened. Not yet. Maybe never."

Chapter Thirty

LUKE

HEARTBREAK HAS a way of turning the world into a personal hell, especially when the rest of the world doesn't get the memo.

I slumped deeper into the metal bench outside the Student Union, watching life unfold around me with the detached interest of someone observing an alien species. Students streamed past in their little clusters—laughing, talking, existing in a parallel universe where everything is normal. Where hearts aren't shattered into a thousand jagged pieces that cut with every breath.

It's been six days since Bebe came home. Six days of seeing her around the house, catching glimpses of her cinnamon hair disappearing around corners, hearing her soft footsteps on the stairs at dawn as she leaves before anyone else wakes up. Six days of torture.

A couple walked past, their fingers intertwined, heads

tilted toward each other in an intimate way that screamed of shared secrets and private jokes. The girl said something that made the guy throw his head back in laughter, his arm sliding around her waist to pull her closer. I looked away; the sight was like salt in an open wound.

I saw her yesterday at the library.

I hadn't meant to find her there—I was just looking for a secluded spot to work on my marketing project. Then I spotted her tucked away in the far corner of the second floor, nestled in one of those oversized armchairs that swallow you whole. Her legs were folded beneath her, textbook balanced on her knee as she dragged a yellow highlighter across the page.

She wasn't alone. Three other students clustered around her—a guy with glasses gesturing animatedly about something in his notes, two girls nodding along. Bebe's eyes were bright with engagement. Her lips curved in that half-smile she gets when she's truly interested in a topic. She leaned forward, tapping her finger against a passage in her book, and the others bent closer to listen.

I stood frozen between the stacks, watching her exist in this perfectly normal college moment. This was exactly what she'd told me she wanted when she first arrived—"the college experience." Simple. Uncomplicated. And seeing her there, highlighting textbooks and debating with study partners, I couldn't help but wonder if this was enough for her. If she was complete in these moments, or missing me as much as I was her.

I closed my textbook and gathered my things, unable to watch anymore. That's how it's been—me retreating when she appears, her disappearing when I enter a room. Two planets in careful orbit, never colliding.

Last night I'd come home exhausted after a grueling day of classes and a mandatory group project meeting that dragged on for hours. Wes and Chase had already ordered pizza and wings, the boxes spread across the coffee table in our living room.

"Action movie night," Wes announced, waving me over.

I hesitated, but the alternative was sitting alone in my room, so I dropped onto the couch beside Chase, who passed me a paper plate loaded with pepperoni pizza and buffalo wings.

The movie had barely started when we heard the front door open. Bebe appeared in the entryway, her bag slung over her shoulder, looking tired but still beautiful.

"Hey, Bebe!" Wes called out, pausing the movie. "We've got plenty of food if you want to join us."

Her eyes flicked to me briefly, as if she wanted to, but couldn't decide if it was a good idea. Something flickered across her face—longing, maybe regret—before she shuttered it away.

"No, but thank you," she said. "I've got a lot of studying to do."

I watched her proceed up the stairs, her footsteps fading until there was the gentle click of her bedroom door closing. This is what it's come to—we're like strangers living in the same home.

I stared at the empty space where she'd stood; the pizza turning to cardboard in my mouth. Neither Wes nor Chase commented on the moment, but I caught them exchanging a look before Wes unpaused the movie. I couldn't focus on the explosions or car chases unfolding on the screen. My pizza sat untouched on my plate, appetite gone. Chase shot me a sympathetic glance but knew better than to say anything.

When I finally went upstairs, I paused outside her door. A thin strip of light shone beneath it, and I could hear the soft scratching of her pen against paper. My hand hovered in the air, ready to knock, to beg her to talk to me, to explain what had changed between us.

But I let my hand fall.

This morning I woke up early, not by choice, but from another restless night of tossing and turning. My room has become a disaster zone—clothes scattered across the floor, empty water bottles crowding my nightstand, sheets tangled from nights of fitful sleep. I drag myself out of bed and start gathering the mess, stuffing everything into my laundry basket.

I heft the basket and make my way downstairs, grateful for the mundane task. The house is quiet; my brothers are likely still asleep. Perfect. I need solitude.

The garage is cool and dim as I shoulder the door open, the familiar scents of motor oil and laundry detergent greeting me. I set the basket on the concrete floor and begin sorting—darks in one pile, lights in another, mindlessly going through the motions that don't require thought or feeling.

I start the washer, the rush of water filling the drum. I hear the door to the house swing open. I don't need to turn around to know who it is—her presence changes the air in the room.

When I look up, Bebe stands just inside the door, hesitant, half-hidden in the shadows of the garage doorway. Her hair is pulled back in a messy bun, wisps of cinnamon framing her face. She wears leggings and an oversized t-shirt that made her look smaller than usual, more vulnerable.

In her hands, she clutches my Dalton U sweatshirt—the one I'd given her that night cosmic bowling. My stomach drops. *This was it.* The final piece of me she's returning, severing the last tangible connection between us.

"I gave that to you," I say, the words coming out rougher than intended. "It's yours."

She shakes her head, her extraordinary eyes downcast. "It doesn't..." she starts, then pauses, swallowing hard. "It doesn't smell like you anymore."

I blink, not understanding.

"Could you..." Her voice is so soft I almost miss it. "I was wondering if you could wash it and... maybe spray some of your cologne on it? To get it back to how it was."

The request catches me off guard. It hits me like a punch to the ribs—soft, but deep. She doesn't want to let go completely. She still wants my scent wrapped around her, even while keeping her distance.

I stare at her standing here, my sweatshirt held to her chest like it was something precious. Her mismatched eyes finally lift to meet mine, and what I see steals my breath—hers were swimming with unshed tears, her lower lip trembling slightly with the effort of holding them back.

"Yeah," I say softly, reaching out to take the sweatshirt from her. "I can do that."

Our fingers brush as she passes the garment to me, and even that fleeting contact sends electricity racing up my arm. I add it to the dark pile beside the washing machine.

"Thank you," she whispers, already backing toward the

door, her voice unsteady. A single tear escapes, trailing down her cheek before she quickly wipes it away with her arm.

"Bebe, wait—" I start, but she's already slipping through the doorway, retreating into the house.

I stand there for a long moment, staring at the sweatshirt among my other clothes. Such a simple request, but loaded with meaning.

Chapter Thirty-One

LUKE

"Still undefeated," Chase brags, slapping me on the back. I smile, but it's forced. The truth? Beating everyone didn't matter when the one person I really wanted wasn't here.

My brothers and I just finished a game of paintball, loading our gear into the Jeep.

Wes slams the Jeep's trunk closed and leans against it, wiping sweat from his forehead. "Have either of you heard from dad lately?"

Chase shakes his head, checking his phone. "Nothing since the dinner last week."

"Not a word," I add, feeling a strange mix of concern and relief. "It's weird, right? Usually he's calling about Keeper business every other day."

"Definitely unusual," Wes agrees, fishing his keys from his pocket. "A week without a lecture or some cryptic assignment? I'm starting to wonder if aliens have abducted him."

I shrug, climbing into the backseat. "Honestly, I'm not

complaining. I've got enough on my plate right now without his society drama."

Wes slides into the driver's seat and adjusts the rearview mirror, catching my eye in the reflection. "How are things with Bebe?"

I shift uncomfortably in my seat, staring out the Jeep as the paintball facility recedes in the distance. "We're still broken up," I finally say, the words still feeling strange in my mouth. "I mean, technically. She's avoiding me—focusing on her classes."

"Damn," Wes murmurs, drumming his fingers on the steering wheel. "That's rough, man."

"Has she at least told you what happened to her face?" Chase asks, turning in his seat to face me. "She looked pretty rough when she came back."

I shake my head, exhaling heavily. "No. She's completely tight-lipped about it."

"Any theories?" Wes asks.

"I thought maybe she was in a car accident," I say, running a hand through my hair. "But her car is perfectly fine, not a scratch on it."

Chase frowns. "Could be something with her brother. Maybe he hit her?"

The suggestion makes my stomach turn, but I can't dismiss it entirely. "That crossed my mind, too."

"You don't think she was—" Wes mutters, his knuckles whitening on the steering wheel.

"No," I say firmly. "She promised me she wasn't. That she did at least say. It's just weird. She's there physically, but emotionally..." I trail off, unsure how to describe the hollow feeling of seeing Bebe every day without really having her. "She leaves early for classes, comes home late. We barely talk."

Wes looks at Chase. "Is she cool with the party tonight?"

"Yeah, she said she's fine with it. She even got a costume." Chase replies. He was in charge of all the party invitations and social media promos. Our first party of the year is our annual Halloween bash. "Oh!" he shouts, his expression brightening. "I invited Ladybug and Wasp over," he adds with a mischievous grin, wiggling his eyebrows teasingly at Wes.

Wes's head whips around so fast I'm surprised he doesn't get whiplash. "You did what?"

Ladybug—Wes's nickname for the pretty brunette next door—has been his not-so-secret crush since the day we moved in. Unfortunately for him, she lives with her husband, who we've dubbed "Wasp" because he's always buzzing around angrily—he's an asshole.

Chase shrugs. "They declined, of course. Wasp gave me his usual speech about noise levels and threatened to call the cops if things aren't quiet by 10 PM."

Wes groans, slumping back in his seat. "That guy is such a douche. Who moves next to a college house and expects noise restrictions?" He shakes his head. "But listen, we do need to keep it relatively tame tonight. Remember, we've got that fundraising gala tomorrow for the football team."

I'd completely forgotten about it. The Dalton U Athletic Foundation was invited last minute to this black-tie event, held by wealthy benefactors looking to donate and sponsor various programs around the state.

"Ugh, do we have to go?" Chase asks, grimacing. "Those things are so boring."

"Yes, you have to," Wes says firmly. "I managed to get plus ones for both of you, so at least we can suffer together."

"Three hours of small talk with rich old people in uncomfortable suits, pretending to care about their investment portfolios." I stare out of the Jeep, watching the buildings pass by. "That's... thoughtful of you."

"Actually," Wes says, catching my eye in the rearview mirror, "I got a ticket for Bebe too, if you want to ask her."

I straighten in my seat. "You did?"

"Could be a nice date night," Chase chimes in, turning to face me. "You know, get out of the house, dress up, reconnect in a different environment."

"She can barely look at me across the breakfast table. I doubt she wants to spend an entire evening in formal wear pretending everything's fine."

Wes shrugs. "Just putting it out there. The ticket's yours if you want it."

The idea settles in my mind, taking an unexpected root. Chase has a point. We've been stuck in this limbo, circling each other in our home like cautious strangers. A change of scenery could help break the ice.

When we pull up at the house, I grab my gym bag and head straight upstairs. I'm halfway up the stairs when I nearly collide with Bebe coming around the corner. Her eyes widen in surprise as she takes a quick step back.

"Sorry," she murmurs.

"No problem," I reply, my voice catching slightly. This is the closest we've been in days.

She's wearing her usual casual clothing—leggings, my Dalton U sweatshirt—and those fuzzy cat slippers. She wears her hair in a ponytail, and she has her laptop tucked under one arm.

She moves to step around me, but before she can escape downstairs, I shift my position, leaning against the wall in what I hope appears casual rather than desperate. My heart hammers against my ribs as I block her path without actually blocking it—giving her the choice to stay or go.

"Hey, I wanted to ask you something," I say, trying to keep my tone light. "So, Wes has a fundraiser event tomorrow night —for the team. Free food. Do you want to go?"

She hesitates, her fingers fidgeting with the sleeve of her sweatshirt. For a moment, I see a flicker of the old Bebe.

"I have plans tomorrow night," she says softly, her eyes dropping to the floor. "With my brothers."

I can't help the sigh that escapes me. Her brothers—the perpetual escape hatch, the excuse I've grown to hate, even if it might be true.

"Right. Of course." I try to keep the disappointment out of my voice, but fail miserably.

Something shifts in her expression. She reaches forward, her fingers tentatively brushing against mine. The contact sends electricity up my arm—it's the first time she's touched me in over a week.

"I really would like to go," she says, her voice barely above a whisper. "If it were any other day, I would."

Her fingers wrap around mine, a gentle pressure that feels like a lifeline thrown across the chasm between us. I search her face, those extraordinary eyes finally meeting mine, and I see sincerity there, mixed with regret.

"What about Sunday?" she asks, her voice soft but steady. "We could do that Star Wars marathon you've been trying to get me to watch." She tucks a strand of hair behind her ear, a gesture so familiar it makes my chest ache. "All of them, in order. Even the prequels you said were terrible."

My heart rate quickens. After days of distance, this small offering feels monumental.

"Sunday works," I say, trying not to sound too eager. "I'll make the caramel popcorn you like."

Her lips curve into a genuine smile—the first I've seen in what feels like forever. The sight of it transforms her face, bringing back the Bebe I fell for. She rises on her tiptoes, balancing herself with a hand on my chest, and presses a soft kiss to my cheek. The kiss is brief, chaste even, but it might as well be fireworks for the way it makes my skin tingle.

"It's a date," she whispers before pulling away.

"Okay, I'll see you at the party tonight."

I watch her descend the stairs, her cat slippers making soft padding sounds against the hardwood. She glances back once, a smile still lingering on her lips, before disappearing around the corner.

For the first time in days, I have hope.

Chapter Thirty-Two

LUKE

Our living room has been transformed with orange and purple string lights zigzagging across the ceiling as our house is packed with fellow students attending the annual Sullivan Halloween party. Fake cobwebs cling to corners and furniture, while plastic skeletons stand guard by the makeshift bar where Wes is playing bartender, mixing drinks with theatrical flair. Chase's playlist pounds through speakers strategically placed throughout, the bass vibrating through the floorboards.

I survey the scene from my position by the fireplace, nursing a beer that's grown warm in my hand. Our normally spacious living room is now a sea of costumes—superheroes mingling with movie villains, obscure pop culture references bumping into classic monsters. The air is thick with excitement and the unmistakable scent of college-party anticipation.

"So that's when Professor Daniels completely lost it,"

continues Brandon. He's dressed as some character from a video game I don't recognize, complete with a foam sword strapped to his back. "He threw his chalk across the room and told everyone to leave. Shortest lecture of my life."

I nod and laugh at the appropriate moment, but my attention isn't really on his story. I've been scanning the room all night, looking for a glimpse of cinnamon hair and mismatched eyes. The party has been going on for hours, and I'm starting to think she might have changed her mind about joining.

A sudden hush falls over the crowd nearest the staircase. Heads turn in unison, conversations pausing mid-sentence. I follow their gaze, and my breath catches in my throat.

Bebe is descending the stairs, and the sight of her makes my heart stutter. She's dressed as a bumblebee—a strapless black and yellow striped dress that goes high on her thigh, hugging every curve, sheer glittering yellow wings attached to her back, catching the light as she moves. Black knee-high leather boots and a headband with short bouncing antennae complete the look, her hair falling in loose waves around her shoulders. The costume is both adorable and undeniably sexy, a perfect play on her name that I can't believe I never thought of before.

I swear the music fades into the background as every eye in the room follows her movement. When she reaches the bottom, her eyes sweep across the crowded room until they find mine.

I offer her a smile. Not the casual one I've been giving everyone else tonight, but something more intimate, a silent acknowledgment of what passed between us on the stairs earlier. She catches it, and her lips curve upward in return, a tentative, fragile thing that makes my chest constrict with longing. Her eyes hold mine, speaking volumes in their silence. I see the same ache reflected there—the painful awareness of our disconnection these past days and the hope that maybe, *just maybe*, we can find our way back.

She takes a step in my direction, her body language open, and I feel a surge of hope. Maybe tonight can be our fresh start. I set my warm beer down on the mantel, preparing to cross the room to her.

"Oh my God, Luke! Your costume is impressive!"

A flash of blonde hair appears in my peripheral vision as Ashley materializes at my side, her voice cutting through the moment as she grabs my arm. She's dressed as a slutty fairy, complete with glittery makeup and a wand that she waves dangerously close to my face.

"The whole Star Wars thing is so retro-cool," she gushes, leaning in too close. "And you totally pull it off. Those pants are very..." her eyes drift downward appreciatively, "authentic."

I gently extricate my arm from her grip, trying to maintain a polite smile while creating some distance between us. "Thanks. Han Solo—classic, not retro," I correct her, my eyes already searching past her for Bebe.

The spot she stood moments ago is now occupied by a group of football players. My heart sinks as I scan the crowded room, trying to catch a glimpse of those yellow and black stripes, the glittering wings that had captured everyone's attention.

"Excuse me," I say to Ashley, who's still talking about

something I haven't been listening to. "I need to find my girlfriend."

I push through the crowd, dodging a vampire making out with a nurse, sidestepping a zombie whose fake blood is dripping on our floor. The living room yields no sign of her, nor does the kitchen when I check there next.

Wes in his ridiculous Superman costume appears at my side, holding two shot glasses filled with amber liquid. Chase flanks him, carrying a third in one hand—a whip in the other, to go with his Indiana Jones costume.

"Tequila," Wes announces, pushing one of the shots into my hand.

I take the shot and down it immediately, wincing as the alcohol burns a path down my throat.

"Have either of you seen Bebe?" I ask, still scanning the packed room. "She was here a minute ago."

Wes's grin widens as he raises his eyebrows suggestively. "Yeah, I've seen her—how could I not? That bee costume is…"

I fix him with a blank stare, my jaw tightening. My expression makes it clear I'm not amused by his appreciation of my girlfriend's appearance, even if we're in this strange limbo.

Wes's smile falters, and he raises his hands in surrender. "Just making an observation, bro."

Chase steps between us. "She's getting herself a drink," he says, clapping me on the shoulder reassuringly. "Saw her heading that way a minute ago." He points toward the garage.

I nod, handing my empty shot glass back to Wes before pushing through the crowd toward the garage door. It's packed with partygoers clustered around a dartboard in the far corner and a shuffleboard table we had brought in. A glance at the second fridge outside, where we keep the bottled drinks, shows no sign of Bebe.

I pivot, remembering the keg we set up earlier in the backyard. I slip through the back door into the cool October night. More string lights crisscross the patio, casting everything in a warm glow.

And there she is...

I spot her near the keg, her bumblebee antennae bobbing as she examines the tap with adorable confusion. She's tilting her head, those mismatched eyes narrowing in concentration as she presses random parts of the mechanism, clearly trying to figure out how the thing works.

Before I can make my way over, Trent materializes beside her. He's dressed as a generic superhero, his muscular frame barely contained by the tight costume. He leans in close to her, pointing at the keg tap with an exaggerated helpfulness that makes my stomach tighten.

Bebe's face brightens with relief as she nods, handing him her empty cup. I hang back near the patio door, watching the interaction unfold. His reputation with women is well known around campus—the guy hits on anything that moves. Part of me wants to intervene, but another part is curious if she recognizes the classic "let me help you with that" move for what it really is.

He expertly pumps the keg and fills her cup, handing it back with a smile that's all white teeth and leaning just a bit too close. His eyes trail down her costume with obvious appreciation. I can see her expression from where I stand— polite but detached as she nods at whatever line he's feeding her. She takes measured sips from her cup but doesn't make direct eye contact with him.

Trent doesn't seem to notice her disinterest, or more likely, doesn't care. He edges closer, one hand braced against the wall behind her. Bebe shifts her weight subtly, creating distance without being obvious about it.

I'm about to intervene when he makes his move. His arm reaches behind her, fingers extended toward the curve of her hip, clearly aiming lower. What happens next unfolds so quickly, I almost miss it.

She captures his wrist mid-air. Her fingers lock around his arm before twisting it at an angle that shouldn't be physically possible. Trent's cocky smile transforms instantly into a grimace of shock and pain.

"AHHH!" His howl cuts through the party chatter. "What the hell?" He staggers back.

The music inside continues pounding, but everyone on the patio freezes, conversations halting mid-sentence as heads turn toward the commotion. His teammates exchange wide-eyed glances while a circle forms around them, party-goers craning their necks to see what's happening.

I elbow my way through the gathering crowd, moving swiftly to them. Bebe's stance shifts when she notices me approaching—her shoulders relaxing as she releases Trent's arm. A dangerous gleam in her eyes softens, replaced by something vulnerable and uncertain.

I extend my hand toward her, palm up—a silent invitation. Without hesitation, she slides her fingers between mine, stepping away from Trent to stand beside me. I curve my arm around her waist, drawing her against my side in a gesture both possessive and protective, though the way she handled him makes it abundantly clear she doesn't need my protection.

Trent rubs his wrist, looking at her with a mixture of shock and embarrassment.

My brothers come to stand by my side, cutting through the ring of onlookers that's formed around us.

"What happened?" Wes asks, his eyes darting between Trent's pained expression and Bebe's composed face.

Trent's face contorts with humiliation and rage. He cradles his wrist against his chest, his superhero costume suddenly looking ridiculous. "This bitch broke my fucking arm!"

Something snaps inside me at the word "bitch." I lunge forward, breaking away from Bebe, my fists already clenching. "What did you call her?"

Wes catches me mid-stride, his arms locking around my chest. "Whoa, easy!" He pulls me back with surprising strength. "Not worth it, Luke."

I struggle against his grip, adrenaline coursing through me. "Let me go, Wes."

"Trent, get out of here," Wes orders, still restraining me, his voice dropping to an authoritative tone he uses on the field. "It's not broken. Go ice it and sober up. And don't you ever speak to Bebe again."

His face flushes as he looks around at the circle of onlookers. "Whatever," he mutters, backing away. "Party sucks anyway."

As he passes by, he pauses next to Bebe who's now standing with Chase, leaning in slightly. "You act all cute and innocent," he hisses, leaning closer, "but I see you."

She doesn't flinch at his words. Her face remains perfectly composed, those mismatched eyes meeting his with unflinching steadiness. The corner of her mouth quirks upward in the slightest hint of a smile, as if his accusation genuinely amuses her rather than offends her.

There's something about her reaction—not embarrassment or anger, but something closer to... recognition. Like she's heard this before. Like she knows exactly what he means.

Chapter Thirty-Three

BEBE

Trent stumbles away, nursing his injured wrist and wounded pride as the crowd disperses, the momentary drama already forgotten as the party resumes.

"Well, that was something," Chase says, breaking the tension. "Remind me never to get on your bad side, Bebe."

I laugh softly. "Trust me, you could never." I give him a playful wink, grateful for the way he's trying to lighten the mood.

Wes runs a hand through his hair, looking genuinely embarrassed. "Bebe, I'm sorry about Trent. He's an ass when he drinks, and..." He sighs heavily. "I should've warned you about him. The guy doesn't understand boundaries."

"The hitting on me part didn't bother me," I say with a dismissive wave. "I gave him no reason to think I was interested." I shrug, adjusting one of my wings that had gotten slightly bent in the commotion. "When he went to grab me, I just... snapped."

Luke's arm slides protectively around my waist again, pulling me closer to his side. I lean into him, savoring the contact I've been denying myself this past week. The warmth of Luke's body against mine sends a flutter through my chest. It's an unfamiliar feeling—being held like something precious, something worth defending.

I glance up at him, noting the protective set of his jaw, the way his eyes still track Trent's retreat across the yard. It's endearing, really. How he lunged forward, ready to defend my honor despite having just witnessed me nearly dislocate a linebacker's wrist without breaking a sweat.

I've spent my entire life being the dangerous one—the weapon, the threat, the protector. Gabriel trained me to stand alone, to need no one. Yet here's Luke, this beautiful man who wants to shield me from harm I'm more than capable of handling myself. The irony isn't lost on me—the Killer Bee being protected by her gentle boyfriend.

The juxtaposition strikes me as I watch Luke—he's not naturally confrontational, not someone who seeks out fights or dominates through physical intimidation. It's one of the countless things I've grown to love about him. Where I was raised to see vulnerability as weakness, Luke embraces his gentle nature openly.

Even now, the tension gradually leaving his body isn't being replaced by the adrenaline high I'm accustomed to after physical confrontations. Instead, his concern shifts entirely to me, his blue eyes searching mine.

"Are you okay?" he asks softly, his thumb tracing small circles against my hip.

The question almost makes me laugh. I'm the one who

nearly broke someone's wrist, and he's asking if *I'm* the one who's okay.

"Those self-defense classes really paid off, huh?" I add with a light laugh, deflecting the intensity of the moment.

Wes's phone chimes with a notification. He checks it, and his face lights up. "The girls from Delta Phi arrived with jello shots," he announces, grabbing Chase by the arm, pulling him away. "We need to make an appearance."

"Duty calls!" Chase calls over his shoulder. "Host responsibilities and all that."

They disappear inside, leaving Luke and me alone on the patio, and the sounds of the party fade into the background. His fingers intertwine with mine, his thumb tracing small circles against my skin. The gentle pressure sends tingles up my arm.

"Come here," he says softly, leading me toward the fire pit where several Adirondack chairs form a semicircle around the dancing flames. He settles into one of them before gently tugging my hand, pulling me down onto his lap.

I hesitate for just a heartbeat before giving in, arranging my bee wings so they don't get crushed as I perch sideways across his thighs. His arms encircle my waist, holding me securely against him.

The warmth of the fire bathes us in a gentle glow, creating our own little island separate from the chaos of the party. I rest my head against his shoulder, breathing in his familiar scent—that mix of something uniquely Luke that always makes my heart race.

"I've missed this," he whispers against my hair. "I've missed you."

His words send a complicated flutter through my chest—equal parts joy and pain. I want nothing more than to melt into him completely, to forget everything else. To forget the impending arranged marriage to Alessandro—the blood on my hands.

But I can't.

My mind spins with contradictions. Every cell in my body wants to be close to him, to reclaim what we had. Yet the rational part of me knows I should maintain distance, protect him from the inevitable heartbreak when I have to leave. I'm caught in this impossible middle ground—unable to fully commit, unable to fully let go. I'm like a moth circling a flame, knowing the burn is coming but unable to resist the light.

His fingers trace a gentle path along my bare arm, and I lean into the touch. When his lips brush against my temple, I turn my face toward him, seeking his warmth like a sunflower turning toward light.

Luke's blue eyes study my face in the firelight, his brow furrowing slightly. "What's going on in that head of yours? You're thinking so hard I can practically hear the gears turning."

I bite my lower lip, knowing I should maintain the walls I've been building, yet finding them crumbling.

"I'm being unfair to you," I murmur, my voice barely audible above the crackling fire. "One minute I'm pushing you away, the next I'm sitting in your lap. I tell you we can't be together, but I'm making movie marathon plans." I shake my head. "I tell you I don't want this, but then I can't stay away. I must be driving you crazy."

His blue eyes search mine, patient and understanding. "A little," he admits with a small smile.

"It's just..." I struggle to find words that won't reveal too much. "My head keeps telling me we shouldn't be doing this —that I should walk away before things get more complicated. But my heart..." I place my hand over his chest, feeling his heartbeat against my palm. "My heart won't let me stay away."

Luke covers my hand with his, pressing it more firmly against him. The steady rhythm of his heart grounds me, anchoring me in this moment despite the storm raging inside me.

"I have faith in us," he says softly, his eyes never leaving mine. "I'm certain we're supposed to be together, Bebe. I feel it here." He taps his chest beneath my palm. "Maybe you can't see the path forward right now, but I do."

His words wrap around me like a warm blanket, offering comfort I know I don't deserve.

"I understand," he continues, brushing a strand of hair from my face. "You're at war with yourself—your mind telling you one thing, your heart another. I see that struggle in your eyes every day." His thumb traces my cheekbone with such tenderness I nearly break. "When you're ready to talk about whatever's holding you back, I'll be here. No pressure, no timeline. Just me... waiting for you."

I stare into the dancing flames, trying to imagine a world where I could tell him everything—about The Killer Bee, about Alessandro. The impossibility of it crushes me.

"What if that's never?" I whisper, my eyes widen at my admission as the implications hang in the air between us. "What if I can never fully give you what you deserve?"

Luke's gaze intensifies, his blue eyes reflecting the firelight as he cups my face between his hands.

"Then I'll fight," he says with quiet determination. "I'll fight for us. For however long it takes."

The simplicity of his declaration steals my breath. No one has ever fought for me before—I've always been the weapon, the asset, the tool to be wielded. Never someone worth fighting for.

"You don't know what you're saying," I whisper, my voice catching.

His finger traces my lower lip, his expression unwavering. "I know exactly what I'm saying," he counters, his thumb gently brushing away a tear I didn't realize I had let fall. "I love you, Bebe. All of you—even the parts you're afraid to show me."

I lean forward, pressing my forehead against his and close my eyes to savor this moment of connection. His hands slide to the back of my neck, fingers threading through my hair as he tilts my face toward his. Our lips meet in a gentle kiss—soft and sweet, yet it leaves a mark, holding the weight of a future neither of us could see yet.

"Hey, lovebirds!" Chase's voice breaks through our bubble, standing a few feet away. "There's a beer pong table with our names on it."

I turn my head in Chase's direction with unexpected enthusiasm. The chance to play a normal college game—something I've seen in movies but never experienced—sends a thrill through me.

"Beer pong?" I ask, perking up instantly. "I've always wanted to try that!"

Luke chuckles against my hair, his breath warm on my neck.

I shift to stand. Chase grins and extends his hand to help me up from Luke's lap. My antennae bounce as I take his offered help, allowing him to pull me to my feet.

"Hold on," Luke protests, reluctantly releasing his hold on my waist. "I thought we were having a moment here."

"Moments can wait," I say over my shoulder with a playful smile. "Beer pong is happening now."

Luke follows us across the patio, where Wes is already arranging plastic cups in perfect triangles at either end of a folding table.

"Teams!" Chase announces, clapping his hands together. "I'm with Bebe."

"Wait, what?" Luke's brow furrows as he looks between us. "I thought I'd be partnering with her."

"Too slow, big brother," Chase says with a grin, throwing his arm around my shoulders. "Bebe and I are going to dominate this table."

Luke turns to me with a wounded expression. "You're teaming with Chase instead of me?"

I bite my lip, trying not to laugh at his exaggerated pout. "Sorry?"

Wes arranges the last cup into formation and straightens. "She's never even played before," he points out, gesturing with the ping-pong ball. "But okay, I'll take Luke. We'll crush them."

"Don't be so sure," Chase says, squeezing my shoulder. "Bebe's basically unbeatable at everything. Bowling, volleyball, paintball, Foosball—"

Luke's head snaps up. "Foosball? How would you know she's good at foosball?"

Chase's face freezes, his arm still around my shoulders. He glances at me with a guilty look before clearing his throat. "Well, um... we might play sometimes. At the Student Union between classes."

"You what?" Luke stares at me, his expression a mix of surprise and betrayal. "You've been hanging out with Chase behind my back?"

I can't help but laugh at his dramatic reaction. "We just play a few games and compete with others when our schedules align."

The truth is, Jake's friendship has been a lifeline this past week. When I've been avoiding Luke, trying to sort through my impossible situation, Jake has quietly filled the void without ever making it awkward. He never pries, never pushes, just offers easy companionship and distraction when I need it most.

Chase turns to me, his hand raised for our pre-game ritual. "Ready to show these losers how it's done?"

"Absolutely," I reply with a grin, slapping my palm against his in our now-practiced sequence—high five, low five, fist bump, elbow touch, and finally, the signature hip bump that always makes me laugh.

Wes watches our routine with raised eyebrows before turning to Luke. "We're completely screwed, aren't we?"

Luke glances between Chase and me, then straightens himself with determination. "No way. They may have their little secret foosball club, but we've got this."

He turns to Wes with a fierce competitive gleam in his eyes and raises his hand. "Oldest Sullivan brothers for the win!"

Wes grins and slaps his palm against Luke's in a resounding high five. "Let's do it!"

As we take our positions at opposite ends of the table, a strange warmth spreads through my chest. I look across at Luke, his face lit with playful determination as he bounces the ping-pong ball in his palm, then at Wes beside him, already talking trash to Chase. My partner throws his arm around my shoulders again, pulling me into a quick side-hug before we strategize in hushed whispers.

The realization comes to me—*I belong here*. I've missed *this*—*them*—*Luke*. These three brothers have folded me into their lives as if I've always been a part of it. The easy banter, the teasing, the unwavering support—it feels like *family*.

Chapter Thirty-Four

LUKE

I REACH across the empty space beside me, still half-asleep, fingers searching for a body that isn't there, leaving only the ghost of her scent on my pillow. Last night floods back in fragments—her whispered, "I'll stay until you fall asleep," the weight of her head on my chest, her fingers tracing lazy patterns across my skin as my eyes grew heavy. She kept her promise, at least that much. We're still technically broken up, existing in this strange limbo.

I roll onto my back, staring at the ceiling where morning light casts shifting patterns through the half-drawn blinds.

Last night had been different. After the Halloween party, after the beer pong game where she and Chase had destroyed Wes and me, she followed me upstairs without hesitation. We'd fallen into bed together, not for sex but for something I've come to crave even more—the simple comfort of her body against mine, her steady breathing lulling me to sleep.

I don't know at what point she went to her room. She had

to get up early anyway and head to the city to meet with her brothers. I'd wanted to ask her to stay, to wake up with her warm body beside me, but I'd fallen asleep before I could form the words.

The door to my bedroom crashes open without warning, startling me out of my half-sleep and the woes of Bebe.

"Rise and shine, sleeping beauty! It's past noon," Wes announces, yanking my curtains fully wide, and I react like a vampire would—hissing in the sunlight.

Chase bounces onto the foot of my bed, making the mattress dip. "The house looks like a war zone, and we've got cleaning to do."

I groan, pulling my pillow over my face. "Five more minutes."

"Nope," Chase says, snatching the pillow away. "Bebe's gone, so you can't use her as an excuse to hide here all day."

Wes crosses his arms, looking at me with mock sternness. "We had a deal, remember? Equal division of post-party labor."

"Fine, fine. I'm up," I mutter, tossing back the covers and swinging my legs over the side of the bed. My head throbs—a mild hangover—the consequence of one too many shots during our beer pong rematch. I pull on a t-shirt and follow my brothers downstairs, squinting against the bright sunlight streaming through the windows.

The aftermath of the Halloween party is even worse than I imagined. Red cups litter every surface, splotches of spilled beer dot the hardwood, and remnants of costumes—a witch's hat, a superhero mask, someone's fake vampire teeth—are scattered throughout the living room.

Chase thrusts a black trash bag into my hands. "Bathroom and kitchen are yours."

I grimace at the assignment. "Seriously? The worst areas?"

"You got to cuddle with your girlfriend all night while we were handling the keg stand disasters," Wes says, already picking up cups from the coffee table.

I don't bother correcting him about the "girlfriend" part. Our relationship status is too complicated to explain, especially with this headache.

The three of us work in silence for a few minutes. The only sounds are the rustle of trash bags and the occasional groan when someone discovers a particularly disgusting mess.

"You know," Wes says, pausing to inspect a mysterious stain on our couch, "we could have used Bebe's rent money to hire a cleaning service. Actually," he adds with a smirk, "we could have hired a sexy maid, the kind with the little French outfit." He mimes an hourglass figure with his hands.

Chase snorts, tossing an empty pizza box into his trash bag. "We could have if someone hadn't blown half our party budget on those ridiculous animatronic zombies for the front yard."

"Excuse me? Those zombies were a hit!" Wes protests. "Did you see how many Instagram posts they were in? The moving arms totally justified the extra hundred bucks."

"A hundred and fifty," Chase corrects. "Plus the fog machine that set off the smoke detector at two am."

"Minor technical issue. The ambiance was worth every penny," Wes insists, dramatically sweeping his arm across the room. "Sullivan Halloween parties are legendary because we don't cut corners."

I roll my eyes as I scrub at a sticky patch on the kitchen

counter. Their bickering is oddly comforting—a slice of normalcy in the chaos of the past week.

"Speaking of Bebe," Chase says, changing subjects as he ties off his trash bag, "how are things with you two? Last night seemed... better."

I shrug, setting down my sponge. "Better, yeah. Not great, but... we're talking again. She stayed with me last night—just to sleep," I add quickly, seeing Wes's eyebrows shoot up. "But she was gone when I woke up."

"That's progress though, right?" Chase asks, leaning against the doorframe.

"I guess." I run a hand through my hair, struggling to articulate the complicated feelings churning inside me. "It's like... she wants to be with me, but something is holding her back. I suspect it's her brothers."

Wes frowns, dropping an armful of empty bottles into the recycling bin. "Her brothers?"

"Yeah." I pick up another red cup, crushing it in my hand. "I believe someone's in her head about us. She told us when we first met her that she came to Dalton U for the 'college experience.' I think her family had expectations for her, plans that didn't include getting serious with someone."

Wes tosses a wadded-up napkin into the trash. "Is she coming to the gala tonight? You never said if you asked her."

"I asked." I shake my head, grabbing another sponge to attack a stubborn stain. "No, she won't be back until tomorrow morning."

Chase pauses mid-sweep, leaning on the broom handle. "Why won't she just tell you what's going on? I mean, you've been together for weeks now. Doesn't she trust you enough to share what's happening?"

"That," I say with a humorless laugh, "is the million-dollar question. She's keeping a secret, and I can't figure out what it is or why."

"Family stuff can be complicated." Wes gives me a pointed look, crossing his arms over his chest. "And how do you expect her to share secrets when you've got one of your own? The Keepers?"

I open my mouth to argue, then close it again.

"He's got you there," Chase says, nodding. "You've been keeping The Keepers from her this whole time."

"I know." I sigh, leaning against the counter. "I was close to telling her everything that night—right before she broke up with me. I had the words on the tip of my tongue, but then she dropped that bomb and..." I trail off, remembering how the moment shattered.

"Ouch," Wes winces, setting his trash bag down.

"Yeah. Kind of hard to share family secrets with someone who's trying to end things," I say, rubbing my temples.

"Actually," Chase says, setting aside his broom, "if that's the case with Bebe's brothers controlling her life, it's really not that different from dad." He shakes his head ruefully.

"True," I admit reluctantly. "He's made it pretty clear he doesn't approve of her."

Wes snorts as he ties off another trash bag. "If he had his way, we'd all be married to proper Keeper society women. Some perfectly bred daughters of his brotherhood with the right pedigrees and connections."

"God, can you imagine?" Chase makes a face. "Those stuffy Keeper's daughters with their perfect posture and conversation topics approved by the Council." He straightens his back and adopts a high-pitched voice. "'Oh, Lucas, I simply adore the new initiatives your father is implementing at Headquarters. Shall we discuss them over cucumber sandwiches and sweet tea?'"

Despite my mood, I laugh. Chase's impression is disturbingly accurate.

Chase groans, setting down his broom. "Ugh, I can't take this anymore. I need a shower, maybe two. I swear this party smell is seeping into my pores." He sniffs his shirt and makes a face. "I feel gross."

"You think you feel gross?" Wes laughs. "I had three different people spill drinks on me last night. But hey—" he gestures dramatically between us "—look at us, going from trashy to classy in under twelve hours. Sullivan Halloween rager to black-tie fundraiser gala. That's range, baby."

I snort at Wes's ridiculous statement, and suddenly we're all cracking up.

Chapter Thirty-Five

BEBE

I GRAB another champagne glass off the waiter's tray as he walks by. It's the third one I've had tonight. I need it if I'm going to survive—using the champagne flute like a life raft as if I'd been tossed into a sea of sequins and shallow conversation.

The bubbles tickle my nose as I take a sip—okay, more like a gulp, scanning the glittering ballroom of the Langford Hotel filled with Los Angeles's elite. Gabriel insisted I attend this "networking opportunity" with him and my other brothers, claiming it was essential for the family business. Meanwhile, across town, Luke, Wes, and Chase are at a football fundraiser —probably laughing, surrounded by people who actually enjoy each other's company.

I shift uncomfortably, feeling the restrictive fabric of my emerald silk gown pull against my ribs. The dress is stunning —backless with a plunging neckline that Gabriel's assistant selected. But the bodice feels like it's crushing my lungs with each breath. Beauty is pain, I suppose. Though I'd trade this designer masterpiece for Luke's Dalton U sweatshirt in a heartbeat.

Across the ballroom, women in couture gowns exchange air kisses while men in tailored tuxedos discuss business ventures and political connections. The chandelier light catches on diamond necklaces and platinum watches—wealth on ostentatious display.

I drift toward the refreshments table, seeking refuge from the endless parade of Gabriel's associates who keep eyeing me like a prize thoroughbred. My brothers are scattered throughout the room, each working their assigned targets—powerful men whose influence or resources he wants to cultivate for our family's enterprises.

As I pop a cheese cube into my mouth, I sense someone approaching. The subtle scent of expensive cologne reaches me before I turn to see him—Alessandro Calabrese, my future husband, standing beside me in a perfectly tailored tuxedo that probably costs more than a semester of college tuition.

"Bebe," he says, his Italian accent caressing my name. "Bellissima, you look absolutely stunning."

His eyes travel slowly down my body, lingering appreciatively on the plunging neckline of my gown. At forty-three, Alessandro is undeniably handsome for his age—salt-and-pepper hair artfully styled, Mediterranean complexion, and a jawline that belongs in luxury watch advertisements. But the twenty-five-year age gap between us makes my skin crawl.

I ignore his greeting, reaching for a halved strawberry and popping it into my mouth. The sweet juice bursts across my tongue as I deliberately focus on arranging a small plate of hors d'oeuvres, selecting a few more cheese cubes and canapés.

Alessandro chuckles, seemingly amused by my cold shoulder. He leans closer, his breath warm against my ear.

"Gabriel tells me you're enjoying a little college adventure until the wedding." He steps closer, his cologne invading my space. "Playing a normal girl, living in a house with roommates." His chuckle is indulgent, patronizing. "It's cute, but you're wasting your time there," Alessandro says, his fingers brushing my bare shoulder. "When we're married, you can continue your education if it amuses you. I'm not opposed to having an educated wife. But perhaps online courses would be more suitable. Especially since you'll likely be pregnant within months of our marriage."

The champagne turns sour in my stomach. I set my glass down with trembling fingers, suddenly feeling lightheaded.

"I'm not even nineteen," I manage to say, my voice barely audible.

Alessandro's eyes narrow, his expression hardening. "I've been patient, Bebe. Delaying the deal for this... experiment of yours." His hand slides possessively to my lower back. "But I do hope you're being careful at that college house of yours." His voice drops to a dangerous whisper. "If you're fucking any of those boys, you better be using protection. I won't raise another man's child." He presses a cold kiss on my cheek before straightening his cufflinks. "Think about what I said. I expect you to fulfill your obligations when the time comes." With that, he nods to someone over my shoulder with a fake smile before walking away, leaving me frozen in place.

The room spins as his words echo in my head. I set my plate down with trembling hands and turn away from the refreshment table. The champagne bubbles that moments ago tickled my nose now churn in my stomach, rising like acid up my throat. The space suddenly feels too crowded, too hot, the surrounding faces blurring into a kaleidoscope of predatory smiles and calculating eyes.

I push through clusters of laughing guests, mumbling apologies as I knock against shoulders and elbows. My heart hammers against my ribs, each beat a panicked rhythm that drowns out the orchestra. I need air. I need space.

I beeline to the single-stall bathroom, barely making it through the door before my stomach revolts. I fall to my knees on the cold marble floor and retch violently into the toilet. The champagne burns worse coming up than it did going down, leaving my throat raw and my eyes watering.

I'm not sure if it's the alcohol or Alessandro's words about getting me pregnant that's making me sick. Probably both. I wipe my mouth with the back of my hand, my breath coming in shallow gasps as I try to regain control.

His words still taunt me—"pregnant within months," "wasting your time," "fulfill your obligations"—each one a nail in the coffin of the brief freedom I've tasted so far.

The memory of Luke's face flashes before me—his gentle blue eyes, the way he looks at me like I'm something precious rather than property to be traded.

My clutch vibrates against the floor where I dropped it. Trembling, I reach inside for my phone, and the screen illuminates with a text.

> Henri: It's time. Gabe needs you on the side stage for the speech.

I pull myself up using the handicap rail, legs unsteady beneath me. The bathroom's harsh fluorescent lighting reveals my reflection in the mirror—mascara smudged under my eyes, lipstick faded, cheeks flushed with fever. I look exactly how I feel: wrecked.

I turn on the faucet and cup my hands below the cool stream, bringing the water to my lips. I rinse and spit, desperate to clear the acidic taste from my mouth. After splashing water on my face, I pat my skin dry with a plush hand towel.

A crystal bowl of mints sits on the marble countertop. I take one, then reconsider and grab three more, popping them into my mouth in quick succession. The sharp peppermint cuts through the bitter aftertaste of vomit and champagne.

I reapply my lipstick with steady hands—a skill perfected through years of training. *Control your breathing. Steady your pulse. Show no weakness.*

With one last look at my reflection, I straighten my spine and exit the bathroom, transforming back into Bebe Laurent, the dutiful sister of the family. The mask slides into place as I navigate through the crowd toward the stage.

My brothers are already assembled, Gabriel looking immaculate in his custom tuxedo. Henri adjusts his cufflinks while Beau checks his phone. They form a picture of power and privilege—the Laurent dynasty in the flesh.

"There you are," Gabe says, his eyes narrowing as they scan my face.

His nostrils flare slightly. He can probably smell the mint trying to mask the lingering scent of sickness.

The announcer's voice booms through the ballroom speakers. "Ladies and gentlemen, please welcome tonight's benefactors, the Laurent family, whose generous donation has made tonight's gala possible."

Polite applause ripples through the crowd as Gabriel leads

our procession onto the stage. Beau follows, then Henri, who stops to take my hand while I climb the steps.

We line up on stage like perfect dolls, Gabe stepping forward to the microphone flashing a practiced smile—the one that's graced countless charity events and business magazines. He taps it twice; the sound's feedback echoes through the ballroom.

"Thank you all for coming tonight," he begins, his voice smooth. "I'm Gabriel Laurent, and I'm honored to continue my father's legacy of service to this city, our communities, and our great state."

I shift my weight from one painful heel to the other, letting my gaze drift across the sea of wealthy faces. I've heard this speech a dozen times before—how our father taught us the importance of giving back, how the Laurent Foundation is committed to making a difference, all carefully crafted words that sound meaningful but reveal nothing of our true business.

The chandeliers blur as I zone out, my brother's voice fading to a distant drone. Blah, blah, blah—something about new initiatives and strengthening communities. Same script, different gala.

I'm mentally counting the minutes until I can escape as I notice a familiar profile. *Trent?* The asshole from last night's party—Wes's teammate. *What's he doing here?* Next to him is another familiar face from Dalton U's football team. I scan the room, and my heart stutters when my eyes lock with *Wes's*, then *Chase's*, and finally *Luke's*. I blink rapidly, certain I'm hallucinating, but no—it's definitely him, standing near the back in a perfectly fitted tuxedo, his expression a mixture of confusion and surprise. *What are they doing here?* This is Los

Angeles, cities away from Dalton's campus. *Is this the fundraiser he invited me to?*

"—which is why the Laurent Foundation is proud to announce a donation of one million dollars to Dalton University's football program," Gabriel's voice cuts through my shock.

My head snaps to Gabriel as the crowd erupts in enthusiastic applause, champagne glasses raised in appreciation of our family's "generosity."

Gabriel turns slightly toward me, his smile never faltering for the audience, but his eyes seek mine for the expected supportive sister's response. I meet his gaze with the iciest stare I can muster, letting every ounce of my fury crystallize in my expression. This isn't a coincidence. This is calculated. He knew exactly what he was doing—arranging for our "family business" to bring my worlds crashing together. He's sending me a message. Or rather—sending Luke one.

Wes's mouth hangs open as Gabriel continues speaking about "fostering excellence in collegiate athletics." Chase whispers something to Luke, who doesn't respond. His gaze fixed entirely on me.

I feel exposed standing on this stage, like Gabriel has deliberately put me on display. The emerald dress that moments ago felt merely uncomfortable now feels like a costume—too revealing, too sophisticated, nothing like the casual girl Luke knows.

Chapter Thirty-Six

LUKE

SO THIS IS HER SECRET...

She's not just a regular college girl—she's rich. Not just
well-off, but one-million-dollar-donation rich. The kind of
wealth that builds wings on hospitals and gets your name
etched in marble.

Bebe's brother wraps up his speech, his polished words
flowing as he gestures toward the Dalton U football coaching
staff seated at a table near the front of the stage. Wes shifts
close to me, whispering something I barely register. My focus
remains locked on Bebe.

She stands rigidly beside her brothers, that dress hugging
curves I know intimately. But beneath the glamour, I see what
others don't—the slight tension in her jaw, the way her fingers
curl too tightly around her clutch, the stiffness in her posture
that speaks of discomfort rather than poise.

"Dude," Wes nudges me, "did you know about this? That
she's an heiress?"

I shake my head, unable to look away from the stage. The pieces start falling into place—her vague references to family business, the mysterious brothers in the city. *But what kind of family drama leaves bruises?*

Chase nudges me. "Think she knew we'd be here? That this is the event you invited her to?"

"I don't believe so," I murmur, watching her eyes widen with recognition when they meet mine. The surprise there seems genuine—too raw to be feigned. "She looks as shocked as we are."

The speech concludes with thunderous applause, champagne flutes clinking as the elite of Los Angeles show their appreciation for the Laurents' generosity. The ovation continues as Gabriel leads his siblings off the stage, his hand at Bebe's elbow. She moves like a marionette, her steps mechanical beneath the flowing silk dress.

Before I realize what I'm doing, I'm pushing through the crowd, weaving between cocktail dresses and dinner jackets. Some primal instinct drives me forward—the need to reach her, to understand, to claim what's mine in this unfamiliar territory.

"Luke, wait up!" Wes calls behind me, but I don't slow down. My brothers' footsteps hurry to catch up as I navigate the maze of tables and guests.

We intercept them near the bottom of the stairs. Bebe freezes when she sees me approaching, her complexion paling beneath the subtle makeup.

"Luke," she breathes, my name barely audible over the orchestra that's resumed playing.

I search her face, looking for the girl who wears my sweatshirts and fuzzy cat slippers, who promised me a Star

like she's a tourist rather than a student. Before I can respond, movement at the edge of our circle catches my attention.

A distinguished man with approaches, his tuxedo is even more impeccable than Gabriel's. He moves with the confident swagger of someone accustomed to commanding rooms. When he reaches us, Bebe's brothers make room for him, and his hand settles possessively on the small of Bebe's back. I suddenly remember that her dress is backless as she flinches at his touch.

"Ah, the Sullivan brothers," the man says, his accent faintly Italian. "I'm Alessandro Calabrese, a close friend of the Laurent family."

He extends his free hand to me, never removing the other from her back.

I reluctantly shake Alessandro's hand. The possessiveness of his touch makes my jaw clench. Something about this man —the way he stands too close to her, the proprietary gleam in his eyes—sends warning signals through my brain.

"I understand you're Bebe's roommate," Alessandro says, his tone implying something more. His eyes assess me with cold calculation. "How... convenient for a young man."

What is that supposed to mean?

"Alessandro is one of our most valued business partners. His family connections in Italy have been instrumental to our European expansion," Gabriel adds.

Bebe hasn't spoken a single word since our initial greeting. Her eyes meet mine briefly, a storm of emotions swirling in those mismatched depths—fear, regret, longing.

Henri, the youngest-looking brother, catches my eye. Unlike Gabriel's calculating stare or Alessandro's predatory gaze, his expression holds something different—a flicker of sympathy, perhaps even apology. It vanishes as quickly as it appeared, his features rearranging into the same neutral mask his older brother wears so well.

"Bebe," Henri says suddenly, his voice softer than Gabriel's, "come with me to the bar. I could use another drink." He offers his arm to her, a gentlemanly gesture that somehow feels like a rescue.

Relief flashes across her face as she takes it. "Excuse us," she murmurs, the first words she's spoken since our awkward reunion began.

Gabriel watches them go before turning back to us with a smile. "Please enjoy the rest of your evening, gentlemen." He gestures to Alessandro. "We have other guests to attend to."

Alessandro's eyes linger on me for a moment longer, his gaze calculating and cold before he follows Gabriel into the crowd. As they walk away, I notice their smooth veneer crack slightly—Gabriel's shoulders tense, Alessandro leaning in to say something that makes Gabriel's jaw tighten. The body language between them shifts from cordial to confrontational once they believe they're out of our sight.

"Well, that was awkward as hell," Wes mutters once they are out of earshot. He tugs at his bow tie like it's suddenly too tight.

Chase runs a hand through his hair, his expression troubled. "Did you see her body language? How tense she was and how they blocked her from us. Man, I'm telling you, she looked like a prisoner. You heard Gabriel—'Thank you for giving her a safe place to experience college life.' Like she's on some kind of fucking work-release program."

"Something's not right," I say, my voice tight. "The way

that guy touched her..." I clench my fists at my sides, the memory making my blood boil.

"Fuck," I mutter, running my hand through my hair as realization crashes over me. "I should have said something. I should have pulled her away from that creep, told him to keep his hands off my girlfriend. I just stood there like an idiot while that guy—" The image of Alessandro's possessive touch on Bebe's bare back replays in my mind, making my stomach turn. Why did I just stand there? Why didn't I step between them, make it clear she wasn't alone or unprotected? "I want to just rewind, walk right up, and knock Alessandro's hand off her back."

"No way, man," Marc says firmly, grabbing my shoulder. "That would've been a disaster."

Jake nods in agreement. "Those guys are sharks in designer suits. One wrong move and they'd have eaten you alive—and probably made things worse for Bebe. It was best if you didn't make a scene."

"You don't understand," I insist. "You didn't see her face when he touched her."

"No, we saw. She looked terrified of him," Wes adds quietly. "Not just uncomfortable—actually afraid."

The orchestra downshifts into something jazzy. The crowd thins out, with a few filtering toward the bar or the terrace outside. I spot Gabriel in conversation with a local politician, Alessandro glued to his side.

A hand touches my shoulder, and I turn to find Henri standing next to me. His expression is guarded, but his eyes hold the same flicker of sympathy I noticed earlier.

"She's in room 2401," he says quietly, nodding toward a

set of French doors at the far end of the ballroom. "West Tower." He gives my shoulder a light pat before walking away.

Chapter Thirty-Seven

BEBE

I SLIDE onto the barstool like it's a sanctuary, exhaling a breath I didn't realize I'd been holding. "Thank you," I say to Henri, grateful for him escorting me away from Gabriel and Alessandro.

"You okay?" Henri asks, ordering me a club soda with lime.

"I'm fine," I saw automatically before taking it back. "I mean, not really. Did you know about this? That they would be here?"

"No," he says quickly. "If I did, I would have warned you."

I down the club soda in three desperate gulps, fury building inside me. That bastard. Gabriel didn't just happen to choose Dalton's football program for his "generous" million-dollar donation. He engineered this entire collision of my worlds with surgical precision. A million dollars just to expose my lie about being a normal college student.

"What hotel room are you staying in?" Henri asks.

"Room 2401–West Tower. Why?"

"I'll tell Luke—send him up, you'll have privacy."

"Why are you helping me?"

"Because I know how terrified you are of Alessandro. And the way you looked at Luke..." Henri squeezes my hand. "Go. I'll run interference with Gabe."

When I reach my room, I kick off my stilettos immediately, leaving them discarded by the door. The dress feels suffocating now, a costume I can't bear to wear another minute. I unzip it with fumbling fingers and let it pool at my feet, stepping away from the expensive fabric like it's contaminated.

In the bathroom, I brush my teeth and pull on my pajamas —my usual shorts and tank top along with my fuzzy cat slippers I brought from home and the hotel's fluffy robe, cinching it tightly around my waist as if it could shield me from the world outside.

Twenty minutes later, I'm pacing the length of the luxurious hotel suite. My hands tremble as I check my reflection for the tenth time. *Will he even come? Would I, if our situations were reversed? What if he's too angry about my secrets?*

I glance at the clock: 9:47 PM. It's been thirty minutes since Henri promised to send him up, and I'm beginning to think he might not come after all. Maybe he's already left the hotel. After seeing me with my brothers, with Alessandro's possessive hand on my back, perhaps he's already written me off as too complicated, too entangled in a world he wants no part of.

My stomach churns as I remember Alessandro's touch, his cold words about pregnancy. I sink onto the edge of the king-

size bed, burying my face in my hands. I can't do this anymore
—live this double life. Most of all, I'm tired of hurting Luke—
the one person who's shown me what life could be like if I
were free to choose. I can't keep lying to him while falling
deeper in love.

The decision crystallizes in my mind with sudden clarity. *I
won't marry Alessandro. I won't be The Killer Bee anymore.* I'll
tell Gabriel I'm done—with the family business, with the
arranged marriage, with all of it. This isn't the life I want. It
never was.

My future stretches before me—uncertain but mine to
choose. I'll tell Luke everything—about my family, about
Alessandro, even about The Bee. No more secrets between us.
No more walls. He deserves the truth, even if it means
losing him.

There's a subtle knock at the door—three consecutive
taps. My heart leaps into my throat, and I freeze, suddenly
paralyzed with uncertainty. *Will it be the one I long for, or the
ones I fear? Is it Luke, ready to support me and listen like he
promised? Or has my oldest brother come to assert his control?
Worse, what if it's Alessandro, coming to remind me I'm
nothing more than a business transaction?*

I take a steadying breath and move toward the door on
trembling legs. With one last silent prayer, I turn the handle.

Luke stands in the hallway, still in his tuxedo, though his
bow tie hangs loosely around his neck. His blue eyes meet
mine, intense and questioning. The relief that floods through
me is so powerful my knees nearly buckle.

"You came," I whisper, unable to hide the wonder in my
voice.

He doesn't respond with words. He steps forward,

backing me into the room. The door swings shut behind him with a soft click as the electronic lock engages. His eyes never leave mine as he cups my face between his palms. Time suspends as we stare at each other, the world narrowing to just this moment, just us.

He hesitates for only a second, then closes the distance between us. His lips capture mine with a hunger that steals my breath. The kiss isn't gentle—it's desperate, claiming, filled with all the words we haven't spoken. My body responds instantly, muscle memory taking over as I melt against him.

This connection between us hasn't faded, hasn't diminished despite my attempts to push him away. If anything, it's grown stronger. His hands slide into my hair, cradling my head as his tongue seeks entrance. I open to him willingly, a soft moan escaping as he deepens the kiss.

His arm wraps around my waist, pulling me flush against him until I can feel his heartbeat thundering against mine. My robe falls open slightly as he holds me tighter, his hand splaying possessively across my lower back.

When we finally break apart, both breathless, I can't suppress the truth anymore.

"I love you," I whisper, my voice trembling with emotion. "I want to be with you. I'll tell you everything."

His eyes soften at my confession. He pulls me closer, pressing his forehead against mine in a gesture so intimate it makes my heart ache.

"I love you too, Bebe," he whispers, his breath warm against my lips. "I need to tell you something too," he says, his voice growing serious. His hands cup my face again, thumbs gently stroking my cheekbones. "I've been keeping a secret from you."

I know what it is—The Keepers, the secret society, his family's legacy. The information Gabriel shared with me that night in his office. And I still refuse to believe that his family is involved with drugs.

"My family... we're part of something—"

I silence him with a kiss, unable to bear the vulnerability in his eyes. He thinks this revelation might change things between us, when my own secrets are so much darker, so much more damning.

Chapter Thirty-Eight

LUKE

OUR MOUTHS COLLIDE with renewed urgency, my confession momentarily forgotten as desire takes over. We stumble backward toward the bedroom area of the suite, never breaking the kiss as my hands find the already loose tie of her robe. With one tug, the plush fabric falls open, revealing her tank top and shorts. Her fingers work at my bow tie, pulling it free completely before moving to the buttons of my dress shirt.

"I need you," she whispers against my mouth, her nimble fingers making quick work of each button. "Now."

The urgency in her voice ignites something primal within me. I shrug out of my jacket, letting it fall forgotten to the floor as her hands push my shirt from my shoulders. Her touch is electric on my bare skin, sending shivers down my spine.

We're frantic now, hands everywhere, tugging and pulling at the barriers between desperate kisses. I lift her tank top over her head, revealing her perfect breasts. Her shorts and underwear follow, sliding down her smooth legs. I kick off my shoes, fumbling with my belt buckle as she works at my zipper.

Within moments, we're both completely bare, our clothing scattered across the hotel room floor. The sight of her naked body in the dim light of the suite steals my breath.

I lift her, carrying her the final steps to the bed. The mattress gives beneath our weight as we settle in. I trail kisses down her throat, across her collarbone, making her arch against me.

My hand slides down her body, tracing the curve of her hip before finding the warmth between her thighs. I can't hold back a deep groan when I find how ready she is for me, slick and inviting against my fingers.

"God, Bebe," I murmur against her neck, my voice hoarse with desire. "So wet for me."

I guide one of her legs up higher around my waist and position myself at her entrance. Our eyes lock as I push forward, claiming her in a single thrust that makes her gasp. Unlike our first time, there's no hesitation, no gentle easing—just raw and urgent need as I thrust into her with possessive intensity.

"Luke," she moans, her fingers digging into my shoulders, urging me deeper.

I establish a relentless rhythm, each thrust harder than the last. The headboard thumps rhythmically against the wall as I drive into her. Nothing else matters. All that matters is Bebe beneath me, her eyes half-lidded with pleasure, her lips parted as soft cries escape with each movement.

I watch her face, captivated by the expressions of ecstasy flickering across her features. Her cheeks are flushed, her cinnamon hair splayed across the pillows like liquid fire. She feels incredible around me—hot, tight, perfect. Every inch of her draws me deeper.

"You feel so good," I whisper in her ear, my voice rough with desire. "So perfect."

This isn't just sex—it's communion, a physical manifestation of everything we've been trying to say with words. Each thrust, each gasp, each shared breath speaks volumes between us. Our bodies communicate what our voices have struggled to express.

Her hips rise to meet mine, matching my rhythm. Her legs wrap tighter around my waist, pulling me impossibly deeper as her nails rake down my back. The slight sting intensifies my pleasure, driving me to move faster, harder.

Something shifts in me—a need to see her, to watch her take control. In one fluid motion, I wrap my arm around her waist and roll us over, never breaking our connection.

She rises above me like a goddess, her eyes gleaming with desire in the soft hotel lighting. Her palms brace against my chest as she adjusts to this new position, her knees sinking into the mattress on either side of my hips. When she begins to move, I nearly lose myself in the way she looks.

"Fuck," I breathe, my hands finding her waist to guide her movements.

She establishes a rhythm that's pure torture—slow, deliberate rises followed by deep, grinding descents that take me entirely inside her. Her head falls back, exposing the elegant column of her throat as she rides me. Her breasts bounce hypnotically with each movement, her nipples in hardened peaks.

Wars marathon tomorrow. She seems both familiar and foreign in this setting, like finding someone you love speaking a language you didn't know they knew.

My attention shifts to the three men standing protectively around her. Her brothers. The family she's mentioned so often but revealed so little about. Gabriel studies me with calculating green eyes, his expression unreadable as he steps forward.

"You must be Luke Sullivan," he says, extending his hand. "I've heard about you."

I take his hand, feeling the firm grip of someone used to power. "And I've heard about you. Just not much."

Gabriel's smile doesn't reach his eyes as he releases my hand and turns toward my brothers. "Wes Sullivan, Dalton's star quarterback." He shakes Wes's hand firmly. "I expect you'll lead your team to the state championship this year."

Wes straightens his shoulders, slipping effortlessly into his public persona. "Yes, sir. That's the plan."

Gabriel nods approvingly before greeting Chase with the same polished charm. The two other brothers—Henri and Beau—exchange handshakes with us as well, their expressions a mixture of curiosity and assessment.

Throughout these introductions, Bebe remains silent behind them, her eyes darting between me and Gabriel. The tension in her shoulders speaks volumes.

"I must thank you and your brothers for opening your home to Bebe this year," Gabriel says, his tone polite but with an undercurrent I can't quite place. "It's comforting to know she has a safe place to stay while *experiencing* college life."

The way he says "experiencing" makes it sound temporary,

"That's it, baby," I encourage, my fingers digging into her hips. "Just like that."

Her pace quickens gradually, her breathing becoming more erratic as she chases her pleasure. I thrust upward to meet her downward motions, the synchronicity of our movements creating a perfect rhythm. The way her body accepts mine, the way we move together—it feels like we've been doing this forever, like our bodies were designed specifically for each other.

"God, you're beautiful," I tell her, mesmerized by watching her take her pleasure. Her movements grow increasingly erratic, her thighs trembling against mine as she grinds down harder. I feel the telltale fluttering around my length, the first signs of her approaching climax.

"Luke," she gasps, her voice breaking on my name.

I reach between us, my thumb finding her sensitive bundle of nerves. The effect is immediate—her body stiffens, back arching as she cries out. Her inner muscles clamping down around me, rhythmically pulsing and squeezing. The sensation is exquisite torture. Her eyes lock with mine, wide and vulnerable as pleasure overwhelms her. The raw emotion on her face—mouth parted, cheeks flushed, eyes glazed with ecstasy—is the most beautiful thing I've ever seen.

Something primal awakens inside me as I watch her come undone. A possessive need surges through my veins—to claim her completely, to mark her from the inside out. With a low growl, I flip us over again, pinning her beneath me as I drive into her with renewed intensity. I grip her hands under her thighs, pushing them up and open as I pound into her with abandon. The new angle allows me to hit that perfect spot inside her, making her cry out with each thrust.

My fingers dig into the sheets beside her head, twisting the cotton in desperate fists as my body tightens with approaching release. She grips my waist, her small hands steadying me with increasingly erratic thrusts. My rhythm falters as the sensation builds to an unbearable peak.

"Bebe," I choke out, the pleasure overwhelming me as my release hits with stunning force.

I bury myself to the hilt, my body shuddering as I empty inside her in long, pulsing waves. The pleasure seems endless, each spurt sending fresh tremors through my entire body that go on forever.

I collapse onto her, my weight supported on trembling forearms as our bodies remain joined. For several moments, we stay like this, hearts thundering together, skin slick with sweat, breath mingling in the small space between us. The world outside this room—with all its complications and secrets—feels impossibly distant, unable to touch us in this sanctuary we've created.

When my breathing finally steadies, I ease myself from her body and roll to my side. She turns toward me naturally, our legs tangling together beneath the rumpled sheets. Her hand finds my cheek, fingertips tracing the line of my jaw with tender curiosity, as if memorizing me by touch.

In the soft golden glow of the hotel lamps, her face is a study in contrasts—the sophisticated heiress I glimpsed downstairs now completely gone, replaced by the girl who stole my heart with her wide-eyed wonder at bowling alleys and paintball courses. Her mismatched eyes reflect the light differently—one catching amber highlights, the other absorbing the warmth into its darker depths.

The realization washes over me with absolute clarity: the

woman who dominated the paintball field, who curls up in my sweatshirts and sleeps with fuzzy cat slippers—that's the real Bebe. Not the silent, controlled woman who stood on stage beside her brothers.

I brush a strand of hair from her face, tucking it behind her ear. "I don't care, you know," I whisper.

Her eyebrows draw together. "About what?"

"The money. The Laurent Foundation. Any of it." I trace the curve of her shoulder with my fingertips. "I fell in love with the girl who gasped in wonder at her first bowling strike, who dominates paintball like a tactical genius but still gets excited about movie marathons."

Her eyes fill with tears, but she doesn't look away. "That's the real me," she whispers. "The rest is just... circumstances."

I nod, understanding more than she realizes. "I know who you are, Bebe."

She swallows hard, her hand finding mine beneath the sheets. "There's more..."

"Alessandro," I say quietly, watching her face carefully. "He's not just a family friend, is he?"

Her face crumples, and she looks away, a single tear escaping down her cheek. The way she tenses at Alessandro's name tells me everything I need to know.

I already suspected it from the way he touched her, the proprietary gleam in his eyes when he looked at her.

It must be a pending arranged marriage. I've heard of such arrangements within The Keepers—old money families preserving bloodlines and merging power through strategic marriages. The practice is archaic but not unheard of in certain circles, especially the wealthy. I just never imagined Bebe would be caught in one.

"Bebe?" I reach for her hand. "Is he who I think he is? The man you're arranged to marry?"

Her face contorts with pain while her anguish makes my chest ache. Her shoulders begin to shake with silent sobs.

"Hey, I'm sorry," I whisper, pulling her against my chest. "I didn't mean to make you cry. We don't have to talk about this now if you don't want to."

I stroke her hair, feeling her tears wet against my skin. She clings to me like I'm a lifeline in a storm, her small body trembling.

"Luke, I—" she begins, her voice breaking.

A sharp knock at the door interrupts her. We both freeze, staring at each other with wide eyes.

"Shit," I mutter, suddenly remembering I told my brothers to give us an hour to talk things through. I glance at the clothing scattered across the floor, the rumpled sheets tangled around our naked bodies. We definitely didn't do much talking.

The knocking becomes more insistent.

"Bebe? Luke? Are you in there?" Wes's voice says.

"Just a second!" I call out reluctantly, disentangling myself from Bebe. Her eyes are wide with panic as I scramble off the bed.

"It's okay," I whisper reassuringly. "It's just Wes and Chase."

I quickly scan the floor, spotting my dress pants near the foot of the bed. I yank them on, nearly losing my balance in my haste. She clutches the sheet to her chest, her cheeks flushed with embarrassment.

I pull the bedroom door closed behind me as another round of knocking starts. Fumbling with my zipper, I manage to fasten it as I reach the hotel room door. I take a deep breath, running a hand through my disheveled hair, trying to look somewhat presentable before opening it.

My brothers stand in the hallway, both still in their tuxedos. Wes's eyes immediately take in my bare chest, the light sheen of sweat still visible on my skin, and the unmistakable flush of recent exertion. A knowing smile spreads across his face.

"Well, well," Wes says. "Looks like you two have worked things out."

I step aside, holding the door open. "Just come in."

Chase whistles as he strolls past me, his eyes widening as he takes in the expansive suite with its panoramic city views and elegant furnishings. "Holy shit, man. This place is nice..." He wanders toward the floor-to-ceiling windows overlooking the Los Angeles skyline. "Check out this view!"

Wes flops onto the luxurious sofa, loosening his bow tie completely. "So this is how the other half lives, huh? The Laurents clearly don't mess around."

The bedroom door opens, and Bebe emerges, her hair slightly tousled, wearing her tank top and shorts with those ridiculous pink fuzzy cat slippers shuffling across the plush carpet. Despite the luxury surrounding her, she looks exactly like the girl I know from home—my Bebe, not the polished heiress from downstairs.

"Hi," she says softly, crossing her arms self-consciously over her chest.

Chase grins, glancing between us. "Glad to see you two made up. The moping was getting unbearable."

She smiles weakly at his comment as she perches on the arm of the sofa, keeping a careful distance from all of us.

Despite our passionate reconnection moments ago, I can sense her retreating again, building those invisible walls. I want to pull her close, to whisper that everything will be okay, but something tells me we're still balancing on a precipice.

Even though we've crossed a physical threshold tonight, emotionally, we're still dancing around the truth. I can feel it hanging between us—all the things left unsaid. Her secret about Alessandro and whatever arrangement binds her to him. My secret about The Keepers and my family's legacy. We both want to be together. That much is clear, but we can't move forward until we lay everything out.

Wes clears his throat, breaking the charged silence, his expression turning serious. "Look, we didn't just come here to interrupt... whatever was happening." He glances at Chase.

Chase steps away from the window, his playful demeanor vanishing. "So, uh, we ran into that creepy guy in the elevator on our way up."

"Alessandro?" I ask, immediately alert. My protective instincts flare as I move closer to Bebe.

He nods, his eyes flicking to Bebe. "Yeah. He wanted us to give you a message the next time we saw you."

"What's the message?" she asks.

"Something about how he and your brother renegotiated a business deal tonight," Wes says. "He's paying ten million more to close it in two weeks instead of the summer."

"Yeah," Chase adds, "he emphasized the two weeks part and said he'd be in touch very soon."

Chapter Thirty-Nine

LUKE

Bebe's face goes completely blank at Wes's words. Whatever this "business deal" is, it clearly involves her. *The marriage, perhaps?* Her body stiffens, and her eyes lose focus, staring at something none of us can see. The transformation is jarring—one moment she's my Bebe in her fuzzy slippers, and the next, she's someone else entirely, someone void of emotion.

Without a word, she slides off the couch and walks deliberately into the bedroom. The three of us exchange confused glances.

"What just happened?" Chase whispers.

Before I can respond, she emerges from the bedroom; her phone clutched in her hand. She dials a number and brings the phone to her ear.

"It's me," she says, her voice stripped of emotion. "Do you have your computer with you?" She pauses, listening. "Henri,

I need you to access the hotel's guest registry. Find Alessandro's room number."

She paces calmly as she listens.

"The security protocol should be standard Saflok. Port 1477 for remote access." Her voice is clinical, detached. "Room 3104," she says into the phone, her voice eerily calm. "Can you get to it?" She nods at whatever her brother says on the other end. "Perfect." Something in her gaze shifts— calculation giving way to resolve. "I'll call you back when I'm ready for the green light," she adds, ending the call abruptly.

She strides to the side table, snatching her room key card and slipping it into her shorts pocket. Her movements are fluid, purposeful—reminding me of how she moved on the paintball field. Without explanation, she heads for the door.

"Where are you going?" I ask, but the door's already closing behind her.

I exchange a quick glance with my brothers before we all scramble to follow her. Chase shoots me a wide-eyed look that clearly asks, 'What the hell is happening?' I can only shrug in response, equally baffled by this sudden transformation.

Wes grabs his jacket, Chase straightens his tie, and I hastily button my shirt, leaving the top three undone in my rush.

By the time we reach the hallway, she is already jabbing the elevator button repeatedly. The doors slide open immediately, as if even the hotel machinery knows better than to keep her waiting. We pile in after her, crowding the small space.

"Bebe, what exactly are you doing?" Wes whispers, leaning closer to her.

She turns, pressing a finger to her lips and shushing him. Her fuzzy cat slippers tap rhythmically against the elevator floor—whether from impatience or to help her focus, it's hard to tell.

The elevator doors slide open with a soft chime. Without hesitation, Bebe steps out and veers right, moving with purpose down the carpeted hallway. We follow behind her like confused ducklings, exchanging bewildered glances as she counts down room numbers under her breath.

A few more doors down, she stops abruptly, causing Chase to nearly collide with her back. Her posture shifts—shoulders squaring, chin lifting slightly—as she pulls her phone from her pocket and dials.

"Ready," she says simply, her voice calm and steady. Nothing more, nothing less.

We watch in stunned silence as the electronic lock on the door before us suddenly illuminates with a green light. *The green light she was asking for.*

She pulls the handle down, pushes it open and strides into the suite, her movements fluid and purposeful. Alessandro looks up from the leather armchair where he's nursing a glass of red wine, his expression shifting from surprise to amusement.

"Bebe, what are you—"

His words die in his throat as her leg snaps upward in a perfect arc, her fuzzy pink slipper connecting with the crystal glass, sending it flying from his hand in a spray of crimson liquid that spatters across the pristine white wall like abstract art.

"Oh shit," Wes breathes behind me while Chase gasps.

Before Alessandro can recover, she pivots, driving her foot directly into his stomach with devastating force. The impact sends him stumbling backward with a grunt, eyes wide with shock.

Chase's fingers dig into my shoulder, his grip tightening reflexively, as if he's physically feeling Alessandro's pain. "Jesus Christ," he whispers.

Alessandro doubles over, gasping for breath, but Bebe still has more to do.

She drops into a crouch and sweeps her leg in a wide arc, her slipper connecting with his ankles. His legs fly out from under him, and he crashes to the floor with a heavy thud that seems to shake the entire room. Despite his physical advantage —he must outweigh her by at least a hundred pounds—she's taken him down with the precision of a trained fighter.

The sight of this tiny woman in pajamas and ridiculous slippers demolishing a man twice her size should be amusing, but none of us laughs. There's something terrifying in the cold efficiency of her movements, in the absolute lack of emotion on her face.

Alessandro attempts to scramble backward, his hands slipping on the plush carpet as he tries to create distance between himself and her. She stalks forward, each step deliberate and predatory.

"You renegotiated?" Her voice is deadly quiet, a controlled fury that sends chills down my spine.

Alessandro's eyes dart between us brothers, perhaps hoping we might intervene. When no help comes, his expression hardens. "It's business, cara mia. Nothing personal."

She steps forward, and crouches again, this time to deliver a precise karate chop to the back of his neck. The blow sends him crashing face-first onto the plush carpet.

I stand frozen, unable to process what I'm witnessing. The woman attacking Alessandro bears little resemblance to the girl who cuddles with me during movie nights. Yet somehow, she's still unmistakably Bebe. There's an effortless grace to her movements I recognize from the paintball field—that same tactical precision now unleashed with devastating effect.

She drops to her knees beside Alessandro's prone form and flips him onto his back like he weighs nothing, her small hands surprisingly strong as she maneuvers his much larger body. Her fingers dive into his front pocket, extracting his cellphone.

"You bitch," he gasps, his accent thickening with desperation. "Gabriel said you'd be compliant. He—"

"Shut up," Bebe interrupts, her voice ice-cold. "You're currently experiencing temporary paralysis from the neck down," she informs him, a chilling smile curving her lips. "Don't worry, circulation will return in about twenty minutes —plenty of time for what we need to do. Now listen carefully," she says, her tone dropping to a dangerous whisper as she leans closer to Alessandro's face. "You will call Gabriel and tell him the deal is off. Completely off. Not postponed, not renegotiated—finished."

Alessandro's eyes narrow with defiance. "I will do no such—"

She presses her thumb into the spot below his ear, causing him to gasp in pain.

"That's your carotid pressure point," she explains calmly. "A little more pressure and you'll black out. A lot more, and you'll never wake up." Her eyes bore into his. "So let me be perfectly clear: you will call him right now and end the

313

arrangement. If I find out you're working with him again—trying to decide my future—I. Will. Kill. You."

I gulp hard while both of my brothers gasp behind me.

"And I promise it won't be quick." Her voice is terrifyingly calm, matter-of-fact.

The cold certainty in her tone sends a chill down my spine. This isn't an empty threat—it's a guarantee from someone who knows exactly how to fulfill it.

She holds his phone in front of his face, using his facial recognition to unlock it. She scrolls through it, pressing a few buttons before dialing and putting the call on speaker.

It rings twice before Gabriel answers. "Alessandro? Is everything alright?"

Bebe leans close to Alessandro's. "Tell him," she mouths.

Alessandro's eyes dart nervously between her and the phone. He clears his throat, voice shaking. "Gabriel, I'm... I'm calling off our arrangement. The deal is terminated."

"What?" his voice crackles through the speaker, sharp with disbelief. "Alessandro, we just agreed to—."

"I've reconsidered," he manages, his face contorting as she applies subtle pressure to his neck. "The marriage is off. I want nothing to do with your sister or your family."

The marriage is off. It makes sense now... That's why she was so desperate to experience college life. To taste freedom before the cage door slammed shut at the end of the school year.

"This is ridiculous. Are you being threatened?" His voice rises with suspicion. "Is Bebe there? Put her on the—"

Bebe's thumb jabs the phone, cutting the call, and Gabriel's questions vanish into silence. She tosses the phone onto Alessandro's chest. It bounces once before settling on his immobilized torso.

She rises from her crouched position with fluid grace, brushing invisible dust from her knees. Her eyes meet mine briefly—those extraordinary mismatched orbs now empty of emotion—before she walks straight past me and my brothers toward the door. We stand frozen for a moment, watching her retreat before we collectively snap into action, hurrying after her.

"Holy shit," Wes whispers as we rush toward the elevator. "That was the most badass thing I've ever seen in my life."

Chase punches the elevator button, his eyes wide with disbelief. "Did you see his face? I've never seen someone look so terrified. He thought she was actually going to kill him."

She stares straight ahead, her expression unreadable, her breathing controlled, shoulders rigid beneath her thin tank top.

The door slides open, and we all step inside. I can't focus on my brothers' chatter. My mind is racing, trying to process what I just witnessed. The clinical precision of Bebe's movements, the way she incapacitated Alessandro without hesitation, the cold calculation in her eyes—this wasn't just self-defense training or paintball skills. This was something else entirely.

But beneath my shock, all I can think about is what Bebe must have been enduring. Being treated like property, sold to a man old enough to be her father, her body and future negotiated like a business transaction. The thought makes my stomach turn with rage.

When we reach her floor, she pulls her key card out of her pocket and fumbles with it, her hands trembling so badly she can't get it in the slot. I lean over gently, taking it from her fingers and unlocking the door in one smooth motion. She doesn't acknowledge me, just stands there, staring at the now-open doorway.

As we step inside, something changes. The steel in her spine seems to melt away all at once. Her shoulders collapse inward, and her entire body begins to shake. She takes two unsteady steps forward before her legs give out.

She crumples to the floor, her knees hitting the plush carpet with a soft thud. A sound escapes her—so raw—that seems to tear through her chest like physical pain. She curls into herself, arms wrapped tightly around her middle as if trying to hold herself together while she falls apart.

I'm at her side instantly, dropping to my knees beside her. I gather her into my arms, cradling her against me as violent sobs wrack her small frame. She clutches at my shirt, her fingers twisting in the fabric as she buries her face against my shoulder. The sound that escapes her is unlike anything I've ever heard—part wounded animal, part terrified child. Her shoulders shake violently as pent-up emotion pours out of her.

"It's okay, I've got you," I whisper against her hair, rocking her gently. "You're safe now."

Chapter Forty

BEBE

I BLINK against the morning sunlight filtering through the hotel curtains, my brain slowly piecing together the events of last night. My body feels heavy; my mind feels foggy. Alessandro's terrified face. The way my voice turned to ice as I threatened him. It wasn't a dream—I did that to him.

What happened wasn't just standing up for myself—I completely lost control. *The Killer Bee took over, the trained assassin emerging when I needed her most.* I couldn't bear another moment of being traded like property for money, of having my future decided by men who see me as nothing more than a business asset.

Luke's arm circles around my waist, his warmth a stark contrast to the cold calculation that possessed me hours ago. His steady breathing grounds me, pulling me back from the edge of my darker thoughts.

A soft snoring sound catches my attention—too distant to

be coming from Luke. I carefully lift my head from Luke's chest, peering over his shoulder toward the other side of the massive hotel bed.

What I see makes my breath catch. There, scrunched up back to back like children at a sleepover, are Wes and Chase, still in their rumpled tuxedo pants and undershirts. Wes's head is buried beneath a pillow, one arm dangling off the mattress as he snores. Chase's blond hair is sticking up in all directions.

A smile tugs at my lips. *They stayed.*

The memory of my collapse, of breaking down completely in front of them, floods back with uncomfortable clarity. After years of controlling every emotion, I'd shattered into pieces. And instead of running, they stayed. All three Sullivan brothers, forming a protective circle beside me until exhaustion finally claimed us.

Luke stirs beside me, his eyes fluttering open. Those blue orbs find mine immediately, softening with tenderness when he realizes I'm awake. A slow, sleepy smile spreads across his face as his arms tightens around my waist, pulling me even closer. His other hand begins a slow exploration up and down my side, fingers trailing from my hip to the underside of my breast and back again.

"Good morning," he murmurs, voice husky with sleep.

Before I can respond, he presses his mouth to mine in a gentle kiss that quickly deepens. His hand slides under my tank top, warm palm against my bare skin as he holds me against him. I melt into him, savoring the softness of his lips, the solid warmth of his body.

I can't believe he's still here after everything he witnessed last night. After seeing Alessandro touch me possessively, after hearing about our arrangement, watching me transform into someone capable of violence—he should have run. *If he knew the full truth—that I wasn't just promised to a monster, but that I am one myself—would he still be here?*

His kisses grow more insistent, his hand sliding higher until his thumb grazes the underside of my breast. Heat pools low in my belly as I press closer, my fingers threading through his hair. Each kiss deepens, our breathing grows heavier as we lose ourselves in the moment. A soft "mmmm" escapes my throat, the sound betraying just how good his touch feels.

"Dude, are they aware we're still in the room?" Chase's soft voice suddenly cuts through our intimate bubble.

"Shhh," Wes says quietly. "Maybe she'll moan again."

Luke lifts his head slightly, not bothering to look over his shoulder. "We can hear you," he calls out, his eyes never leaving mine.

I can't help the giggle that bubbles from my chest, pressing my forehead against Luke's as embarrassment and amusement war within me.

"You guys could have slept on the couches, you know," Luke adds, his thumb still tracing lazy circles on my skin.

"And wreck my back right before the regional championship game?" Wes grumbles, his voice muffled by the pillow. "Coach would kill me."

I hear rustling as Wes sits up, followed by more movement. Shortly after, he lets out a string of curses.

"Shit! Guys, check your phones," Wes's voice cuts urgently, suddenly alert. "Dad called me like six times."

Chase groans loudly, the mattress shifting as he fumbles for his phone. "Me too. Three missed calls."

Luke reluctantly pulls away from me, reaching for his on the nightstand. I immediately feel the loss of his warmth as he sits up, his expression changing as he looks at his screen.

"We have to go," Wes says, standing and gathering his things. "Mom left a voicemail. She's saying he's hysterical about something. She needs us home now."

Chase runs a hand through his messy hair, already heading for his shoes. "What happened? Is she okay?"

"I don't know. She just said it's urgent," he replies, tucking in his wrinkled shirt.

Luke's eyes meet mine, filled with reluctance and worry. He squeezes mine gently. "I should..."

"Go," I tell him, forcing a reassuring smile. "Your family needs you. I'll be fine here."

He hesitates, clearly torn. "Are you sure? I don't want to leave you alone. After everything last night—"

"I'm positive," I say, touching his cheek. "Go take care of your parents. Besides," I add, "I have my own family situation to handle."

The truth of those words settles over me. Gabriel will be furious after what happened with Alessandro. The call I ended prematurely won't be the end of it.

Luke's eyes search mine, concern etched across his features. "You're going to confront your brother, aren't you?"

I nod, suddenly feeling more resolute than I have in years. "It's time."

He leans forward, pressing his forehead against mine. "Call me as soon as you're finished? Promise you'll come home to me?"

"Nothing could stop me from coming back to you," I whisper, sealing the words with a quick kiss.

"We still have a lot to talk about."

I nod, squeezing his hand.

"I love you," Luke says suddenly, his voice soft but certain.

My heart swells, and I can't fight the smile that spreads across my face. Despite everything—the chaos of last night, the uncertainty ahead—his words feel like an anchor.

"I love you too," I whisper back, rising onto my tiptoes to seal the declaration with a quick kiss.

Luke sighs, reluctantly joining his brothers while they gather their belongings and straighten their rumpled formal wear as best they can.

"Thanks for the sleepover," Chase says with a wink, trying to lighten the mood despite the urgency of their departure. "Next time, separate beds maybe?"

Wes claps a hand on Luke's shoulder, guiding him toward the door. "Let's move. Bye Bebe!"

With one last concerned glance, Luke follows his brothers out the door. The soft click as it closes behind them feels oddly final, leaving me alone in the suddenly too-large hotel suite.

The elevator ride to Gabriel's penthouse feels endless. The doors slide open with a soft chime, and I step into the marble foyer, my Converses incongruously squeaking across the polished stone. My body is charged with purpose, each step propelling me forward despite the exhaustion weighing on my limbs.

I bypass the living room where Beau sits with a drink, ignoring his startled "Bebe?" as I rush down the hallway. Henri appears in a doorway, worry creasing his face. Our eyes meet briefly—his filled with understanding, mine with determination.

Gabe's office door is ajar. I don't knock. I push it open and stride in, finding him standing behind his massive desk, phone pressed to his ear. He looks up, his expression darkening when he sees me.

"I'll call you back," he says into the phone before throwing it down. "What the hell have you done?" Gabriel's voice explodes through the room, his fist slamming against the desk. "Do you have any idea what you've destroyed? Two years of negotiations! A multi-million dollar partnership that would have secured our family's position for generations—gone!" His face contorts with rage. "And for what? So you could play house with your college boyfriend?"

His words hit like physical blows, but instead of shrinking back, something ignited inside me.

"Is that all you care about?" I scream back, my voice matching his in volume. "The money? The deal? Is that all I am to you—a bargaining chip? A transaction?"

His eyes widen, clearly shocked by my outburst.

"I am a person, Gabriel! A human being with feelings and dreams of my own. I'm your sister! Your blood!" My hands tremble as I gesture wildly between us. "Not once—not a single time—did you ask me what I wanted. How I felt about being sold to a man twice my age, who all he talks about is getting me pregnant."

My breath comes in short gasps as tears suddenly flood my eyes, spilling down my cheeks. My knees weaken and I collapse into the chair across from his desk, my body shaking with sobs I can no longer contain.

"I'm so tired." I whisper through my tears. "I've done everything you've asked of me. I've trained until my body broke. I've killed for you. I've become The Killer Bee because I thought that's what I had to do for our family. I thought that's what I had to *be* to belong in this family."

I look at him through blurred vision, watching his expression shift from anger to something unreadable.

"All I've ever wanted was to make you proud. To please you. You're the only family I have left." My voice cracks as the words tumble out. "But do you know what I realized? While I was doing everything to earn your love, I've been missing out on living."

He remains frozen behind his desk, his knuckles white where they grip the edge.

"I know you never wanted this," I continue, wiping at my tears with trembling fingers. "You had to raise me when mom and dad died. I was just a burden dropped in your lap when you were barely an adult. I've spent years trying to earn the love of someone who resents my very existence," I say, my voice growing steadier despite the tears streaming down my face. "You never wished for a sister. You had your whole life ahead of you, and suddenly you were responsible for raising a child."

His jaw tightens.

"But instead of being honest about that, you turned me into something useful. Not a sister, not family—a weapon." I rise to my feet, finding strength in finally speaking these truths aloud. "The Bee was never about protecting our family's interests. It was about justifying my presence in your life." I straighten my shoulders, wiping the last tears from my face.

"I'm done, Gabriel. I won't kill for you, I won't marry for you."

His eyes narrow. "And how exactly do you plan to survive? Your tuition, your rent, your clothes—everything comes from family money."

"I'll get a job—take out student loans. I'm not helpless, Gabriel. I never was—*you* made sure of that." I turn and walk toward the door. "I'm taking my life back, starting now." My hand reaches for the doorknob.

"Bebe."

I pause, my fingers hovering over the brass handle. Part of me wants to keep walking, to not give him the satisfaction of my attention. But something in his tone saying my name—a vulnerability I've rarely heard—makes me turn around.

Gabriel's face has lost its hardness. He looks suddenly tired, the weight of his years visible in the lines near his eyes.

"That call I just ended," he says, gesturing to his phone. "It was our intelligence team. They've uncovered evidence about The Keepers. It's pointing to Wesley Sullivan Sr."

"No," I say immediately, shaking my head. "Luke's family—"

"It's planted evidence," he interrupts, his voice level. "The L.A. Chapter is setting them up, redirecting it."

My heart freezes. "What are you saying?"

"They know we've been targeting them. They're desperate." His voice grows urgent. "They've fabricated evidence against the Sullivans, the entire family, clearly for the police, but also to draw out The Bee—it's another trap."

Luke's worried face flashes in my mind—the urgent calls from their parents, their hasty departure this morning. A cold dread washes over me.

"I have to go," I say, already turning toward the door. "Luke and his brothers—they were called home. Their mom said it was urgent."

Gabriel moves with surprising speed, blocking my path. "Bebe, listen to me. This is exactly what they want. They've already rounded up Luke and his family just now. They're hoping The Killer Bee will come for the Sullivans, thinking they're guilty. They want you to eliminate them."

"Then it's a trap I need to walk into," I say. "I can't let them hurt the Sullivans."

"You can't just charge in there." He grabs my arm. "Not as yourself. Not as Bebe Laurent."

"What are you suggesting?" I ask, though I already know the answer.

"The Killer Bee. One last mission."

I laugh, but it's humorless—the irony of it. After everything I just said about being done, about reclaiming my life, here I am considering putting on that black suit one more time.

His grip on my arm loosens, his eyes softening as they meet mine. "I know what you think, Bebe, but you're wrong about one thing. I do love you—even if I'm shit at showing it."

The unexpected confession stuns me.

"I never resented you," he continues, his voice rough with emotion I've never heard before. "I was terrified of failing you. Protecting you and training you was the only way I knew how to show you I cared—to keep you safe. I couldn't imagine a world where you could be happy without all this," Gabriel gestures around us, to the penthouse, the wealth. "Our father taught me that power and money were the only true protection in this life. The marriage to Alessandro—" his voice falters, "I genuinely believed he was the best choice. A man with enough resources and influence to shield you from our enemies when I couldn't anymore."

Something shifts in his expression—a vulnerability I've never seen before.

"It never occurred to me you could just... leave. That there was another option." He shakes his head, looking almost bewildered. "That you could build a life outside of all this or that there was another way. I was trying to prepare you for our word. I never considered you might find your own."

I stare at my brother, seeing him clearly for perhaps the first time. His words ring with a truth I'd never considered— that his control came from fear rather than malice, that his manipulation stemmed from a warped sense of protection. His vision of safety was so narrow, so confined to the world we were raised in, that he couldn't imagine security existing outside wealth and power.

It makes a terrible kind of sense. Gabriel was barely an adult himself when our parents died, thrust into a position of responsibility for which he had no preparation beyond our father's twisted lessons about power. He did what he thought was right—what he'd been taught was right.

But understanding doesn't equal forgiveness. The years of control, of being molded into a weapon, of having my autonomy stripped away, body bargained to secure a business deal—those wounds won't heal with a single moment of honesty.

"I understand why," I say finally, my voice steady despite the storm of emotions inside me. "But good intentions don't erase what you did to me."

Gabriel nods, accepting this without argument, stepping away from the door; no longer blocking my path. "Go," he says simply.

I stand frozen, unable to process this moment of clarity from my brother. After years of control, he's finally letting me go.

Chapter Forty-One

LUKE

THE CAR IS silent as we pull into our parents' driveway. I'm still processing everything that happened at the hotel with Bebe, the revelation of her family's wealth, and Alessandro.

But none of it matters to me—it doesn't change a thing. I still want to be with her. There is still the question of how she got those bruises, which is even more mysterious now that I'm convinced she can defend herself. But I'm certain she'll tell me —she promised to come home to me.

The house looks peaceful from the outside, but as we approach the front door, a raised voice filters through the windows. Dad sounds agitated, frantic—nothing like his usual controlled demeanor.

"Something's wrong," I mutter, exchanging concerned glances with my brothers.

The shouting grows louder as Wes reaches for the doorknob. The moment we step inside, I freeze. Dad stands in the middle of the living room, a pistol gripped in his hand, which he immediately swings toward us. My heart nearly stops as I stare down the barrel.

"Jesus Christ!" Wes yells instinctively, throwing his hands up.

Dad's eyes widen with recognition, and he instantly lowers the weapon. "For God's sake, boys! You should announce yourselves!"

My chest pounds against my ribs as we cautiously step inside. The living room is in disarray—papers scattered across the coffee table, dad's laptop open with multiple windows displayed, and empty coffee mugs littering every surface.

"What the hell is going on, Dad?" Chase asks, stepping forward warily. "Why do you have a gun?"

He paces back and forth in the living room, running his free hand through his disheveled hair. His usual composed demeanor has completely vanished, replaced by a wild-eyed nervousness I've never seen in him before.

"It's all falling apart," he mutters, more to himself than to us. "They're setting me up. I was trying to help them, and they turned on me the moment I found out what was really happening."

My brothers exchange worried glances. Mom is nowhere to be seen, which heightens my concern.

"Found out what, Dad?" I ask. "What's happening?"

He stops pacing and looks at me, his eyes suddenly focusing with frightening intensity.

"The L.A. Chapter has been distributing drugs, Luke. That's why The Killer Bee is targeting them." His voice drops to a harsh whisper. "They've been selling synthetic opioids; people are dying."

The room goes completely silent. I feel like I've been punched in the gut. The L.A. Chapter dealing drugs?

"What do you mean 'setting you up'?" Wes questions, stepping closer to him.

Dad's eyes dart nervously toward the windows before he responds. "They're framing me—us, our family. They've been doctoring financial records, planting evidence, and a paper trail that leads directly here!"

"Let's go to the police." Chase says, his voice steady despite the tension filling the room. "Show them what you've found, explain that we're being framed."

He lets out a harsh laugh that borders on hysteria. "The police? We are the police, Chase! Their Chapter has officers on the payroll, judges in their pocket. The Commissioner himself is a Keeper!" His eyes are wild now, darting between us. "We can't trust anyone. And now The Killer Bee will come."

I exchange worried glances with Wes. Dad sounds unhinged, paranoid. I've never seen him like this before.

I take a cautious step forward. "Dad, you need to calm down. The Killer Bee won't come after us—we're good people. We haven't done anything wrong."

"You don't understand," Dad snaps, pacing again. "The Bee is going after everyone connected to the drugs. It doesn't matter if we're innocent! She won't know! She'll just see the evidence pointing to us!"

I freeze, the word catching in my mind. "She? You said 'she'?"

Dad stares at me momentarily confused by my question. Then, understanding dawns on his face. "Yes, *she*. The Killer Bee is a *woman*." He moves to his laptop, clicking through files with shaking fingers. "We set a trap, remember? The night

Archibald agreed to be bait. He's dead, along with the mercenaries we hired. But I caught her on camera."

"You have footage of The Bee?" I ask, my voice barely above a whisper. "Even the police don't have that."

He hesitates, then nods grimly. "I had set up a nanny-cam. You should see it. You need to understand who we're dealing with."

We gather around his laptop as he pulls up a video file and cues the recording for us. The video is grainy, a wide angle showing a dimly lit bedroom. A figure—small, clearly female despite the poor quality, dressed in black—moves with lethal precision, taking down three larger men in tactical gear.

There's something familiar about the way she moves, the way she carries herself. Her movements are fluid, graceful even. My eyes dart curiously to the timestamp in the screen's corner. My heart stops—the exact night Bebe disappeared for three days. I recall the evening she came back with that bruise on her jaw, a cut lip, the way she winced when she moved.

Bebe's paintball skills. The perfect aim. How she incapacitated Alessandro with such clinical precision.

Bebe is The Killer Bee.

Has she known I'm a Keeper this whole time?

Chase stiffens beside me, his sharp intake of breath telling me he's made the same connection. Before he can speak, I shoot him a warning look, a silent plea to keep quiet. Wes catches on immediately, his hand subtly gripping Chase's arm.

"What do you notice, Son?" Dad asks suddenly, turning to Chase.

Chase's eyes meet mine briefly before he shrugs with forced casualness. "Uh, those moves look like Japanese martial arts. Reminds me of the aikido demonstration we saw at the cultural festival last year."

Dad's expression shifts, his paranoia momentarily replaced by academic interest. "Japanese? You think she could be Asian?" he nods eagerly, suddenly energized by this new theory. He grabs a second laptop from the side table, opening it with renewed purpose. "That makes sense. The L.A. Chapter has enemies in international syndicates." His fingers fly across the keyboard. "Japanese martial arts... aikido... jujitsu..."

With Dad thoroughly distracted, Wes leans closer to me, his mouth inches from my ear. "Tell me you're seeing what we're seeing," he whispers, his voice barely audible. "That's her, isn't it?"

I swallow hard, my throat dry as sandpaper. "Yes," I whisper. "Almost certain."

My attention returns to the screen just as the video shows something unexpected. After dispatching the men, the woman in black doesn't immediately flee. Instead, she collapses against the wall, her body folding inward.

The Killer Bee—Bebe—draws her knees to her chest, her shoulders shaking. Even through the grainy footage, the raw emotion is unmistakable. She's sobbing, her small frame convulsing with each silent cry. Her hands cover her face as she rocks back and forth, completely broken in the aftermath of violence.

My chest tightens painfully. This isn't a cold-blooded assassin reveling in death. This is someone shattered by what she's done—someone trapped in circumstances I can't even imagine.

Chase opens his mouth to say something when a

deafening crash interrupts. The bay window explodes inward, glass shards spraying across the living room floor. A metallic cylinder tumbles along the hardwood, coming to rest at my feet.

"Get down!" Dad screams, diving behind the sofa.

Before any of us can react, the canister hisses open. Thick purple-gray smoke billows out, instantly filling the room. The acrid chemical stench burns my nostrils and throat. My lungs seize as I inhale the gas, sending me into a violent coughing fit.

I drop to my knees, eyes watering uncontrollably. Through the haze, Wes collapses beside me, his body convulsing with desperate coughs. Chase stumbles backward, hand clutched to his neck, before sliding down the wall to the floor.

My vision blurs, and it's getting harder to breathe, which makes it hard to think. The room spins around me as I struggle to maintain consciousness. If Bebe is truly The Killer Bee, then she might be the one attacking us right now. But something doesn't add up—why use gas? The Bee in that video was direct, efficient with her kills.

My vision darkens at the edges as I fight to crawl to the door. Dad's gun lies abandoned on the floor, just out of reach. I stretch my arm toward it, fingers trembling, when a silhouette appears in the doorway.

The figure's face is obscured by what looks like a gas mask. He moves with purposeful strides through the smoke, scanning the room systematically. Not Bebe's movements. Too large, too rigid. Male.

Relief and terror war within me as I realize this isn't Bebe —but if not her, who?

Chapter Forty-Two

LUKE

THE FOG in my head slowly lifts as I blink several times, trying to focus. My mouth feels like sandpaper, and there's a metallic taste on my tongue. I test my restraints—duct tape wound tight, cutting into my wrists with each subtle movement.

As the room becomes clear, I notice my family similarly bound to dining chairs arranged in a perfect circle. Mom and dad directly across from me, his head lolling against his chest, her quietly sobbing. To my right sits Wes, awake and struggling against his restraints, while Chase is on my left breathing heavily.

We're in the great room now. A formal space usually reserved for holiday gatherings and important Keeper meetings.

"Luke," Wes whispers urgently when he notices I'm awake. "Thank God."

"What's happening?" I rasp, my throat raw from the gas fumes.

Before Wes can answer, the double doors swing open. A tall figure enters, draped in a midnight blue Keeper cloak that sweeps the floor, hood obscuring his face. He moves to the center of our circle. With theatrical flair, he raises his hands and pushes back the hood to reveal himself. My breath catches in my throat as recognition hits me instantly—Richard Maxwell, the L.A. Chapter's Grand Master, my father's superior in the Keeper hierarchy.

"You're all awake," Maxwell observes, his aristocratic features arranged in a bitter smile. "Good. I was hoping you'd all be conscious for this."

"Is all this necessary?" Wes asks, jerking his head toward the duct tape binding his wrists. "You've already framed our family. Why the theatrics?"

Maxwell's eyebrows rise, impressed by Wes's directness. "Yes, Mr. Sullivan, it is absolutely necessary. While the digital evidence has been planted thoroughly, we still must leave physical evidence." His voice carries a polished cadence. "The authorities need a complete picture, something tangible in your home."

As if on cue, a younger man in our Keeper robe enters, carrying a large plastic container. He sets it on the floor and removes the lid, revealing dozens of small packets filled with white powder.

"Our synthetic opioid," the Grand Master explains, nodding toward the box. "Very potent. We'll make sure the police find it hidden throughout your lovely home."

"You're insane," Dad croaks.

He circles our chairs like a predator, his robe swishing against the hardwood floor. "I would love nothing more than to kill you myself, Wesley Sullivan. Our Chapter reached out to yours for an outside look; instead, you did what you always do and inserted yourself—took control. You've put your nose where it didn't belong, finding our Chapter's secret," he says to my dad. "Killing you would be... messy. No, your deaths need to appear as part of a pattern." He stops behind my father's chair, placing his hands on his shoulders. "You see, when The Killer Bee's victims are discovered, they all have one thing in common—traces of a specific honey in their bloodstream and a piece of honeycomb in their mouth..."

Dad's head begins to shake. A broken sound escapes his lips.

"Yes," Maxwell continues, clearly enjoying my father's fear. "Without that signature toxin, the authorities would question whether these deaths were truly the work of The Bee. So you see, The Bee herself will have to do the honors."

My father lets out a sob, a sound so raw and terrified that it shocks me. I've never seen him afraid of anything, but the mere mention of The Bee has reduced him to this.

Something inside me cracks. A laugh bubbles from my chest, small at first, then growing until I'm genuinely laughing.

Everyone—including my family, stares at me like I've lost my mind.

"What's so funny?" Maxwell demands as he stalks toward me. He leans in, bringing his face inches from mine, his breath smelling of expensive scotch. "You find your impending death amusing?"

"The Bee isn't going to kill us," I say, still chuckling despite the tape digging into my wrists.

He straightens, genuine curiosity flickering across his features. "And how could you possibly know that?"

I just smile at him, a calm certainty washing over me. His eyes narrow, confusion replacing his smug superiority.

Suddenly, the room plunges into darkness. The security system beeps once before going silent—a complete power cut. Maxwell's sharp intake of breath tells me this blackout wasn't part of his plan.

"What's happening?" his robed associate hisses from the hallway.

"She's here," I say, my voice carrying in the sudden silence.

Even in the shadows, I can make out Maxwell's face, illuminated faintly by moonlight filtering through the windows. The confident mask has slipped completely, replaced by raw terror. The light catches on the silver of his Keeper ring as his hand trembles.

"No, she's early. Her marks are usually later than this... secure the perimeter!" Maxwell barks at his associate. "Find her before—"

A man's scream echoes from upstairs, followed by a heavy thud against the wall. Then another. And another. The sound of bodies hitting the floor in rapid succession sends Maxwell scrambling backward.

"She can't possibly—" Maxwell's voice cracks as more screams filter through the darkness.

"You fucked with the wrong family," Wes says, his voice dripping with satisfaction despite our dire situation.

Chase lets out a low whistle. "Man, she is going to kick your ass."

"Shut up!" Maxwell shouts.

Emotion surges through me—hope, pride, and a strange sense of calm certainty. Bebe is here, and despite being The Killer Bee, she would never harm us. I can feel it in my bones.

"The Bee won't touch us," I state, my voice unwavering and filled with conviction. "But she will kill you, Maxwell. The reason I know this... is that she's my girlfriend."

Maxwell's eyebrows shoot up, his mouth falling open in shock.

At the same time, I hear my father's choked "What?" as he struggles against his restraints.

"That's impossible," Maxwell sputters, his composure shattering. "The Bee is a—"

"A highly trained assassin who's been systematically eliminating members of your drug operation," I finish for him.

Maxwell's eyes widen in terror as he fumbles in his robe pocket. A small black device emerges in his trembling hand—rectangular, with a single red button in the center. A panic button?

A soft beep echoes through the room as Maxwell lunges toward the double doors, desperation giving his movements an awkward urgency. He makes it three steps before a blur of movement erupts from the shadows. Something—no, someone—connects with his chest, a devastating kick that sends him airborne. His body flies backward, arms windmilling helplessly before his spine crashes against the coffee table—the wooden surface splintering beneath his weight.

Maxwell lies sprawled amid the wreckage, wheezing for

breath, his elegant robe twisted around his legs like a fallen flag.

A dark silhouette materializes in the doorway, fitted in a black suit, backlit by the faint glow of moonlight from the windows. My heart pounds against my ribs as the figure steps forward, gradually revealing her form. The silver light catches first on hair—light reddish brown, then illuminates the curve of her cheek, and finally, those extraordinary eyes find mine—one green, one brown with blue—holding a question I answer without words.

I smile at her, pouring every ounce of acceptance and love I feel into that single expression. The uncertainty in her gaze softens, relief washing over her features as she realizes I'm seeing her—*truly seeing her.*

Bebe steps into the room, moving with that fluid precision I've come to know so well, though now I understand its deadly origin.

She stalks toward Maxwell, her movements predatory and precise. Without taking her eyes off him, she reaches into a concealed pocket on her tactical jumpsuit and extracts a syringe filled with amber liquid.

"Mr. Sullivan," she says, her voice eerily calm as she addresses my father directly. "Your call since he set you up. Honey toxin or police?"

My father stares at Bebe with wide eyes, recognition and fear battling across his features.

"I—I—" he stammers, swallowing hard. "Police. Call the police."

Something softens in her expression—approval, perhaps relief. She nods once, acknowledging his choice.

She crouches beside Maxwell. Her boot presses firmly

against his throat, pinning him to the floor. He claws weakly at her ankle, face reddening.

"This will knock him out until the police get here," she explains. His body jerks once, then goes still. His eyelids flutter, fighting against the inevitable, before finally closing as unconsciousness claims him.

She rises, scanning the room with tactical awareness. Her gaze drops to the floor, where something catches her attention. "Shit," she hisses, spotting the small black panic button lying several feet away from where it had fallen from Maxwell's hand.

She moves swiftly to Chase—the closest to her. From a holster strapped to her thigh, she extracts a matte black tactical knife and slices through the duct tape.

Chase flexes his freed hands, wincing as blood rushes back into his fingertips.

"Free the others," she instructs, pressing the knife into his palm.

A thunderous noise echoes from the back of the house— heavy footsteps, multiple sets, descending upon us. Backup responding to Maxwell's panic signal.

Bebe's head snaps to the sound. "I'll hold them off, gather what weapons you have and keep the room secure," she says, already moving toward the doorway.

"Wait!" I call out to her, my voice urgent despite my raw throat. Chase works quickly to free me from my restraints.

She freezes at the threshold, one hand already on the doorframe. She turns back, those extraordinary eyes finding mine across the room.

"I love you," I say, rubbing my wrists as Chase slices through the last of my bindings.

A ghost of a smile touches her lips—not the deadly Killer Bee but my Bebe.

"I love you too," she says, the smile widening enough to make my heart skip. Then she's gone, slipping into the darkened hallway.

Chapter Forty-Three

BEBE

My attack on the two mercenaries I find in the kitchen is very much as you might see in a Jason Statham or Jackie Chan movie. In my training, I was taught that everything around you can be used as a weapon.

The first one turns, surprise registering on his face as I grab a ceramic mixing bowl from the counter and smash it against his temple. He staggers, blood trickling down his cheek, but recovers quickly. Too quickly. His hand moves toward his holster.

I don't give him time to draw. Dropping low, I sweep his legs with a spinning kick, sending him crashing into the kitchen island. As he falls, I snatch a bottle of olive oil, uncapping it and splashing the contents across the tile floor.

The second mercenary charges at me, tactical baton raised high. I sidestep his swing; the weapon whistles past my ear close enough that I feel the air displacement. When his boot hits the slick oil, he loses his footing before he crashes down hard, propelling him into the pantry shelves. Rice, flour, and canned goods rain on him as I land in a crouch.

"Sorry, Mrs. Sullivan," I whisper, noting the mess in her kitchen.

I grab a heavy cast-iron skillet from the stove. The first mercenary struggles to his feet, reaching again for his weapon. I swing the skillet like a baseball bat, connecting with his jaw. The sickening crack tells me it's broken, and he drops unconscious before he hits the ground.

The second man rises, blood streaming from his nose where the shelving hit him. He lunges at me with surprising speed, tackling me against the refrigerator. His forearm presses against my throat, cutting off my air. I slam my knee upward into his groin. He grunts but doesn't release his hold.

Spots dance in my vision as I frantically reach behind me, fingers scrambling against the side of the refrigerator. They connect to something metal—a magnetic knife strip. I wrench a chef's knife free and drive it into his thigh. He howls, his grip loosening enough for me to twist away.

I don't wait for him to recover. One precise strike to his temple with the butt of the knife handle, and he joins his partner on the floor.

I pause briefly to catch my breath before moving into the hallway. The narrow corridor stretches ahead, dimly lit by light filtering through other rooms. Footsteps pound toward me—heavy, purposeful. Another mercenary appears at the end of the hall, assault rifle raised.

"Don't move!" he shouts.

I sprint toward him instead. He fires, but I'm already in motion and the bullets whiz past me. The hallway is narrow, barely wide enough for his broad shoulders. I use this to my advantage, leaping upward and planting my feet against the opposing walls. With the walls supporting my weight, I launch myself forward, both feet connecting squarely with his chest. The impact sends him flying backward, his massive frame crashing into the drywall.

The mercenary slumps to the floor, groaning. I don't wait to see if he'll get up again. Adrenaline courses through my veins as I move deeper into the house, my footsteps silent despite my racing heart.

A door stands ajar at the far end of the hallway—Mr. Sullivan's home office. Light spills from inside, casting long shadows across the hardwood floor. I approach cautiously, back pressed against the wall.

Through the gap, I spot another man in tactical gear. He's hunched over the desk, rifling through papers, muttering into a radio clipped to his shoulder. The Sullivan family's personal files are spread on the polished mahogany surface.

I slip inside unnoticed, my eyes scanning the room for a weapon. A silver letter opener glints on the desk's edge. Perfect.

In one fluid motion, I snatch it and strike. The mercenary barely has time to register my presence before the metal pierces his throat. His eyes widen in shock, blood bubbling from his lips as he clutches frantically at the wound. The radio clatters to the floor.

Before I can process what I've done, firm grips seize me from behind. A gasp escapes my lips as I'm yanked backward, arms pinned against my sides. More hands grab my legs as I kick wildly, trying to break free.

"Got her!" a gruff voice shouts. "The Bee is secured!"

I thrash violently, but three—no, four—mercenaries have

me now, lifting me off my feet. My elbow connects with someone's face, earning a pained grunt, but their grip tightens.

"She's stronger than she looks," one of them growls as they manhandle me through the doorway.

I twist and buck against their hold while they convey me down the hallway toward the front entrance.

The cool night air hits my face as they drag me across the threshold. Moonlight bathes the front lawn in silver as they carry me. My lungs burn with exertion, muscles screaming as I continue fighting.

They lower me onto the grass, pressing my body against the cool earth. I taste dirt as one of them presses my head down harder. My cheek scrapes against the ground, forcing my gaze sideways toward the house. Through the iron bars of the side gate, I notice a commotion—Luke bursting through it, his face contorted with anguish as he spots me pinned.

"Bebe!" His voice carries across the lawn, raw with desperation.

He lunges forward, but Wes and Chase immediately catch him. They grab his arms, restraining him as he struggles wildly against their grip.

I want nothing more than for Luke to come to me, but I know that will only get him killed—his brothers know that too.

"Let me go!" Luke roars, fighting against Wes and Chase. "They're hurting her!"

One mercenary shifts his weight, allowing me to breathe easier. "Check her equipment," he orders. "The Bee always carries the honey toxin."

Rough hands search my tactical gear, patting at my sides

until they reach my utility belt. I feel a slight tug as they locate the hidden compartment.

"Jackpot," another announces triumphantly. "Got the Bee's stinger right here."

"Perfect," a deep voice says from somewhere behind me. "Inject her."

"And what about the others?" one asks, and I assume they are talking about the Sullivans.

"Our employers need them alive. We're going to Plan B."

I struggle harder, but there are too many of them, their combined weight keeping me immobilized against the damp grass.

Luke's face contorts with horror as he realizes what's about to happen. He renews his efforts to break free, nearly dragging Wes and Chase forward with his desperate lunges.

"No!" he screams, his voice cracking. "We have to stop them!"

At this moment, facing my own weapon, all I can think about is Luke. Not the missions, the college experience, not even my own survival—*just Luke*. My handsome, kind-hearted Luke, who showed me what real love feels like. Who made me believe I deserved something better than the life I'd been forced into. I turn my face toward him, our eyes locking across the distance. The mercenary's grip on my hair loosens just enough for me to lift my head.

"It's okay," I mouth silently, willing him to understand with my eyes what my voice can't reach. "I love you."

His face crumples, tears streaming down his cheeks as he reads my lips. The sight of his anguish cuts through me more painful than any physical wound. He shakes his head violently, still battling his brothers' restraint.

The cold press of the metal needle pierces my neck with a sharp sting. But it barely registers compared to the agony of watching Luke's desperation.

A strange warmth spreads from the injection site, radiating outward through my body. The toxin—*my toxin*—floods my veins. My vision blurs, but one thing remains clear—*his face*. My limbs grow heavy, muscles relaxing against my will. I fight to keep my eyes open, to hold Luke's gaze with every ounce of willpower I have left. If these are my last breaths—final moments, I want his face to be the last thing I see—I want to be at peace.

His mouth forms my name over and over. My chest rises and falls unevenly, my body growing weaker with labored breath. I try to—

Chapter Forty-Four

LUKE

ONCE BEBE'S body goes limp, no longer fighting them, the mercenaries step back. One of them kicks her still form with his boot, checking for any response. Nothing. She lies motionless on the grass, her cinnamon hair fanned out around her head like a halo against the dark green.

With a roar that doesn't sound human even to my own ears, I wrench myself free from my brother's grip. Their fingers slip from my arms as I surge forward, fueled by pure adrenaline and desperation. *But it's too late.*

"Luke, no!" Dad shouts behind me, but his voice sounds distant, underwater.

I sprint across the lawn, my focus narrowing to her still form. The mercenaries react instantly, weapons swinging toward me, laser sights marking my body. I don't slow down. If they're going to shoot me, so be it.

"Stop or we'll shoot!" one of them barks, but I'm already

diving, sliding across the damp grass on my knees until I reach her.

I gather her into my arms, cradling her head against my chest. Her body is terrifyingly limp, deadweight in my embrace.

"Bebe," I whisper, my voice breaking. "Wake up. Baby, please wake up." Her skin is already growing cool to the touch, her mismatched eyes closed as if in peaceful sleep. "You can't do this. Not now. Not when I finally understand."

The mercenaries circle around us, weapons trained on my back, but I barely register their presence. Nothing matters or exists beyond the woman in my arms.

Suddenly, the night erupts with the squeal of tires on asphalt. Headlights slice through the darkness as multiple black SUVs come barreling down the street, cutting across the lawn with military precision. They screech to a halt, forming a protective semicircle around us.

"What the—" one mercenary shouts before the doors fly open and men in tactical gear pour out, weapons raised.

The mercenaries spin toward this new threat, momentarily forgetting about me as they shift into defensive positions.

"Drop your weapons!" someone yells.

I clutch Bebe tighter, shielding her body with mine as the standoff unfolds and tension escalates.

From the lead SUV, a door swings open. Gabriel Laurent emerges, his face a stone mask of fury. Henri and Beau flank him, each armed and moving with lethal purpose.

Gabriel raises his hand, fingers extended in a precise gesture. His men respond instantly—silenced weapons discharge in perfect unison. The mercenaries drop one by one, their bodies hitting the grass with dull thuds. No warning, no chance to surrender. Clinical. Efficient. Exactly like Bebe's fighting style.

"No!" I scream, my voice raw. "You're too late! Five minutes! If you'd been here five minutes sooner!"

Gabriel's eyes find mine, then drop to his sister's still form in my arms. He strides toward us, dropping to his knees beside me while his team sweeps past, heading for the house.

"Bebe," he whispers, reaching out to touch her cheek. His hand trembles—the first sign of genuine emotion I've seen from him.

I clutch her tighter, irrationally protective even now.

"Give her to me," he says, arms extended.

I tighten my grip. "No."

His jaw tightens, but he doesn't press further.

"What happened?" he asks, his voice steady despite the storm of emotions in his eyes. His fingers find the pulse point on Bebe's neck, pressing firmly.

"They injected her with the honey toxin," I say, the words tasting like ash in my mouth.

Wes and Chase appear at my sides, their hands gripping my shoulders in silent support.

"She wasn't scared," I tell them, recalling her eyes meeting mine in those final moments. "When they stuck her with the needle. She just... looked at me."

Henri kneels beside his brother, gently brushing a strand of hair from Bebe's forehead. "She didn't feel pain," he says softly. "Just sleepy."

Tears stream down my face, falling onto Bebe's still features. I can't stop them, can't even try. The grief is too raw, too overwhelming to contain.

Gabriel watches me for a long moment, his calculating

eyes studying my face. Then, something shifts in his expression.

"You love her," he whispers. Not a question—a realization.

I look up at him, vision blurred. "Of course I do. I've loved her from the first day I met her."

He continues to assess me, this ordinary college boy holding his extraordinary sister.

"I may not come from wealth," I tell him, my voice breaking but growing stronger. "I may not know a hundred ways to kill someone or have connections in high places. But I'm a decent man who would have never broken her heart. Never." My voice cracks on the last word. "I would have protected her." I laugh. "Scratch that—she would have protected me. But I would have given her the life she wanted."

Something that might be respect flickers across Gabriel's face.

"He's right," Beau says suddenly, stepping forward. "I approve of him, Gabe."

Henri nods emphatically. "So do I. Quit torturing the poor guy already."

I look between the three brothers, confusion replacing my grief for a moment. "What are you talking about?"

Gabriel sighs, running a hand through his hair. "They're not the first ones to try using her toxin against her," he admits, his voice softer now. "She's encountered this situation before."

"Before she ever started using it on targets, we made sure there was an antidote," Henri says, his expression gentler than his older brother's.

"Antidote?" I repeat, the word barely a whisper as hope flickers to life inside my chest.

Beau kneels with us, producing a black case from his jacket pocket. "She takes it before every job. It protects her from exactly this situation." He flips open the case, revealing a small vial filled with clear liquid and a syringe. "Standard protocol."

My hands shake so badly I can barely maintain my grip on Bebe. "She's alive?"

"Her pulse is there, but it's weak—hard to detect," Gabriel confirms. "She needs medical attention soon, but yes, she's alive."

Alive. She's alive. I hold her closer, afraid to believe it's true, afraid that if I loosen my hold for even a moment, she'll slip away forever.

My brothers hug each other beside me. Chase wipes tears from his face while Wes claps him on the back, both of them processing the emotional whiplash of the last few minutes.

"Luke," Gabriel says, his voice uncharacteristically gentle. "May I have my sister now? We need to get her to our medical team."

I hesitate, my arms still protectively cradling her. Every instinct screams at me not to let her go, but reason prevails. He has resources I don't—doctors, antidotes, everything she needs. Reluctantly, I nod.

"You can come with us," he says as slides his arms beneath her, and I feel the weight of her lifting away from mine.

Gabriel cradles Bebe in his arms, her body unnervingly still as he carries her toward the waiting SUV. Henri rushes ahead, pulling open the rear door and preparing the backseat.

I stand and stumble forward on weak legs.

"We'll take her to our private medical facility," Beau says, his voice surprisingly gentle. "The doctors there understand her unique physiology and the toxin's effects."

"Wait," I call out, my voice hoarse.

Gabriel pauses, his expression softening slightly as he recognizes the desperation in my eyes. He nods once, allowing me a moment.

I step closer, gently brushing my fingers across her cheek, cold and damp from my tears. Her cinnamon hair catches the moonlight, and even now, unconscious, she's the most beautiful thing I've ever seen. Leaning close to her ear, I whisper, "I love you." The words catch in my throat, half-prayer and half-promise.

Something flutters beneath her eyelids—the faintest movement, so slight I might have imagined it. But I know I didn't. *She's fighting*, clinging to life with the same determination she brings to everything.

Epilogue

BEBE

A YEAR AND A HALF LATER...

The wind whips through my hair as we cruise down Route 66. Luke's profile is golden in the late afternoon sun, his blond hair tousled, a content smile playing on his lips.

"I can't believe we actually did it," he says, eyes fixed on the winding road ahead. "Three weeks, seven states, and not a single regret."

This summer road trip has been just what we needed after the chaos of the end of the school year for me and his graduation.

I slide my hand onto his thigh. "Best summer of my life."

His smile widens as he places his hand over mine. "Mine too."

The setting sun casts everything in amber light, turning the corn stalks into liquid gold. In a few days we'll be back in Ambrose, returning to our home by campus, real life resuming. It's funny that I can call it that now. There was a time when my 'real life' meant something else.

My hand travels higher up his thigh, my fingers tracing small circles on the denim. Luke's breath catches, his grip tightening on the steering wheel.

"Bebe," he warns playfully, "I'm driving."

"Then keep your eyes on the road," I say teasingly.

I slide my hand to the button of his shorts, feeling the hard outline of him. He sucks in a breath as I work the button free, then slowly drag the zipper down.

"Anyone could drive by," he murmurs.

I glance around at the endless cornfields stretching in every direction. "We haven't seen another car for at least thirty minutes."

I tug his shirt up, exposing his tanned stomach, then work his shorts down just enough. He lifts his hips to help, keeping one hand steady on the wheel. Despite my teasing touches, he's already fully aroused, straining against his boxers.

I free him completely, wrapping my fingers around his length before lowering my head. The wind rushing through the open Jeep almost drowns his groan of pleasure. His thighs tense as I work him with my tongue, his breathing growing ragged. His hand settles gently in my hair.

The car swerves slightly, tires rumbling over the rough edge of the shoulder. I pull back immediately, my hand still wrapped around him.

"Sorry," Luke says with a sheepish smile, his cheeks flushed. He adjusts his grip on the wheel, guiding us safely back to the center of the lane. "That just felt really good."

I can't help laughing, my hair wild around my face from the wind. "I'll take that as a compliment."

His eyes are dark with desire as they flick briefly from the road to my face. "Please don't stop."

I lean down again, taking him between my lips. There's something intoxicating about this—the taste of him, the vibration of the engine beneath us, the openness of the endless sky above. I swirl my tongue around his tip before sliding my mouth down his length.

The thrill of being so exposed adds an edge to everything. Though the road remains empty, the possibility of being seen sends electricity through my veins. My body responds, heat pooling between my thighs as my tongue runs up and down his cock.

His hips start to rise beneath me, pushing himself deeper into my mouth. His fingers thread through my hair, grip tightening. I recognize the signs immediately—the way his thighs tense under my hands, the subtle tremor in his breathing. He's close.

The car swerves again, tires crunching over gravel. This time when I lift my head, Luke is already turning the wheel sharply, guiding us onto a narrow dirt path that cuts between towering rows of corn. The Jeep bounces over the uneven terrain before coming to an abrupt stop, engine still running.

"What are you—"

"I can't take it anymore," he says, voice rough with need. "I need you. Now."

The engine falls silent as he turns it off, leaving only our heavy breathing and the rustle of cornstalks in the breeze. He reaches for me, pulling me across the console to the driver's seat and straddling him. His mouth finds mine in a hungry kiss that steals my breath, and I gasp against his lips.

His hands slide up my thighs, pushing the yellow fabric of

my sundress higher until it bunches around my waist. His fingers hook into the thin strip of my thong, tugging it aside with gentle urgency. When I lower myself onto him, I'm already slick, taking him inside me in one fluid motion that makes us both gasp.

Luke fumbles with the lever on his seat's side, reclining it back several inches. The new angle lets me sink deeper, taking all of him as I adjust my knees on either side of his thighs. My hands brace against his chest as I begin to rock my hips, establishing a rhythm that has him groaning beneath me.

"God, Bebe," he murmurs, his voice thick with desire.

His fingers hook into the straps of my sundress, sliding them off my shoulder to expose my breasts to the warm summer air. When his mouth closes around a nipple, warm and wet, I arch into him, a moan escaping my lips that seems to echo across the empty fields surrounding us.

I increase my pace, grinding against him as sweat begins to bead along my hairline. The rhythm of our bodies becomes primal, desperate, as if we're racing against the setting sun. Luke's hands grip my hips, guiding me as I ride him with increasing urgency. There's a familiar tightening low in my belly, the pleasure building with each movement.

Suddenly, he pulls me down against his chest, one hand tangling in my hair as his lips find mine again. The kiss is deep, consuming, his tongue sliding against mine in perfect synchrony with our bodies. I've experienced pleasure in so many ways with Luke, but there's something about the intimacy of our kisses that speaks volumes. This connection—the way our lips speak without words—unleashes the wave I've been chasing.

"Luke," I gasp against his mouth as pleasure crashes

through me. My back arches involuntarily as my eyes flutter open to the sky above. The sunset has painted the heavens in breathtaking streaks of orange and purple, bleeding into deep blue at the edges. The beauty above mirrors the sensation pulsing through me, colors blurring as my body trembles.

Luke follows immediately, his hands gripping my hips as he surges upward. I feel each pulse inside me as he finds his release, his eyes never leaving mine even as pleasure overtakes him.

"You're incredible," he whispers, his thumb tracing my cheekbone as we both catch our breath. He looks over my flushed skin, my disheveled hair dancing in the breeze. "So beautiful like this—completely free." He pulls the straps back up my arms, and I adjust the top of my dress, re-covering my breasts.

I collapse against his chest, feeling his heartbeat gradually slow beneath my cheek. My fingers trace lazy patterns across his collarbone as contentment washes over me.

"It's because of you," I murmur, pressing a kiss to his sternum. "You make me feel safe enough to be free. To just... be me."

His arms tighten around me, one hand stroking my back in gentle circles. We stay like this for several minutes, connected in every way possible as the sunset deepens around us.

"Bebe," he says finally, his voice taking on a serious tone that makes me lift my head to look at him.

Something in his expression shifts—a vulnerability mixed with determination. His eyes search mine with an intensity that causes my breath to catch. "Marry me."

The words hang in the air between us. I stare at him, waiting for the laughter, the "just kidding".

There's something in his movements—a nervous energy I rarely see in him. He turns toward the center console, fumbling with the latch.

"Luke? What are you—"

He turns back to me, holding a small velvet box in his palm. My heart stops.

"I've been carrying this around for weeks," he says, voice slightly unsteady, "waiting for the perfect moment."

He opens the box, revealing a simple diamond catching the last rays of the sunset. My breath hitches in my throat as I recognize it immediately—a delicate gold band with a modest princess cut that somehow seems to hold galaxies within its facets. It was my mother's ring.

"How did you...?" I whisper, unable to complete the sentence as tears spring to my eyes.

I stare at the familiar glint of gold and reach out with trembling fingers to touch it.

Luke's smile is gentle, almost shy. "Gabriel gave it to me. Last month when we had dinner with our brothers." His thumb caresses my wrist.

I can hardly believe it. Gabe giving Luke our mother's ring isn't just a gesture—it's his blessing, his acknowledgment of what Luke means to me. After everything we've been through, after the near-disaster with the Sullivans being framed by their own brotherhood, after my brother finally accepted that I needed to build my own life—this feels like the last piece falling into place.

"We'll be in Vegas the day after tomorrow," he continues, his voice gaining confidence. "I know it's not the traditional way, but I don't want to wait. We could do it there—find a chapel—or we could have Elvis officiate, or even do it at one of those drive-thrus—"

I silence him with a kiss, pouring every ounce of love I feel into it. When we break apart, I'm nodding through tears.

"Yes," I whisper against his lips. "Yes, I'll marry you."

His smile could outshine the setting sun as he slips the ring onto my finger. It fits perfectly. The weight of it feels right —a connection to my past that now points toward my future.

I stare at the ring, marveling at how far I've come. Just two years ago, I was The Killer Bee. A weapon rather than a person. Now, sitting in Luke's lap as the last rays of sunset paint the sky, I'm simply Bebe—a college student, a woman in love, someone with dreams and choices that belong to me.

That night at the Sullivan house feels like a lifetime ago now—the L.A. Chapter's trap, the fabricated evidence against Luke's family, the moment I chose to *protect* rather than destroy.

In the end, officers took the L.A. Chapter members away in handcuffs and secured the actual evidence of their crimes. Gabriel used his resources to help clear the Sullivans of any wrongdoing. And now, The Keepers have found a friendship and alliance with the Laurent family.

How strange it had felt to strip off the Bee suit for the last time, to leave it crumpled on the family doctor's medical bed —only to be incinerated. I didn't need that armor anymore— didn't need to hide behind The Killer Bee's reputation. I could just be Bebe, with all my flaws, hopes and ordinary dreams.

The skills remain, of course. I still notice exits when I enter rooms, still catalog potential weapons without thinking. I tend to get a little overzealous on the paintball field with Luke and his brothers... but those instincts serve me now, rather than control me. They're tools I own, not chains that bind me.

The Bee met her end that night on the Sullivans' lawn. She will always be a part of me, her essence forever intertwined with mine. But it felt freeing to let *her* go.

The moment I woke up in the hospital with Luke by my side—Bebe had been *reborn*...

The end.

About the Author

Lulu Hart

Lulu Hart is a passionate storyteller who has been fascinated by the written word since childhood. From the whimsical worlds of Disney and Dr. Seuss to the thrilling adventures of Goosebumps and Sweet Valley High and the literary classics studied in high school. While in college, she dabbled in poetry, eventually publishing a collection that captured her creative spirit.

Lulu decided to bring her own love stories to life and share them with the world. Her debut novel, *Punches & Pirouettes*, marks the beginning of an exciting chapter in her writing journey. With its emotional depth, unforgettable characters, and engaging storytelling, this love story will keep lovers of contemporary romance captivated and yearning for more.

Lulu is a full-time professional in administrative healthcare and lives in Las Vegas, Nevada, with her loving husband and adorable daughter. In her free time, she finds fulfillment in watching horror movies, reading romance novels, and celebrating the joy of the holidays—Christmas being her favorite.

Also by Lulu Hart

The Fitzpatrick Clan

Punches & Pirouettes

Whiskey & Wine

Interludes with Insects

The Killer Bee

TBD Book 2

TBD Book 3

www.ingramcontent.com/pod-product-compliance
Lightning Source LLC
Chambersburg PA
CBHW071224250626
47163CB00001B/90